TEN YEARS TAKEN

Susannah B. Lewis

Billy Brown and Charles
You're forever in my heart.

ONE

Truck stop ahead. Boiled peanuts ahead. Detour ahead. Free Wi-Fi and HBO at the Holiday Inn on Exit 56.

I'd grown bored with the billboards, the same songs on every radio station and the endless fields of corn. I'd grown impatient with the other drivers, the semi-trucks that roared alongside me, the gray Buick that continued to pump the brakes in the fast lane and the mini-van that held up traffic- the frazzled father not realizing he had dropped below the speed limit as children yelled and threw candy in the back seat, ignoring their mother's pleading requests to be quiet.

I'd grown tired of it all as my body, my mind and my car raced away from something and to something, just the same.

In the ten hours of travel, I'd only stopped once at a gas station in Texarkana. I'd been longing to stop again, and when the low gas light illuminated on the dash board, I was happy to exit the interstate and pull into the small convenience store just east of Memphis. My legs needed to stretch, my eyes needed to focus and I needed a change of scenery, if only just for a moment.

I waited in line at the Tennessee store and stared at a photo above the cashier's head. A man stood knee deep in muddy water as he held a large catfish and smiled down at me. It reminded me of the old black and white photograph in my grandmother's kitchen. My grandfather posed next to a boat load of fish, cigarette hanging from the smile covering his face as my grandmother glanced over at the photo, flipped pancakes in an iron skillet and declared that Tennessee was the best place in the country to catch those whiskered monsters.

I'm pretty sure the man in the picture at the general store would agree with her.

As I waited on the elderly lady in front of me to find fourteen pennies in her purse, I looked around the small store. I noticed a relic rear-projection television in the corner, rabbit ears and all, and I was startled at the sight of Jonathan's face on the screen. A blonde newscaster with gorgeous diamond earrings and beautiful plum lipstick appeared to tell my story, but the volume was so low that I couldn't hear what she was saying.

The photograph of Jonathan was replaced with one of me in a stunning black gown at some random charity event, gorgeous diamond earrings of my own. A phone number scrolled along the bottom of the screen, followed by the word "MISSING" in large red letters.

No one was going to see that girl on the television. My long blonde hair had been haphazardly cut and dyed a cheap reddish hue. My blue eyes had been changed to green and for extra measure, the prosthetic pregnancy belly had been placed under my t-shirt.

"Fifty on pump three?" the cashier, an older woman with her own haphazard haircut, asked me between fierce smacks of gum.

I nodded and asked for a pack of cigarettes.

"Not good for the baby, dear," she scowled at me.

"They are for my husband," I lied.

"Ought not be smoking around an expecting woman, either," she mumbled and reached for the cigarettes on a shelf above her head. "Can I see some I.D.?"

My heart fluttered. "I left it in the car. I'm exhausted. Please don't make me walk all the way back out there."

She eyed me, my fake hair, my fake eyes, and my fake baby.

"You don't think I look eighteen?" I smiled. "I'm flattered, but I've been eighteen for a *long* time."

"Birthday?" she asked, the gum snapping between her teeth.

I blurted out a date, threw the cash at her and retrieved my nicotine.

Once the Land Rover was out of the parking lot, I threw the foam baby belly to the passenger seat and inhaled the smoke.

I knew my disappearance would be featured on the local Houston news. I had no idea it would be broadcast across the nation. This made me nervous.

Someone I knew in Nashville was bound to see my face on national news. In the television photo, I was a decade older than I was when I lived in my hometown. My short and naturally brown hair had been replaced by long, yellow locks. My breasts were larger, my waistline smaller, my arms toned, age had settled around my eyes, but it was still me. An old neighbor, old friend or certainly my family would all still recognize me.

The time had come. I had to call my parents.

It's so difficult to find a working payphone today. I pulled over at half a dozen gas stations and truck stops only to discover cement poles and square boxes where payphones once lived- wires cut and receivers missing. My cell phone was undoubtedly in custody of the Houston Police Department, so I continued to search for some untraceable way to contact my parents, my home.

I finally found one at a truck stop nearly fifty miles from the small general store. The receiver was greasy and smelled of fried chicken, the #3 button was missing, and the dial tone was fuzzy. I exhaled, inserted what seemed to be an ungodly amount of change, and I dialed the number that I had longed to dial for years.

One ring. Two. Three. Finally, ring number four was interrupted by the sound of my mother's sweet, slow, southern drawl.

I lost my breath. I literally lost my breath at the sound of her voice. It was the same voice that solaced me when lightning struck and thunder roared; the same voice that scolded me when I drank red Kool-Aid on the white carpet, the only voice that could correct me and comfort me simultaneously.

"Mama," I breathed helplessly into the dirty receiver.

Out of habit, my eyes scanned my surroundings to make sure that I wasn't being watched or heard. I kept my voice low. My hand covered the receiver and my mouth so no one could make out what I was saying. I pressed my body against the cold brick of the busy truck stop, and my eyes continued to search.

"Mama?" I repeated quietly, softly.

"My God," my mother's voice cracked. "Elle?"

"Yes, Mama."

"My God, Elle. Is that really you? Is it really you?" I could hear the hope and the happiness rise in her voice.

"Mama, I have to be quick. Are you listening?"

"Yes, I'm listening. I'm listening!" she exclaimed.

"Have you seen the news?" I asked as my eyes fixated on a burly truck driver pumping gas and loudly whistling an Allman Brothers tune over the roaring of diesel engines.

"No, baby, I haven't. No, what is it?" my mother was on the border of hysteria. Her slow southern inflection was now fast and frantic.

"If you see me on the news, don't call anyone. Do not call the police. I am fine. I am okay. Don't contact anyone. Tell everyone the same," I gave quick instructions as I watched a pickup truck of young boys. "You're still on Pine Hills? You haven't moved?"

"Of course we are still here! What's going on Elle? Why are you on the news?" Mama panicked.

"I'm fine, Mama. I will see you soon. Don't call anyone. Kiss Vaiden for me. I will see you soon," I hung up the phone. I raced back to the Land Rover, locked the doors, and I sped away.

Mama knew I was okay. She would tell Daddy, Vaiden, Emma, Nathan. I would see them all soon. I was so relieved to be going home. I was finally going home.

TWO

By the time I crossed the river, the orange moon had set fire to the night sky. When I left Texas so many hours before, I knew I was coming home to Tennessee. I'd planned to drive straight to my childhood home, oak trees shading the yard, ivy climbing the north side of the house, ferns setting on the long front porch. I'd planned to speed up the steep driveway, run through the kitchen door and scoop them all into my arms. However, once I saw my photo on the national news, I knew this would be too dangerous. Our neighbor, old lady Lancaster, could be on the phone with Houston right now, giving them information, giving them my parent's address. Someone could be giving me away.

After seeing the picture of the smiling fisherman outside of Memphis, the image in my grandmother's kitchen began to weigh heavily on my mind. That photo impelled me to go to the river, the familiar place where I'd spent so much of my childhood, but I didn't make the final decision to stay there until I had crossed the bridge and saw the sign.

The Land Rover kicked up gravel and dirt as I slowly navigated down the winding road. I had no idea where it went, what was waiting at the end, but the "camper for rent" sign prompted me to turn. Who would think to look for Texas socialite, Claire Marsh, in a camper on the muddy banks of the Tennessee River?

The SUV pulled up a steep hill, and the car lights shone on a couple of campers nestled between thick pine trees on the banks of the water. A mobile home sat at the end of the gravel cove with several faded signs indicating that it was the office. The trailer's porch light was lit, and a TV flickered inside. I got out and stretched my legs.

I left the fake stomach in the car. I didn't know how long I would be staying on the river. I didn't think I could pretend to be pregnant in the August heat, lugging around that stupid prosthetic belly every day for an extended period of time.

I walked onto the mobile home's creaky porch, nearly tripped over a cooler, and I rapped on the screen door. I heard a recliner slam shut inside, and an older gentleman appeared in plaid pajama pants and a white t-shirt. His eyes squinted to see me through the door, under the bright porch light, as moths swarmed my head.

I had rehearsed my story as I drove down the dusty gravel road. I'd been a professional liar for years. Stories came easy to me.

"What can I do you for?" he opened the screen door, toothpick sticking out of his mouth. His thick gray hair was messy on his head.

"Hey, there," I smiled. "I saw a sign on the main road that you have a camper for rent."

"I sure do. You interested?" he eyed my shoddy haircut, my cheap clothes and then the expensive vehicle parked behind me. I knew it didn't add up.

"Yes, sir, I am. I just lost my house in a divorce. I would've never married a lawyer for money if I knew I'd end up divorcing him," I chuckled. "He knew all the tricks in the book. He took everything from me but that car. He took it all."

"You from around here? Any lawyer I might know?" he chewed on his toothpick, eyes still squinting from the bright porch bulb.

"No, sir, I'm from St. Louis. My grandfather used to spend his summers fishing close to here, though. I spent a lot of time here with him when I was a kid. Maybe you knew him? Albert Hershey?" I replied.

Albert Hershey wasn't my grandfather's name, but I'd passed Albert's Tackle before I crossed the bridge, and I had eaten a Hershey bar earlier.

"Don't ring a bell. He still come around here?" the old man questioned.

"No, sir, he died a few years ago. Now that I'm divorced and going through so many emotions, I feel like I need to be someplace that reminds me of him. We were so close. I just need to be someplace where I had a lot of happy childhood memories with him. Oh, that sounds crazy, doesn't it?" I shifted my weight and shook my head.

"Why, no, that ain't crazy. My wife been dead thirteen years now, but sometimes I still get out on my boat just to feel close to her. We spent a lot of time in that boat over the course of thirty eight years. I did a lot of fishing, and she did a lot of complaining. I never knew how much I'd miss that complaining," he grinned at me. "Let me get a flashlight, and I'll show you the camper."

"Thanks," I moved aside as he grabbed a light, put on his slippers, and then walked onto the creaky porch.

"How long you think you'll be staying?" he asked as we walked past the dusty Land Rover and several campers as I kicked pine cones out of the way.

"I'm not quite sure. I just wanted to get away from St. Louis for a while, clear my head, do some thinking. I may stay a week or two if that's okay?" I swatted at a mosquito.

"That ain't no problem. I've rented this camper out to an old fishing buddy of mine every summer for the last couple of years, but he had a stroke a few weeks ago. They got him up at the V.A. hospital in Nashville now. He won't be staying here anymore this year," he coughed as we reached the camper, and he unlocked the door.

"How many campers do you have here?" I looked around the small, dark campground.

"I only got three others besides this one. My brother and his wife stay in that one up closest to me. She sits outside eating and reading all day while he's gone fishing and then she fries his catch when he gets back. She's big as a barn, but she's a sweet gal. She probably won't bother you none," he replied as we stepped into the small camper. He switched on a light and moths swarmed to it from the open screen door.

"The other two campers are fishermen, too. One feller, Gus, lost his wife to the cancer a few months ago. I reckon he is here for kind of the same reasons you are. Says he comes here to clear his head. The other feller is named Monroe. He only comes down on weekends to get away from his old lady. I guess he come here to clear his head, too. River is a good place for that."

I looked around the small space. The camper was old as I was, but it was well kept and clean. There was a small kitchen sink, countertop, gas range and mini fridge. An old massive brown microwave, with a huge turn-knob dial, took up most of the counter space.

"Now, there's a double bed behind that curtain there," he pointed behind me as I pulled the sheet back and saw the double bed covered in a yellow and brown corduroy quilt. "And I just washed them covers a few days ago, too," he added as if it was a special bonus.

"Great," I nodded.

There was a small black and white hound's tooth card table and two orange chairs across from the kitchen area, and an AC unit was stuck in the window above the table. Beyond that was another yellow sheet.

"Behind this curtain is a little cot, see?" He pulled it back for me to look. "You also got you a toilet, sink and stand up shower back here. Everything works just right."

"It looks great," I grinned. I meant it. It didn't compare to the 12,000 square foot home I left in Texas, but it was perfect.

"I take rent by the week. It's seventy five, and that includes water and sewage, electricity. There's a television hooked up back there by the double bed, and we get local channels."

"Seventy five sounds perfect. I sure do appreciate it," I nodded at him as I looked around my new place.

"There's a great view, too. Wait until the sun comes up. The water is right here out your front door. Best view on the river," he pointed out the window.

"I can't wait to see it. I bet it's beautiful, just like I remember with my Papa," I gave an Oscar-winning performance.

"Well, I'm going to need to see some identification and go ahead and get your first week's payment. We can go back up to my house and get all that squared away," he headed out the door.

"Well, there's a little problem there," I sighed.

"Problem?" he turned to me as I made my way down the wobbly camper steps.

"My purse was stolen this afternoon. They got my wallet, my cell phone, everything," I groaned over the chirping of crickets and croaking of bullfrogs.

"Pity," he said.

"I do have cash, though. Thankfully I kept some in my car. I can pay you the rent, but I sure don't have any I.D. with me. I'm going to make some phone calls and get it all squared away tomorrow," I batted sad eyes at him. I looked pitiable, divorced, mourning my dead grandfather, recently robbed and just wanting to clear my head and find myself in a camper on the banks of the Tennessee River.

"Well," he sighed. "I reckon that will be alright. You don't seem like the type to cause no trouble."

"No, sir, scouts honor," I held up my fingers and awkwardly, wrongly, did some kind of scout salute.

"Let's get back up to the house and get some information and that rent then," he turned on the flashlight, and I followed him to his trailer.

I gave him a fake name, the second alias I'd ever used, Charley Dahl, after Charlotte, my favorite childhood ragdoll. I handed him the rent and thanked him again. I grabbed the suitcase from the car, kicked more pine cones in the dark, and I threw myself onto the 70s corduroy quilt. I heaved a collective sigh of relief.

I was free.

THREE

I didn't dream that night. I didn't wake. I slept peacefully as the sounds of nature roared outside. The next morning, when I sat up in the hard bed smothered in a sea of corduroy, I realized Mr. Walter was right. The view was lovely.

The early sun shone down on several fishing boats sitting in the middle of the cove of calm glass-like water. I smiled at the sight and welcomed the peace that accompanied it.

I washed up, threw on another cheap t-shirt and khaki shorts, and I went outside. Pine trees partially blocked my view of the other campers, but as I walked to my car parked on the gravel drive, I saw Mr. Walter's sister-in-law sitting in a lawn chair next to her place. She wore a moo-moo straight out of 1978. Her butt hung over both sides of a poor weak lawn chair as she held a book in one hand and a donut in the other.

I walked quickly to the car, in no mood to introduce myself or exchange pleasantries. I had to get into town and buy some food and toiletries.

My eyes caught the Missouri plates on the back of the Land Rover. I had taken them off of a van at a McDonald's outside of Houston the night that I left. I had my pick of Missouri or Minnesota in the fast food parking lot that evening, but I knew my skin was too tan, my voice too southern to convince anyone I was from Minnesota.

My shopping trip was uneventful. I went to a Wal-Mart and picked up all of the supplies that I needed. I stopped by the clothing section and got Vaiden a Hello Kitty t-shirt. She was twelve now. I didn't know if Hello Kitty was too babyish for her. I didn't know anything about her anymore, but I got the shirt anyway. I had longed to buy her something, anything, for years.

I wanted to buy a pre-paid cell phone, but I figured I probably couldn't get service at the campground, and I didn't want to take any chances of it being traced. I decided I would use the historical payphone that I had spotted at a pharmacy parking lot on my way into town.

I wanted to call home again. I wanted to hear my mother's voice. I wanted to hear Vaiden breathe over the line. I wanted to hear my father's laugh. I needed to hear those things, but I was too scared to call again so soon.

Mr. Walter's sister-in-law was hovering over a smoking grill when I pulled into the campground. I gave her a quick wave as she eyed my dusty car. I pulled closer to the camper this time, and I began lugging the sacks of groceries inside.

"Hello there," she stuck her head through the camper door as I stocked the small cabinets with junk food.

"Hi, how are you?" I smiled at her, dreading having to lie to someone else.

"I'm Clarence's sister-in-law, Dora Walter. Clarence said you'se from Missouri?" she grinned at me, sweat pouring down her round cheeks, her short brown perm damp from the humidity.

"That's right. Charley Dahl," I stuck my hand out to shake hers. Her pudgy fingers gripped mine, and then she used the mint green apron covering her pink and lime striped moo-moo to wipe the perspiration from her brow.

"I just wanted to introduce myself. You and I are the only ladies around these parts. Feel free to stop by and chat any time, okay, dear?" she nodded at me.

"I sure will. Thank you," I replied, relieved that this wasn't going to be a long, drawn out, nosey conversation.

"Clarence said you'se recently divorced?" she continued.

I was wrong.

"Yes, mam, for about three weeks now. I decided to come down here where my grandfather and I used to fish when I was younger," the lies began.

"Who was your grandpappy?" she continued to wipe sweat, her eyes begging me to invite her inside the air-conditioned camper to talk for hours.

"Clark Hershey."

Damn, I'd given the wrong name. I'd given the name of two candy bars. I needed to focus. Getting my lies mixed up was a sure way to get into trouble.

"Don't ring no bells. Where did he fish, exactly? At the resort?" she inquired.

"I don't remember exactly where. It was somewhere close to here. I remember we passed over the bridge and took a few turns. It was kind of a large campground. He passed away years ago so it's been a long time since I've been down here," I said.

"Well, I'm sure he knew my Paul. He's been fishing this stretch of the river for over fifty years. Ain't no one fish around here that didn't know my Paul Walter," she boasted.

"I'm sure he did," I nervously nodded. I really didn't need any fat ladies or old fishermen inquiring about my family tree.

"What was his name again?" she asked.

"Albert Hershey," I redeemed myself.

A confused look covered her chubby face.

"Albert Clark Hershey. I may have said Clark earlier. A lot of folks called him Clark," I said. I was relieved when she appeared to have bought it.

"I will have to ask my Paul. Who knows? They could've been big buddies. My Paul might have great stories about your grandpappy. Wouldn't that be fun?" she chuckled, her belly jiggling, her jowls jiggling and the ground beneath her jiggling.

"That would be wonderful," I giggled. "Well, I better get this place cleaned up. I have a lot of groceries to put away. I appreciate you stopping by. Hopefully we can have a girls chat before I head out."

"When you think you're gonna be heading on, dear?" she questioned.

I sighed.

"I'm not sure yet. I just need to clear my head. I'm probably going to go back to my parent's house in St. Louis once I figure out a couple of things and take some time for myself," I fibbed, wishing she would leave. Mr. Walter said she probably wouldn't bother me none. Mr. Walter was obviously wrong. I had a feeling this lady would be bothering me plenty.

"Well, that's good, honey. Take all the time you need. If I can help you with anything, just holler at me, alright?" she headed towards her camper and gave me a wave.

"Thank you!" I called out to her. I shut the camper door and ripped open a bag of Doritos.

Surprisingly, Mrs. Walter didn't worry me anymore that day. She walked around eating, reading, and cleaning fish once her husband pulled in that afternoon. I was thankful she didn't drag her Paul Walter down to inquire about my fictional candy bar grandfather.

I watched Gus and Monroe pull up on a bass boat before sunset and part ways. I figured out who was who when Gus headed inside his trailer, and Monroe climbed into his pickup truck and, I assume, headed home to his old lady. This was seeming to be the perfect place to hide, to recuperate, to rest; just me, a bunch of old fishermen that kept to themselves, and Dora. Hopefully Dora would take a lesson from the fishermen and keep to herself, too.

I'd been waiting to see the 5 o'clock news all day. Once it was on, I stretched across the double bed, ham sandwich in my hand, and I waited.

Ten minutes in and nothing was said about Jonathan or me. Terrorists, the economy, and the brewing storm in the Gulf all took precedence over a missing housewife from Texas. I felt relieved. I smoked a cigarette and looked around the small place and the decades old décor. I actually laughed out loud. I hadn't laughed out loud in so long.

I laughed because I was free, because the news didn't show his photo, my photo, our story. Because being in that old camper made me feel like I was in a scene from *Urban Cowboy*.

FOUR

September 4, 2001 was a rainy Tuesday in Nashville. I'd fixed Vaiden's lunch, a peanut butter and jelly sandwich and cheese crackers. I remember her sitting in her booster seat, blonde ringlets covering her head, jelly covering her lips and her hands as she watched *Blue's Clues* on the television setting on the kitchen counter. She was wearing a pink t-shirt with an elephant on it. I remember Mama wiping a glob of purple jelly from the elephant's ear as I waved goodbye and walked out the door.

I had only been at the mall for a few minutes, browsing the children's section at Dillard's, when I noticed him smiling at me from the shoe department. He was gorgeous and tall with dark hair and aqua eyes. I gave a bashful grin as he walked towards me. He used adjectives like "gorgeous" and "stunning". Since Vaiden had been born and left my once athletic body soft with stretch marks, compliments like his were just the self-esteem boost I needed.

"Why is such a young beautiful girl shopping in the children's department? You can't be a mother. You must be a big sister."

"I have a daughter. She's two," I blushed. "I also have a boyfriend. He's twenty."

"Well," he smiled, "how lucky they both are, to always be in *your* presence."

I smiled nervously.

"Have a good day," he winked at me and walked away.

An hour had passed. I quickly threw the bags of my daughter's clothes into the trunk as the rain poured down and soaked me to the bone. I just knew that my hair was going to frizz. It was going to look terrible for dinner with Nathan that evening.

I jumped into the car, the rain sticking to my clothes and my legs sticking to the leather seats of my Camry. I checked my hair in the rear-view mirror and sighed in disgust at my brown bob growing in the humidity.

The passenger side door flung open, and there he was again.

I didn't know whether to scream, to blow the horn, to dig my fingernails into his attractive face and his strong cheekbones. I just sat there, silent. I was stunned that there was a stranger in my car.

"Listen carefully to me, Elle," he threw a duffel bag into the back seat.

"How do you know my name?" my heart pounded through my shirt.

"Listen to me. You are going to drive now. You are not going to do anything crazy. Do you understand? You are merely going to drive where I tell you to drive, do you understand?"

First rule of survival: never drive. Never leave. I knew this. I knew I was supposed to jump out of the car- running, screaming, causing as much attention as possible. I reached for the door handle, prepared to do what I knew would keep me alive.

"Vaiden Bingham, two-year-old. Nathan Bingham, twenty-year-old. Your mother is Judith Holley. Your father is Martin Holley, retired History teacher at Hillsboro High. You have a younger sister, Emma, who is in Algebra class right now. You are a student at Tennessee State. You skipped English Lit this morning. Your address is 542 Pine Hills. Do you understand what I am saying? If you run out of this car, I can find you. I know all about you. If you want to save your family and your daughter then you will not get out of this car. You will do exactly as I say," he replied, calm, cool, his dark hair damp from the rain, his black jacket strikingly contrast against the car seat's light tan leather.

My heart continued to race. Tears blinded my eyes. I knew I was going to die. I knew I wasn't going to jump out of the car- running, screaming, causing as much attention as possible. I knew I had been defeated.

"How- how do you know all of this?"

"Drive," he instructed.

I drove, fighting the urge to urinate on myself, my legs trembling and my arms numb. I drove further and further away from my parents, my Nathan and my reason for living, my precious Vaiden.

He didn't flash a weapon. He didn't put a gun to my head or a knife to my throat. He actually turned on the radio and sang along to Alice in Chains. A smile covered his face as we hit the interstate and traveled miles and hours away from Nashville.

"Here's what's going to happen, Elle Marie Holley."

He was disassembling my cell phone, crunching pieces of it beneath his shiny black shoes, and then he rolled down the window and tossed it into the rain. "You are going to be my wife now."

"What?" I asked. "You aren't going to kill me?"

He laughed.

"I'm not going to kill you, pretty girl. I'm going to save you. I'm going to save you from a life of monotony. I'm going to save you from being a mother, being a slave to Nathan who could never provide you the kind of life you deserve. I'm giving you a life, don't you see that?" he reached over and grazed my cheek with his thumb. I shuddered.

"I don't understand," I stared at the road ahead.

"I saw you in the Miami airport back in June. You were waiting on your flight home after your family vacation. Little Vaiden was in your arms. Your mother bought her a stuffed dolphin, I think it was, in the gift shop? From the moment I first saw you, I knew I had to make you mine," he smiled at me.

"Where are we going?" I asked, still confused, still shaking, still scared, but somehow not as terrified.

"Houston, Texas," he rapped his fingers on the console to the tune on the radio.

"Why?" I asked, my eyes darting along the road. I wanted to rear-end someone, cause an accident or flash my lights. I wanted to open the door and roll out of my car as we sailed eighty miles per hour down the interstate.

"You really have no idea who I am, do you?" he asked, surprised.

"Should I?" I glanced at him.

I knew he was crazy and psychotic, but I couldn't overlook the fact that he was handsome as well.

"My name is Jonathan Marsh. My father is Thomas Marsh. You know, Thomas Marsh, the former mayor of the great city of Houston, Texas? We are a very prominent family, do you understand?"

I didn't know who in hell Thomas Marsh was. I didn't know a damn thing about Houston, Texas. I didn't know why he thought I should know such things.

"Why do you want me? It sounds like you can have anyone. Why do you want me?" I begged for answers.

"I don't know. When I saw you, I just wanted you. I didn't come to Miami with some crazy plan to see a girl in the airport, research her and bring her home, but I've never looked at a woman and just had to have her. I had to have you," he tried to make it sound romantic.

"You can't just take me away. I have a family. I have a child. I am a child! I am only twenty-years-old!" I exclaimed as tears streamed down my face.

I had to crash the car. I had to cause a diversion. I had to get home.

"I am Jonathan Marsh. I can do whatever I damn well please," he said.

I didn't wreck the car. I didn't throw open the door and jump out as we flew down I-40. I did exactly what he said because he made it clear that if I caused any problems he would hurt my family. I believed him. He seemed powerful. He seemed like he could do whatever he damn well pleased.

When he told me to pull over at a gas station in Wynne, Arkansas, he finally revealed the weapon. It was a shiny handgun, concealed in his jacket pocket. He instructed me to walk to the payphone, dial my parent's number and tell them exactly what we had rehearsed in the car. I held back sobs when my father's voice came over the line.

"Keep it together," he put his arm around my waist, "and sound convincing."

"Daddy," I cleared my throat.

"Elle, where are you? Nathan is already here. Your mother tried to call your cellular phone," Daddy said sternly over the sound of the television roaring in the background.

"Daddy, I've got some news," I looked at Jonathan as he nodded in approval.

"What is it? We are supposed to be at the restaurant in-"

"I'm not coming home, Daddy," I interrupted him as I fought back tears.

"What?"

"Listen, I've met someone else. I'm in love, and we are getting married," I said as convincingly as possible. I knew my daddy wasn't going to believe this story.

"Elle, be serious. What's going on?" he asked.

I startled as Jonathan pressed the gun into my side.

"Daddy, I'm not coming home! I mean it! Do not come looking for me, do you understand!" I exclaimed, frightened at the feel of the weapon against my flesh.

"Elle, are you in trouble? Are you? Answer me!" Daddy yelled into the phone.

"No, Daddy, I'm not in trouble. I've decided not to come home. Don't come looking for me, do you understand? Tell me you understand!" I shouted.

Jonathan nudged me and mouthed for me to keep my voice down.

"Elle? I just can't- I can't believe. I can't- what about Vaiden and Nathan? What about us, Elle? Who the hell is this guy? Where are you going? Are you in trouble!?" Daddy was furious.

I struggled to remember the fake name, the fake city, the fake love story that we had practiced in the car. I was no good at lying then.

"His name is Michael Kee. He's from Chicago. I met him at a club months ago. We are in love, Daddy."

"This is absolutely damn ridiculous, Elle! I refuse to believe this. You need to get home right this minute, do you hear me?" I knew Daddy's face was red. I knew that vein in his shiny forehead was bulging.

"I'm sorry, Daddy," I began to cry. "Kiss Mama for me. Kiss my Vaiden."

Jonathan pried the phone from my hand.

"Mr. Holley, your baby girl is fine. I will take care of her now," he said as he hung up on my screaming father.

"My daddy won't settle for this," I cried softly. "He will search for me. He will find me."

"Get in the car," he walked me to the driver's door, placed me in the car, and we merged onto the interstate.

FIVE

Once we reached Little Rock, I was forced to take a sedative. Jonathan said I needed to rest. He said I had a busy schedule ahead of me.

He was very intimidating. He seemed powerful. He seemed intelligent. And aside from the kidnapping, he didn't seem all *that* crazy. He was also very convincing, and I believed it when he said that he wasn't going to kill me. Of course I was terrified of what waited in my future. I didn't know if I would ever see my parents or my daughter again. I was frightened, I was anxious, but I believed this psychopath. I believed that he was going to take care of me.

When I woke, the sky was dark. I didn't jerk or wake hysterical. I glanced at Jonathan in the driver seat singing Neil Young quietly. He looked at me, and he smiled. He smiled at me like we were old lovers. He smiled at me like stealing a girl from her family was a completely normal thing to do.

"Where are we?" my voice was groggy and hoarse.

"Houston. We have to make a stop at my dealership," he said as he turned on the blinker.

"Dealership?" I asked, looking out the window as beautiful homes whizzed by. The streets were damp from an earlier rain.

"I own the most successful Jaguar and Land Rover dealership in Houston," he boasted.

"Great. I'm so glad some psycho with a used Honda car lot didn't kidnap me," I said dryly.

"You're funny, Elle. I'm so glad that you're funny," he grinned.

We pulled into the dealership, the expensive cars wet with rain under the bright lights. Jonathan typed in some numbers on a key pad, a gate opened, and my car circled to the back of the building.

When he got out of my Camry, I knew I should run. Before I could open the door and take off down streets in an unknown city, he opened the passenger door, and he gently took my hand.

"You want to do some car shopping?"

"I want to go home," I replied.

"You are home," he walked me to the back of the building and unlocked the door.

We stepped into a dark room. He switched on the lights and an enormous office was revealed. It was decorated elegantly. Tapestries hung from the walls. A large cherry desk sat in the middle of a Persian rug, surrounded by leather chairs.

"Sit down," he pointed me to one of the plush seats.

I did as I was told, taking in my surroundings, not believing that this was really happening to me.

"I have all new documentation for you," he winked at me, as if I should thank him for taking care of everything.

He tossed a manila envelope into my lap, and I was instructed to open it. He sat at his desk and began clicking on his computer.

In the envelope was a birth certificate.

"How did you do this?" I asked.

"I can do anything," he said, confidently, his eyes never leaving the computer screen.

"Claire Harper?" I asked.

"I think Claire is a beautiful name, don't you? You look like a Claire," he continued to tap on the keyboard.

It looked legitimate. Claire Elise Harper, born in Oklahoma County, Oklahoma on March 23, 1981, to Robert and Ann Franklin Harper.

"I don't understand. How can you get away with this? How can you just invent someone like this?" I held up the birth certificate, stunned.

"I told you that I can do anything, Claire. Now, we have to get a couple of things straight. You have to memorize a new past. You have to start all over. I know this is going to be hard for you, but you can do it," he reassured me.

"Please let me go home," I begged.

"Your parents died in a car accident when you were small. You had no living grandparents or close relatives. You were put into foster care when you were four. I have all of the documentation to back that up if anyone ever asks, which they won't," he finally looked away from his computer screen and reclined in his chair.

"You did well in foster care. A wonderful English lady by the name of Marion Stewart took you into her home in Oklahoma City. She loved you. She was your mother figure, you understand? You had a wonderful childhood with her. Say her name. Marion."

"Marion," I repeated, tears welling up in my eyes.

"You did not attend college. You've never held a real job aside from babysitting for neighbors. It just seemed easier that way, not having to produce W2 forms and whatnot."

I was pretty sure he could have come up with W2 forms, any forms, if he wanted.

"I met you several months ago while I was in Oklahoma City looking at a shipment of Jaguars. Our eyes caught at the Bordeaux Club. It was love at first sight. Isn't that sweet?" he stood and walked behind me and squeezed my shoulders.

"Your beloved Marion passed away a few weeks ago from a sudden heart attack. You and I have been talking on the phone and the computer every day for weeks. I have copies of all of our emails. I've finally convinced you to move to Texas to be with me. As of," he looked at his watch, "forty five minutes ago, you finally arrived in Houston. We are both ecstatic!" he exclaimed.

"I can't do this," I mumbled.

"Of course you can, Elle," he knelt beside me and covered my hands with his. "I have all of this written down for you. Cliff's Notes if you will."

"You don't have children?" I studied his face.

He shook his head.

"Then you don't know the love between a parent and child. I cannot survive without my daughter, do you understand?" I pleaded with him.

"I know it's going to be hard, but she is in good hands with your parents. You will learn to live without her," he said as if this was supposed to comfort me.

"I will kill myself," I stated.

His face turned rigid and he removed his hands from mine.

"You won't do that, do you understand? You will not bring that kind of shame upon me or my family. If you do that, your family will suffer. I will make sure of it," he promised. "I am going to throw you into the lap of luxury. I am going to mold you into the ultimate socialite. You are going to have a good life."

My eyes fell to my lap. He could see how distraught I was.

"Look," he cleared his throat. "Maybe later I can work something out with your kid, okay?"

"What do you mean?" I wiped tears from my cheeks.

"I mean," he stood up, "maybe we can bring her out here. I don't know. I have to think on it. You just obey the rules, and I will work something out."

"Thank you," I said. I wanted to be in his good graces. I knew conforming to his plan would be the only way to see my daughter again.

He sat back at his desk across from me.

"Okay, a tap has been placed on your parent's home phone. I was surprised to learn that they don't own cell phones, it being 21st century and all," he snickered. "However, I've got Nathan's home and mobile tapped and several other family members and friends have surveillance on their phones as well. Do you understand this?"

"I can't call anyone," I stated.

"Right. I also have some people in Nashville keeping a close watch on your family. I will know if you contact them. Please understand that if you attempt to contact them, you and your family will be punished. If you run away, they will be punished. If you tell anyone about this, if you do anything to ruin this, if you ever smear my name, my reputation, if you ever act any other way than as an obedient, loving wife, your family will suffer. I don't want to do that, Elle, but I will if I have to," he said.

Again, I believed him.

"I'm a high-profile person in this area. You will be attending parties, charities, auctions, and all kinds of events with me. Your photo will likely be in the paper and local magazines. Our wedding alone will be the social event of the season. We have to keep this closely monitored. I mean, the last thing I need is for your family or friends back home to see your photographs, to know where you are. From day one of our marriage, you are going to let it be known how much you hate being photographed. We are going to make a public statement about how we want our privacy, blah blah blah. It's always going to be that way. You are going to portray yourself as a classy woman who values her privacy. Understood?" he asked.

I nodded silently.

"You've got to meet my family. They've been hearing about you for months. They know you are in Houston tonight. They know that we are in love and that I have every intention of marrying you," he reached across his desk and tossed a stack of stapled papers to me.

"That is all of the information about my parents, my brother, my extended family, best friends. Everything that you would have learned about me during our long-distance relationship can be found in that packet," he stated. "We will go over all of it later."

I flipped through the pages, my head spinning.

"Now you need a car. You can pick anything on the lot," he smiled.

"Awesome," I dryly replied.

"Come on, Elle. How many twenty-year-old girls get to drive away in a new Land Rover, hmm?" he clicked his tongue.

"A Land Rover in exchange for my family? You sure know how to cheer a girl up," I stated.

"Okay, come over here and let's look out the window," he stood and pulled back the heavy burgundy drapes. The wall-length window overlooked the showroom of luxurious British cars.

"I don't really care," I said, uninterested.

"Do you like the black Range Rover there?" he pointed through the glass to the shiny SUV. "I think you'd look good in that one."

"You trust me to drive? You don't think I will run?" I asked.

"I know you won't go anywhere. You will be followed closely, and there will be a tracking device on the car anyway. If you leave this city, I will know. If you leave this city, if you stray from your designated route, your family will suffer the consequences," he put his arm around me and pulled me close. I took in the scent of Coolwater Cologne. The same cologne my Nathan wore.

I pulled away.

"Black it is," he turned away from the window.

He drove my Camry into a garage and removed the tags. He said it would be impounded.

"Wait!" I exclaimed as we began to pull away in my new vehicle. "Can I have the clothing out of the trunk? The clothing I bought for my daughter? Can I have my purse, the pictures of her in my wallet? Please?" I begged.

He stopped the Range Rover, heavy with that new car smell, and he stared ahead into the dark. He thought for a moment, and then he answered.

"No."

I sobbed quietly as we pulled away.

SIX

It was nearly 4 AM when we pulled through the mansion gate. I stared out the window in awe at the elegant home. I was born and raised a middle-class girl. Aside from the other shocks I had suffered throughout the day, I was now in culture shock.

He parked the Range Rover in the five car garage next to other luxurious makes and models I'd never seen before. He opened the passenger door and took my hand to help me out of the car. I followed him into the house and immediately shivered and wrapped my arms around myself.

"I'm very hot natured, and I keep the house pretty cold. That's something else you are going to have to adapt to, I suppose," he said as I trailed behind him down the dim, frigid hallway.

He began flicking switches and gorgeous chandeliers came to life. Oversized furniture filled the home and gigantic paintings covered the walls.

We stopped in the large kitchen lined with white cabinets and black granite counter tops. I eyed the shiny, stainless Sub-Zero refrigerator and vent hood, which both looked very commercial.

"I can't cook. What am I supposed to do with all of this?" I looked around the gourmet kitchen.

"You can learn," he winked at me and gently pulled me out of the kitchen and down another hallway.

We passed many doors, tables, lamps, artwork, my head still spinning. We walked up the winding staircase in the front foyer and down another hall. There were more doors, tables, lamps, artwork. We finally entered a room at the end of the hallway. The light turned on to reveal a plush, girly bedroom.

"Do you like it?" he smiled at me and searched my face for approval.

"It's nice," I said, eying the mint green walls, the pink eyelet bedding, flowery chenille rugs covering the dark hardwood. The poster bed was bulky and white. The matching dresser and chest were covered in vases of fresh flowers, crystal figurines and popular fashion magazines.

"I want you to be comfortable," he walked around the room.

"You aren't forcing me to sleep with you?"

"I knew you wouldn't be comfortable with that. Not yet, anyway," he opened the bathroom door and motioned for me to look.

I slowly walked over to the door and peeked inside at the marble tub, walk-in shower, and the pink hydrangea blooms on the vanity.

"Check this out," he walked into the bathroom and opened another door. It was a huge walk-in closet stocked with clothing, shoes, purses and accessories.

"I have everything you need, down to the underwear and earrings," he said, opening a drawer in one of the built-ins. He held up a pair of white underwear. They weren't trampy or slinky. They were plain old granny panty underwear, probably out of a Hanes 12 pack.

I didn't know what to say. Was I supposed to thank this man for doing all of this for me? Was I supposed to thank him for bringing me here, decorating a room for me, buying me clothing and jewelry? Was I supposed to thank him for taking me away from my family?

"You could say thank you, Claire," he said.

"Thank you," I looked down at my feet.

I wanted to shout to him that Claire wasn't my name. I wanted to run down the winding staircase, through the lavish home and scream for help. Instead, I thanked him.

"You're welcome," he passed me and went back into the bedroom. "You need to get ready for bed. Don't think about trying to escape, Claire. Don't do it. This room is being watched. We aren't alone in this house. If you think of running, you will be caught."

As if being there alone with him wasn't frightening enough, the thought of someone else in the house terrified me.

"There are pajamas in one of the dresser drawers. I have all of the toiletries you need in the bathroom," he walked out of the room. "Good night."

I dressed in a silk turquoise gown. I went into the bathroom to wash my face and noticed there were no razors in any of the drawers. I assumed this was a precaution in case I wanted to slit my wrists. I stood in the middle of the bedroom, taking in my surroundings. I examined the windows, wishing I could open them and jump to safety. Instead I discovered a bolt-like lock secured to them. The fall to the concrete below would probably kill me, anyway, and he didn't want me to escape *or* die.

I crawled into the tall soft bed. I lie there freezing, motionless, staring at the ceiling. I didn't sleep, not for a moment. I spent the long, cold hours weeping, missing my family and formulating a plan to see them again.

When the sun had been peeking through the locked bay windows for hours, I decided to sit up in the bed. I didn't know if I was allowed to roam the house and go downstairs to find some food, or if I was locked away in the East Wing like Belle in "Beauty and the Beast".

I'd only been sitting up for a few moments, looking around the room, my face still damp from the crying I had done throughout the night, when the door opened and a man stood before me.

"Good morning, Miss Claire," he nodded to me.

He was a middle-aged Hispanic man with more of a Texan accent than a Spanish one. He was tall, broad-shouldered, clean shaven. His jet-black pompadour was slicked back on his head. He wore khaki pants, a white button-down shirt, and a tan jacket. He reminded me of Lou Diamond Phillips.

I pulled the covers close to my body, unsure if this man was sent to hurt me, kill me or offer me breakfast in bed.

"I'm not going to hurt you," he noticed my anxiety and gave me a comforting grin.

I unclenched the blankets.

"My name is Ernesto. I am Mr. Jonathan's personal assistant," he tilted his head from side to side as if to relieve a crick in his neck. "Mr. Jonathan would like you to join him for breakfast."

I nodded.

"Feel free to shower or whatever you need to do and then join him in the kitchen. Take your time," he spoke kindly as he left the room, closing the door behind him.

I hesitantly got out of the bed and walked to the bathroom. I looked around, wondering if cameras were watching me, wondering if my naked body was being broadcast on a television monitor somewhere in the home. I covered myself with one of the oversized towels on the vanity, and I jumped into the walk-in shower, slamming the glass door behind me.

The chrome shower caddy was filled with many body washes, shampoos, and loofa sponges. I felt like I did the time my father was a contestant on *Wheel of Fortune* and we stayed in some posh hotel. I had stood in that California shower trying all of the different gels, soaps and lotions until the bathroom smelled like a flower shop and citrus farm had collided. That morning was different, though, as I quickly scrubbed my body with a bar of plain soap and rinsed my hair.

I dressed in blue jeans and a pink tank top, both of which fit perfectly. I scanned the shoes on the shelf before me-heels, flip flops, shoes for every occasion, all in the right size eight. I trembled at how he had obtained so many details about me-all the way down to my shoe size.

I didn't know my way around the home, but I slowly navigated the stairs and hallways and managed to find the kitchen. There he was, with Ernesto, sitting on a wrought iron pub stool at the kitchen bar. He was dressed in light blue cotton pajama pants, a plain white t-shirt, and his bare feet were resting on a bar at the bottom of the stool. His hair was dark and messy on his head, and stubble covered his cheeks and chin. He turned to look at me, a broad smile covering his face, as he held a piece of toast and told me to come eat.

I cautiously sat on a stool at the opposite end of the bar.

"I won't bite, Claire," he slid a dish of scrambled eggs, bacon, hash browns and biscuits down to me. "Eat up."

I began shoving the food into my mouth, famished after not eating for twenty four hours.

"You didn't sleep well?" he asked.

I shook my head.

"You did a lot of crying last night," he glanced at me and took a swig of orange juice.

He'd seen me crying. There were a million nooks and crannies in that room. Now I was sure cameras were hidden everywhere.

"I expect you are going to be doing a lot of crying at first, but you will learn to love it here," he nodded.

Ernesto nodded as well, eating bacon and watching me closely.

"You have a busy day. Ernesto is going to take you into town for a makeover. You are also going to study and prepare to meet my parents this weekend. You really need to get some sleep tonight. You have a lot to learn over the next few days," he replied.

I rode silently in the passenger seat of Ernesto's Ford truck. I gazed out the window at the beautiful homes passing by and the mothers pushing their children in strollers down the shady streets.

I thought about my family and what they were doing at that moment. It was Wednesday morning. Vaiden had her Tunes for Tots music class at the church. I wondered if my mother had taken her, as to not disrupt her routine.

Surely my mother was too distraught to focus on the Hokey Pokey. I knew she was probably curled up on the couch, surrounded by wads of Kleenex, praying I would walk through the door.

Vaiden was probably asking where I was. "Mama be back?" she would say when I was gone for more than a few minutes. Although my mother cared for her while I spent so many hours at school and studying, Vaiden was very much a mama's girl.

Vaiden loved her daddy, too. Nathan was a wonderful father. He had a demanding schedule helping his father work their farm and studying Agricultural Education at Tennessee State, along with driving a forklift on the night shift at Thomas Plastics, but he spent every free moment with Vaiden and me.

My father was surely reclined in his worn leather chair, watching *The Price is Right*. Daddy was loud. His overbearing voice roared throughout the house as he screamed out prices and called people idiots when they overbid by thousands on a cheap compact car.

Vaiden would crawl onto his lap and shake her fist at the television and say, "Id-yut, Papa! Id-yut!" My daddy was so proud of his granddaughter for calling idiots "id-yut" at the tender age of two.

My baby sister, Emma, had most likely stayed home from school. She hated school. She hated waking early. She hated doing anything besides watching MTV and talking on the phone to boys. She was probably ecstatic that I'd gone missing. It gave her a legitimate reason to miss her math quiz.

No, that wasn't true. Although we often argued, Emma loved me dearly, as I loved her. I'm sure she had sad, puffy eyes and anxiety about my absence (but secretly enjoyed the day off).

I wondered if my family and Nathan had bought the story about running away with some stranger from Chicago. Surely they hadn't. They knew I couldn't leave any of them, especially Vaiden. The police were probably camped out in my front yard at that moment. Some detective in a gray suit was asking my father questions about the mysterious phone call. My photo was on the Nashville news. A search party, complete with bloodhounds, was combing the woods behind my house. No one would believe that I would leave everything behind and run away with some stranger.

I had no idea how Jonathan Marsh would get away with this or why he thought taking someone was so easy.

As we rode in the truck, Ernesto remained silent. He knew what was going on. He knew I had been stolen from a life very different than this. He knew I didn't belong here. He was privy to the crimes that were being committed, but he drove calmly, slowly, and we pulled into the parking lot of a boutique on a bustling street.

He walked to the passenger side and let me out of the truck.

"Play along, Miss Claire," he mumbled as we walked across the parking lot. "Please play along."

Ernesto was an intimidating man. His size, his stature, his slick black hair all seemed threatening. As intimidating as he was, he continued to address me in a kind tone; but I could easily picture him sliding a razor blade across my throat if I got out of line.

When we walked inside the salon, the smell of hair dye and a young girl with a bright red pixie cut greeted us.

"Claire," she smiled, a small silver ring hanging from her bottom lip, charcoal-colored make up heavy around her blue eyes. A bright tattoo of a fish covered her entire right arm extending from the black tank top.

I gave a pitifully convincing smile.

"It's so great to meet you!" she exclaimed. "Jonathan has told me so much about you."

I nodded silently.

"Well, let's get you started," she motioned for me to follow her to the back of the salon. "Ernesto, I'll work as quickly as I can.
"

"Take your time," Ernesto replied as he sat down in a chair and picked up *Harper's Bazaar.*

"Silly me, I didn't even introduce myself. I am Camilla Cross," she smiled.

"Hi," I said quietly, sitting in the chair, looking at myself in the mirror.

I looked tired. I looked scared. I didn't look like I was ecstatic to finally be in Houston, Texas with the love of my life.

"So, Jonathan said you wanted blonde extensions, right?"

"That's the plan," I replied.

I wanted to beg this girl for help, but the shop was small and empty. Ernesto was still in earshot.

"You have lovely hair," she ran her fingers through my short, layered, caramel locks. "Is this your natural color?"

"My natural is a little darker. I get it foiled back home," I stopped myself before I started talking about Abby, my hairstylist in Nashville.

"Well, Jonathan said you wanted a change. Long and blonde is certainly going to be a change," she began mixing up color in a small plastic bowl.

"Sure is."

"I'm mixing up a honey blonde. That's what Jonathan said you wanted. Does that still sound okay? It won't look bleached out in any way. It will be subtle."

"Honey blonde sounds fine," I continued staring at myself in the mirror, then at Ernesto behind us in the waiting area. He glanced at me several times and went back to reading the ladies' magazine.

"So, tell me all about yourself, Claire," Camilla said as she applied the color to my hair, dripping it onto the leopard print shawl around my neck.

Ernesto immediately looked at me as I tried to remember what I was supposed to say.

"Not much to tell, really," I answered.

Camilla gave me a confused look. She wasn't an idiot. She knew something wasn't right with my demeanor. I was supposed to be in love with Jonathan, happy to change my hair, my life. My face, my voice, and my attitude all screamed the opposite.

"I'm sorry if I'm a little out of sorts. I'm just dealing with a lot of change right now," I tried to redeem myself as Ernesto continued to watch me.

Camilla's face softened.

"It's completely understandable. Jonathan told me about your foster mother dying suddenly and how you just packed up and moved out here to be with him. That's a lot to deal with at one time."

I nodded.

"Well, I've been cutting Jonathan's hair for a few months now. My mother was the Marsh family stylist for years until she passed away in April," she continued to douse my hair in chemicals.

"Sorry to hear that," I solemnly said.

"He was telling me all about you at his appointment last week. How you met in the club in Oklahoma City, how he was so thrilled that you were coming out here to be with him. He said you were just beautiful. He was right," she grinned at me in the mirror.

"Thank you," I shifted my eyes down to my lap.

"He just lit up when he spoke about you. Jonathan is such a great guy. I'm so glad he's finally found someone. That you found each other," she said.

"Tell me about him."

"Like what?" she asked, wiping color from my earlobe with a hand towel.

"Well, we are still learning so much about each other. I'm anxious to hear things about him from the people that have known him for a long time," I said, Ernesto still watching me, monitoring my attitude, my questions.

"Well, I used to have the biggest crush on him!" she chuckled. "My mother did his mother's hair and makeup when his father was in office. I used to tag along to their house, and I thought Jonathan was the bee's knees. I mean, he's quite a bit older than me, but he sure is a handsome devil, isn't he?"

Devil for certain.

"Now, how old are you?" I inquired when it occurred to me that I had no idea how old Jonathan was.

"I just turned twenty one. Jonathan says you are twenty, is that right?" she asked.

I nodded.

"Well, if I'd had known that he liked such younger women, I would have made more of an effort to go after him!" she nudged my shoulder and laughed again.

I pretended to laugh. I wished she had pursued him, that they had fallen in love and that I was still at home.

"How old was he when you thought he was the 'bee's knees'?" I asked, still trying to determine my future husband's age.

"Well, I was about thirteen so he was maybe twenty three or so," she worked quickly on my hair.

My God. The man was at least thirty one-years-old. What did he want with a twenty-year-old child? And what did I want with an old man? Nothing. I wanted absolutely nothing with him.

"He's just such a nice guy, too. I mean, he's always in the paper for the kind things he's done. You know, donating money to churches and the homeless and personally delivering coats to those poor kids at Christmas. The man is a saint. You've really lucked out, girl," Camilla nodded.

The man was giving poor kids warmth, homeless people soup, appearing to be a saint to the entire city of Houston, Texas, and yet, he was a thief. He was a monster.

Camilla finished applying the hair color, and then she sewed fourteen –inch blonde hair to my head. She continued to babble about what a wonderful man Jonathan was, to the point that I was certain that she was in love with him. For all I knew, she was included in this crazy arrangement. I began to wonder if she knew I had been kidnapped, but was so enamored with Jonathan that she would go along with his plan and keep her mouth shut.

However, my suspicions about her knowledge of the situation soon faded. Her questions were genuine, as if she had no idea who I really was. She seemed to sincerely believe the love story that Jonathan had told her about us. She gazed at me with jealousy, as if she wished she were me. She wished she were the one marrying Jonathan Marsh. I wished it was her, too.

When she spun me around to face the mirror, my jaw dropped. I looked completely different with long, straight, blonde hair. In fact, I looked great. The lengthy light locks complimented my dark skin, my pale blue eyes and my oval shaped face. Wispy bangs swept across my forehead and the fake hair blended in perfectly with my natural mane. I thought my short, brown layers had looked good for so many years until I saw the new me.

But as nice as I thought I looked, I wasn't going to be giddy and overjoyed because I finally had long and beautiful hair. I still longed for my daughter and loathed my situation. New hair could never change that.

"You look gorgeous, Claire!" Camilla patted herself on the back.

"Thank you."

I wasn't Claire, this wasn't my real hair, but I thanked her.

Ernesto nodded in approval, "You look great, Miss Claire. Nice job, Miss Camilla."

Camilla waxed my eyebrows, my legs and my bikini line. She gave me a manicure and pedicure while I drank sparkling cider and snacked on some kind of pretty crackers topped with a fancy cheese spread. She covered my face in creams and makeup until my complexion was fresh.

"Come see me again soon!" she shouted, hours later, as Ernesto and I walked out the door. "Tell Jonathan I said hello!"

As Ernesto drove us back to the house, I kept looking at my reflection in the truck's passenger side window. I couldn't believe the girl in the glass was me.

"Mr. Jonathan is going to take good care of you, Miss Claire," Ernesto glanced over at me.

I said nothing.

"He asked Camilla to clear her calendar for the day so she could do all of this for you. He paid her extra just so you could have the place to yourselves and get the pampering that you deserve. He's a good man, Miss Claire."

I still said nothing.

"I can imagine that this experience will be difficult for you in the beginning, but you will see how much he loves you."

"I have a family and a child. I belong with them," I looked at Ernesto, my face rigid and angry.

He looked back at the highway.

"Well, your hair looks nice."

SEVEN

When I walked into the freezing mansion, chill bumps immediately formed on my arms. If this man was going to hold me hostage, he would have to put a heater in my room and stock my closet with sweatshirts and robes.

"Mr. Jonathan!" Ernesto called as we rounded the corner and entered the kitchen.

"Coming!" I heard his voice call from somewhere in the house. I caught a glimpse of myself in the kitchen cupboard glass, and I still couldn't believe it was me. I was certain that Nathan would think I looked beautiful. I missed my Nathan terribly.

"My God!" he said when he entered the kitchen, his face and hair wet with perspiration. Sweat stains covered his gray t-shirt. He must have been exercising because there was no possible way any human could sweat in a house so cold. Maybe he wasn't human. Maybe he was some vile and evil creature from another planet, another dimension. It would explain much.

"You look absolutely stunning, Claire!" he gawked at me as I became embarrassed and looked to the floor.

"Hey," he walked to me. "Don't ever underestimate how beautiful you are."

I thought his words were gentle, comforting. I hated that I thought such a thing about him. He was a monster. He was a dagger dipped in honey.

"Thank you," I said quietly, still looking to my freshly painted toenails.

"Look at me," he softly took my chin in his hands and tilted my face so that my eyes caught his. "You are beautiful. You are absolutely beautiful."

His complimentary words sounded as gentle and sincere as the first time he spoke them to me in the department store, but now they made me cringe.

I was instructed to shower and wear something nice to dinner. I searched the closet, tears streaming down my cheeks at the heartache of missing Vaiden, and I selected a red fitted top and black linen pants. I applied my makeup, brushed my new hair, and I went to the dining room.

When I entered, Jonathan stood from the large table. He wore a pink Oxford cloth button down, the sleeves loosely rolled to his elbows. His shirt tail hung casually over his neatly pressed khaki shorts. His face was clean shaven, his dark hair still wet from the shower. He walked over and pulled the heavy cherry chair from the table as I sat down.

"You look amazing, of course," he replied as he sat next to me at the head of the table.

"Thank you," I looked at the feast before me.

"I can't take credit for this," he smiled. "I had it catered."

"It looks delicious," I said, dryly, as I put the linen napkin in my lap.

"Do you like wine, Elle?" he held up a bottle.

"I'm too young to drink," I said. "And you called me Elle. You better catch yourself next time."

He gave a quiet grin.

"You're correct. I better."

The parmesan chicken was scrumptious, and the mashed potatoes were almost as delicious as my mother's.

"So, after dinner, we need to begin studying. Have you looked over anything in the family packet that I gave you?"

"No."

"Well, we better get started. My mother has called me three times today inquiring about you. You will meet my family at a barbeque on Saturday night," he drank his wine.

"How am I supposed to learn everything in three days?"

"You're a smart girl. I have faith in you, *Claire*."

Once our plates were clean, Jonathan cleared the table. I sat there watching his bare feet shuffle back and forth across the beautiful hand-scraped hardwood. He may have been eleven years older than me, but he had the confident stride and the appearance of a young man. Not that thirty one was really old, but he just seemed much more youthful to me than any other thirty something's that I knew, which weren't too many.

The scent of his Coolwater cologne reached my nostrils as he walked about, and I began to quietly cry again. I hated myself for crying every fifteen minutes. I wished I could compose myself and be strong.

"I'm a patient man, Claire. You can cry in front of me," he sat back at the table with a thick stack of papers.

I wiped my eyes and noticed dark and wet mascara on my fingers.

"You can cry all you want here, but you can't do this in front of other people. You can't mope around crying like-like-"

"Like a kidnapped child?" I finished his sentence.

He sighed.

"Listen to me," his voice was stern. "I love you, dammit. You are here because I love you. I know I've taken you away from everything that matters to you, but my love has to count for something. Is there any possible way that you can dig deep and find some joy in the fact that I love you?"

I nearly laughed aloud. There was no way in hell that I would ever find joy in Jonathan loving me. He was my enemy. He had stolen me. He had stolen everything from me. He had stolen my joy.

"Give me time," I played along, only to keep my family safe.

He took my hand into his and planted a kiss on my knuckles. I nearly gagged.

We studied so long that my head was spinning. I felt like I did when I was memorizing lines for the character of Rizzo in our high school's production of *Grease*.

Thomas Marsh, father. He served two terms as the mayor of Houston. He was three years retired now, devoting most of his time to charity work and hob-knobbing with the big shots around town. Thomas liked his whiskey, his grill and his guns. He was turning sixty on Saturday. Jonathan said introducing me to Thomas on his birthday was the best present he could give the man. He'd been waiting a long time for Jonathan to find "the one".

Caroline Killebrew Marsh, mother. She was heavily involved with the Houston Humane Society and served on countless boards and committees. She loved throwing parties, playing Bunko, bossing ladies at the Review Club. She was born into money and appreciated fine jewelry, fine clothes, and fine living. Her Thanksgiving turkey and dressing was also "to die for."

Casey James Marsh, brother. He'd just turned twenty nine, the wild and reckless one. He drank too much, smoked too much, cussed like a sailor. He had embarrassed the family on several occasions, and he'd been thrown out of Baylor College of Medicine for skipping classes and using drugs. He was currently working for Jonathan as sales manager at the Jaguar dealership, and he was trying to get his act together. He'd been engaged to his high school sweetheart, Adrienne Brown, for years.

There was an aunt and uncle and a couple of cousins, but I was relieved to learn that most of his extended family and all of his grandparents were dead. I knew that this was a harsh thought, but I was thankful that the family was relatively small and there were a minimum number of people to study.

I lapsed into verse of Rizzo's "There Are Worse Things I Could Do", while trying to remember his father's hobbies, his mother's favorite foods, and the name of the uncle who nearly let him drown on a camping trip when he was ten.

Jonathan Marsh, kidnapper. He attended Alexander Academy, class of 1988. He received his high school diploma while I was eating Flintstone push pops on my back porch at the age of seven.

He was very intelligent, graduating at the top of his class at Rice University. Not just any dummy could kidnap a girl, re-invent her, and get away with it.

Jonathan was briefly engaged to his college sweetheart, Suzanne Simmons, but she broke his heart by drunkenly sleeping with his best friend, Grant, after a silent auction in 1995.

Grant Mallory, best friend. Grant was born with a silver spoon in his mouth. He was handsome, athletic, and successfully practiced law in New Orleans. He and Jonathan grew up together. They were inseparable throughout school. He was Jonathan's best friend, but Jonathan spoke of him with disdain.

Apparently Suzanne wasn't the first of Jonathan's women to be seduced by Grant. Jonathan described Grant as a selfish and loathsome creature, taking whatever he wanted, not caring who he hurt in the process.

"Like you?" I commented.

He looked hurt, as if that wasn't *exactly* what he was doing by stealing me from my family.

"I'm not like him. Grant is a bastard," he said.

"And yet he's your best friend?" I flipped through the stack of notes.

Jonathan turned to me, a stern look covering his face. He took my hands into his and said, "Stay away from him, Claire."

Jonathan hoped I would be frightened of Grant Mallory, but I wasn't. Maybe Grant Mallory was the very one who could save me.

EIGHT

When Saturday, September 8, 2001 arrived, I had begged him to let me call home numerous times. I was hoping that the Nashville police could trace the phone call and I would be found. Jonathan was no idiot. He knew what I was hoping.

"It's too soon to call, Claire," he said as we walked around the beautiful garden.

A rock waterfall emptied into the kidney-shaped pool. Shady trees and flowering bushes lined the property. The grass was thick and plush to my bare feet, birds were singing in the decades old limbs above our heads as we sat on a wrought iron bench at the back of the yard.

I hung my head low and picked at my French manicure.

"Quit picking your nails," he sounded like my mother as he turned to me on the small bench. "Look at me."

I did, but our stare was interrupted by the long locks blowing into my eyes.

"Claire, I love you," he dropped one knee to the Bermuda grass, gazing at me like we were long time lovers, soul mates.

I knew the proposal stance. I knew it was coming. My heart began to pound, not for the same reasons my heart would pound if Nathan was kneeling before me, but because I knew this man really had every intention of marrying me and forbidding me to ever return to my home.

"Will you marry me?" he pulled a black velvet box from the back pocket of his khaki shorts.

"You are asking? You are giving me an option?" I asked him as he opened the box to reveal the largest diamond I had ever seen.

"I'm trying to be romantic," he stated as I stared at the ring.

"You know my answer," I looked away and pulled the long strands of hair away from my eyes.

He sighed loudly and sat back on the bench.

"Here," he grabbed my left hand and roughly shoved the heavy diamond on my finger.

It was a gorgeous ring. I didn't know how many carats it was, but I was betting it cost more than all of my school loans and the now impounded Camry that I had driven for four years.

"Do you like it?" he asked, annoyed.

"It's pretty," I looked away from the ring.

He pulled his cell phone from his pocket and dialed a number. I looked to him, hoping he was calling my parents.

"Ernesto, bring the camera out back," he said into the phone and then flipped it closed.

I hung my head again and ran my finger over the sparkling square diamond.

"Is it too much to ask for a little appreciation?" he murmured.

"What am I supposed to appreciate?" I became angry. "I don't appreciate being ripped away from my family. You should have found a woman who would love you on her own. That's the kind of person who would appreciate this!"

"I want it to be you."

"You're wasting your time. I will never love you. Do you want to live your life with a person who will never love you?" I felt him staring at me as I watched the water ripple in the pool.

"You'll love me," he stated.

He believed it.

Ernesto exited the French doors at the back of the house and walked across the thick grass to us, camera in hand.

"Take some photos of us, Ernesto," he moved closer to me on the small bench. "My parents will want to see photos of the happy engagement."

I rolled my eyes.

"Look ecstatic, Claire," he warned.

Ernesto pointed the camera at us as Jonathan took my hand in his, wrapped his other arm around my shoulder and commanded me to smile. I did the best that I could.

"Kiss me," he said.

"No," I shook my head.

"Dammit, Claire, kiss me one time for a picture. I haven't asked *anything* of you in the romantic department of this relationship. The least you can do is kiss me for a damn picture," he was irritated.

I turned my head towards him as he placed his lips on top of mine. It was merely a peck. I'd experienced more passionate kisses on the middle school playground.

The camera shuttered as I pulled away from him. He stood up and walked to the house, Ernesto following. I remained on the bench, looking at the ring and inspecting the yard for a way to escape.

Before getting ready for the barbeque, I'd spent most of the day studying in my room. Jonathan had placed my clothes on the bed, an orange and green paisley sundress, brown sandals, matching jewelry. I was dressed and sitting at the foot of the poster bed, surrounded by papers of Marsh family information, when he entered.

"Are you ready?" he asked me, standing in the doorway, rolling the sleeves of his yellow Ralph Lauren shirt to his elbows. His silver Rolex watch clinked against his arm as he walked over and checked his appearance in the dresser mirror.

He situated a few pieces of hair around his forehead, rubbed his hands across his freshly shaven face and adjusted the wide brown belt looped through his blue jeans.

"Are you ready?" he repeated as I nodded and followed him downstairs.

As he drove the white Jaguar to his parent's house, he quizzed me.

"1970," I answered.

"Aunt Junie," I answered.

"Texans and Astros," I answered.

"You broke your arm in the 5th grade," I answered.

I was nervous. I knew playing along would keep me and my family safe as long as I did it well. Jonathan never let me forget that there was surveillance at my home in Nashville and that he would take drastic measures if my performance wasn't up to par.

Mr. and Mrs. Marsh's house was even larger than Jonathan's. It was nestled on a steep green hill outside of the bustling city and the property was surrounded by a white wooden rail fence. The long driveway passed a huge pond, ducks floating.

"The same ducks have come back every year since I was a child," Jonathan nodded towards the water.

I stayed silent.

"When we step out of this car, you better be the hap-hap-happiest little woman this side of California. Do you hear me?" he demanded.

"I hear you," I snapped.

We followed the circle drive to the front door, and he walked around to let me out of the car. I knew by now to stay in the passenger seat until I was let out, either by him or Ernesto.

"You look beautiful," he put his hand at the small of my back as we walked up the wide white steps to the front porch of the plantation-like home.

The doorbell chimed, Jonathan shifted from one foot to the other, and the door opened.

"Well by God, she's pretty as a picture, Jon!" a heavy set man declared when the door opened, cigar hanging from his mouth. His voice was thunderous, just like my father's. "Caroline, get in here!"

I produced the biggest smile that I could muster as the large man pulled me into his arms and hugged me tightly.

"She *is* a young one," he eyed me like an animal on display and then looked to Jonathan.

Jonathan nodded, "Claire, this is my father, Thomas Marsh."

I had no idea, I thought.

"It's so nice to meet you, Mr. Marsh," I declared, my smile wide, my voice cheerful.

Jonathan glanced at me and looked pleased. I knew he was surprised that I sounded so genuine.

"The pleasure is all mine, sweet girl. Come in, come in," he motioned us into the large foyer, a chandelier the size of Pluto hanging over our heads.

"Happy birthday," I added.

Jonathan's head whipped towards me, an amazed look of approval on his face.

"Thank you, my dear. Jonathan bringing you here is the best present I could receive!" He laughed, and his large belly jiggled beneath the white Brooks Brothers shirt.

"Where's Mom?" Jonathan kept his hand on my back as he pressed me through the home.

"Potato salad, son. You know the woman takes her sweet time in the kitchen," he replied as we walked into an enormous kitchen and there stood Jonathan's mother, her short blonde hair perfectly styled, a cream colored apron covering her bright floral dress.

"They have arrived!" Jonathan's loud father proclaimed.

His mother startled and nearly dropped the bowl in her hands.

When she looked at me, she looked at peace. I wasn't sure why, but she looked relieved.

"Oh, Jon was right, Claire. You're beautiful," she put the bowl on the granite countertop, wiped her hands on her apron, and she came to me. She held me close and the scent of her fresh perfume engulfed me. She smelled wonderful, and for some reason, I felt safe in this woman's arms. Maybe it was from missing my own mother so.

She pulled away and studied my face. She was still a beautiful woman, in her sixties, but I could tell she must have been stunning as a young lady.

"I'm so glad to meet you, honey," she said.

"Thank you," I smiled at her and nodded my head.

"So?" she asked, looking at Jonathan, then back at me.

Jonathan looked embarrassed and then said, "Show them the ring, sweetheart."

I held out my hand for his parents to see the rock on my finger, and his mother squealed loudly like a little girl.

"By God, Jon! What did that set you back?" his father's loud southern drawl boomed throughout the open floor plan.

"Thomas!" his mother lightly slapped his shoulder. "That's the rudest question I've ever heard."

They both hugged and congratulated us, and his mother wiped tears from her eyes. I liked Jonathan Marsh's parents. If these were normal circumstances, I would enjoy being in their company.

We assembled on the large patio as Jonathan's father sauced the chicken and pork chops on the grill. I even offered to help Jonathan's mother in the kitchen. He nodded at me in approval, gave a little wink, and went about drinking whiskey and talking to his father about Houston politics.

Mrs. Caroline declined my help, though. She told me to stay put on the patio and enjoy myself. I looked across the acreage surrounding the house and thought how much Nathan would love this place. He'd always said he wanted lots of land when we got married.

Jonathan would casually reach over and touch my hand and ask if I needed anything. I smiled at him, laughed at his jokes, put on an award-winning performance that we were contently in love although I was overwhelmed by it all. He continued to smile and wink at me because he was so astonished at my presentation.

His brother bustled out the back door, a bottle of Jack Daniels in his hand and a perturbed- looking woman following behind him.

"Robbing cradles, I see," was Casey's reply when Jonathan introduced us. Jonathan punched him in the arm.

Casey didn't resemble Jonathan at all. He was short, kind of squirrely, and looked like an idiot. He was far from handsome.

"I'm kidding. You must be crazy for marrying this son of a bitch, but welcome to the family," he gave my cheek a peck and laughed, whiskey rolling off his breath.

The troubled looking woman following him was Adrienne, Casey's high school sweetheart and fiancé of seven years.

"Pay him no mind. He's half-drunk already," she scoffed at Casey.

She was in her late twenties and naturally pretty with olive skin and long dark hair. Her eyes were green and almost cat-like. She seemed nice enough as she introduced herself, badmouthed her drunken fiancé, and then returned inside the house.

I swatted at mosquitoes, sipped my iced tea and listened to the men of the family talk. Uncle Jim and Aunt Junie had arrived, lugging around presents and a casserole.

Aunt Junie reminded me of one of my great aunts, long dead and gone, with her haphazardly applied rouge and her smell of old perfume. She held my hand in hers, put on her spectacles and gawked at my ring for fifteen minutes.

I laughed at their jokes, I answered their questions, and I spoke solemnly when I discussed my parent's car accident and Marion's heart attack. I exuded joy as we passed around the engagement photos taken in the garden that day. I didn't resist when Jonathan took my hand. I did the best that I could to conceal the hurt and heartache that was boiling inside of me.

"Tell us how you met, Claire," Aunt Junie asked as I wiped potato salad from my lips. Jonathan peered at me from behind his corn on the cob and gave me a look of encouragement.

"Well," I looked around the manicured lawn, shifted my weight in the comfortable patio chair and my heart fluttered, "back in May, I was with some girlfriends at the Bordeaux Club in Oklahoma City."

"Now, the Bordeaux Club isn't your average nightclub. It's a high-end place," Jonathan explained.

He didn't want his family to think he'd picked up some trashy girl taking shots and dancing to Def Leppard on the bar of a regular old night club. "Think 1950's New York. Jazz band. Guys in suits. It's a classy joint."

"Well, aren't you Mr. Cary Grant?" his mother chuckled.

His wasted brother hiccupped loudly, and his father kicked his foot under the table. "The girl's telling a love story, Casey. Listen up. You may learn a thing or two about sweeping a woman off her feet!"

I looked to Adrienne.

"He hasn't swept me off my feet since his senior prom twelve years ago, Mr. Thomas," she stated between chews. "And even then he was drunk."

"Shut it," Casey said to her and took another drink.

"Go on, dear," Aunt Junie said.

I cleared my throat.

"So, here he comes, strutting up in his three piece suit, chest puffed out," I giggled in a loving way as Jonathan gave a sheepish nod. "He asked if I was in the market to trade vehicles. He told me I would look great in a British car," I shot loving eyes at him.

"She said, 'I'd love a British car if you're buying.' and I said 'I wouldn't have it any other way,'" Jonathan laughed.

I thought the story made me sound like a gold-digging floozy, but the family didn't seem to mind. They all chuckled and grinned and adoringly looked at us. All of them except Casey, who was half asleep with barbecue sauce on his chin.

I had such an urge to yell out the true story of how we met. I could imagine the look on Aunt Junie's face when I told her Jonathan had jumped into my Toyota, held a gun to my side and then forced me to memorize the random fact that she loved cross-stitching.

After dinner, the men had another drink at the patio table while Caroline and Aunt Junie invited me to join them in the kitchen. They began pressing me about wedding plans, to which I replied, "We haven't gotten that far yet."

"Don't wait too long or you'll never get married. Trust me," Adrienne chimed in, as she sat in the keeping room and flipped through a magazine.

"Poor Adrienne got stuck with the slacker Marsh. Bless her heart," Aunt Junie said quietly and winked at me.

"Am I in time for cake?" I heard a voice call from the front of the house.

"That must be Grant. You'll just love him, Claire. He's the best friend Jonathan has ever known," Mrs. Caroline patted my hand and stood to greet Grant walking into the kitchen.

He was tall and handsome, even favoring Jonathan a little. He held a present in one arm as he wrapped the other around Mrs. Caroline and pulled her close.

"You smell refreshing as ever," he said to her and then his eyes shifted to me. "Now, what have we here?"

"Oh, Grant, come meet Claire," she said, excitement rising in her voice, as he sat the present on the counter and strutted my way.

I felt uncomfortable as he peered at me like he was undressing me with his eyes. I pulled the sundress over my crossed legs and covered my knee.

"Get up, girl. Hug my neck," he reached for me.

He smelled fresh, like soap, as he gave me a good squeeze.

"Show him the ring!" Aunt Junie exclaimed, holding her coffee cup tightly in her hand.

"Well, my Lord. You're really going through with it, huh?" he held my hand, observed the ring and then gave me a flirtatious wink.

"I couldn't be happier," I lied.

"And I couldn't be happier for you," he lied.

He hugged Aunt Junie and Adrienne, but he kept his eyes focused on me.

"I thought I heard you in here," Jonathan busted through the back door, shook Grant's hand and patted him on the shoulder. Then he immediately came to my side as if to protect me.

"You've got a pretty one here, Jon. Congratulations," Grant beamed.

"I think so. Thank you," he replied.

Old man Marsh blew out sixty candles on the yellow cake with chocolate icing. He opened his presents- books, grilling accessories, a bottle of aged whiskey. Several times he hugged me for no reason except to tell me he was glad I was joining the family.

The men drank more bourbon, the women asked me about life in Oklahoma City. Jonathan seemed content with all of my answers, randomly giving my hand a soft squeeze and nodding in approval. I felt like I had done everything right. Maybe I would be rewarded by getting to call home, or better yet, being allowed to see Vaiden.

Jonathan drank two cups of coffee before we headed home so he wouldn't be too drunk to drive, give me the keys, and end up back in Nashville.

"You did excellent, Claire," he reached over and patted my knee as we drove home in the dark. "Thank you."

I nodded silently, staring out the window, wondering if Vaiden was asleep yet or wanting to read *Cat in the Hat* one more time.

"My family loves you. My father pulled me aside and really expressed his approval. They don't care how young you are. They think you're going to make a wonderful wife. Thank you for giving them a wonderful first impression," he said again.

Again, I nodded quietly.

"I saw the way Grant was looking at you. I know he's eaten up with jealousy," he boasted.

"He seemed nice enough."

"Yeah, well, don't get too friendly with him. I'd hate to slit your mother's throat because you took a liking to my best friend."

His comment disturbed me on so many levels. Yes, he'd threatened harm to my family, but he had never said anything so specifically wicked. I shuddered with fear, and I wrapped my arms around myself as we rode in the cold Jaguar.

NINE

I'd been at the camper for a week. I woke each morning the same way that I'd woken back in Houston over the years, with thoughts of my daughter and pain in my left breast from the aging implant. I'd begged Jonathan to let me have the breast implants removed, or at least redone, but he was against it. He liked my fake breasts. He liked the size, the shape. He didn't want some doctor hacking into my chest and them not looking the same. I'd always planned to have the damn things removed once I reached freedom. Thankfully I was now closer to my family, my old home, my old life and my old breasts.

Dora invited me to dinner each night, a feast of crappie or catfish always on the table. I was so sick of fried fish and hushpuppies that I nearly vomited at the thought of them. Besides, my once toned body was already turning to mush.

I hadn't called home again, but I was getting anxious to do so. I continued to check the news each night, but there was no sight of our story, which gave me a great sense of peace.

"We're having burgers tonight, honey," Mrs. Dora called down to me as I relaxed in a lawn chair overlooking the river, making a list of things that needed to be done once I returned to Nashville.

#1. Have boobs ripped out.

"That sounds great! Thanks!" I called back to her, relieved that fish wasn't on the menu.

I walked down to the Walter camper at around six that evening, mosquitoes feasting on my arms and legs, even though I had doused myself in repellent several times that day.

Dora and Paul sat at the picnic table and loaded their paper plates with burgers, baked beans and potato salad. Gus sat across from them doing the same. It was Monday and Monroe was back at home with his nagging wife.

"Paul, you tell Clarence supper was on?" Dora asked as I sat down, and she handed me a paper plate.

"He'll be out shortly," Paul shoved food into his mouth.

"Fish just ain't bitin' today," Gus shook his head and stared at the river.

"That's fine with me. I think Charley and I are sick of fish, aren't we, honey?" Dora laughed.

"I'll eat what I can take. I sure thank you all for helping keep me fed," I stated.

"Glad to do it," Dora slapped potato salad on her plate. "Where's Clarence?"

"Dammit, woman, he will be out when he's ready. I told him to come on," Paul replied and wiped sweat from his forehead.

I took a bite of potato salad, remembering Mrs. Caroline's delicious recipe. Dora's was missing something, maybe green pepper.

Mr. Walter came out of his trailer and shuffled over to us.

"It's about time, Clarence!" Dora motioned for him to hurry.

We'd only been sitting there for a few minutes so I didn't know why she was making such a big deal about him being late. But Dora made a big deal about everything.

"I'm a-comin," Mr. Walter sat next to me and filled his plate.

"How was your day, Mr. Walter?" I asked him.

"Call me Clarence, girl. I've told you that a hundred times," he said. "Day was good and lazy. Yours?"

"Mine was pretty lazy, too," I answered.

"Your head getting cleared?" he asked.

"Clarence, the girl has only been here a week. Can't nobody completely clear a head in a week," Dora proclaimed.

"I'm feeling better," I nodded. "I sure do enjoy being out here. I have next week's rent at the camper."

"I'll get it tomorrow. That'll be fine," Clarence replied.

He hadn't inquired anymore about my stolen identification, and I surely wasn't going to bring it up.

"You need to come fishing with us, girl. Don't nothing clear the head like fishing," Gus chimed in.

"I might do that. Thanks."

"As long as you don't talk, now. Can't have no woman gabbing in the boat all day. That's why Dora don't come," Paul said seriously.

"Shut your mouth, Paul Walter," Dora smiled at me as she reached for the mustard bottle.

"Quiet as a mouse," I took a drink of tea and watched flies skim across the calm water.

"I met a feller once that said his wife talked so much in the boat that one day he just shoved her out. He shoved her right out into the water. She was there just a-screaming for help and he told her to pipe down all that screaming or she'd scare the fish away," Paul laughed aloud.

"I've had a mind to shove a few people out of a boat but ain't ever done it," Gus laughed, ketchup caught in his gray beard.

"Well, this feller," Paul continued to laugh, "he let her sit in that water for nearly an hour. He threw her down a life jacket. She floated in there so long that he tied some stink bait to her big toe. Said she caught a six pound catfish that day!"

The men all laughed while Dora shook her head. "Well, I declare. That's abuse. Downright abuse!"

"That ain't no abuse, woman. That couple loved each other. Hell, she sat right along with him laughing when he told me that story. Said it was the first fish she ever caught and boy was she proud!" Paul held his burger, laughing too hard to eat.

"You don't want to catch a catfish with your big toe, girl, so you best be quiet if you come with us," Gus nudged me, smiling.

"Boy, what was that feller's name? He was a good ole guy. He always had a funny story about something or another. Do you remember him, Gus?" Paul asked.

"Don't reckon so. Where was he from?"

"That's that feller from up around Nashville, ain't it? He used to fish over at Landry's Resort. He had that nice bass boat?" Clarence interrupted.

"Yeah, that's him, Clarence. Funny guy. Always telling a story you wouldn't never believe!" Paul shook his head.

"Now I remember," Gus said. "Said he was Buddy Holly's big brother, remember that?"

"Why hell yes!" Paul exclaimed. "He had some stories."

"Eddie Holley, by God. His name was Eddie Holley!" Clarence remembered aloud.

My heart skipped, the pickle fell off my burger, and I shifted my eyes as these men talked about my grandfather.

Once I was alone in the camper that night, tears poured from my eyes. I hadn't heard stories about my Papa in so long. He'd only died a year before Jonathan had taken me. One of the last things he told me, as he lay in his bed, lungs riddled with emphysema was, "Elle, did you know Buddy Holly was my baby brother? I bought him those glasses." We laughed together, and he died not two hours later.

I was so close to my family, yet so far away. I longed to be sitting at our dining table while my daddy told stories about his daddy. I wanted to see my mother roll her eyes at tales she had heard a million times.

I began to wonder what my sister looked like now. She was twenty six. Was she married with children of her own? My Vaiden was twelve. Was she as boy crazy as my younger sister was at that age?

Did my mother still look young? She'd always been so beautiful, looking years younger than she really was. Had my father upgraded his bulky glasses to sleek little frames? Had he finally lost the baldness battle? How had time taken a toll on their appearance? How had the grief of losing me taken a toll on their appearance and their health?

My parents tried to conceive for years, but it wasn't until they were both thirty eight that I was born, followed by my sister four years later. They would be nearly seventy now. Had my parents turned into old people?

I sobbed at the thought of Nathan. I recollected the way we met at the local skating rink when we were fourteen. He asked me to dance with him to a Red Hot Chili Peppers song. I fell and bruised my tailbone.

I got pregnant with Vaiden the first time that Nathan and I ever slept together. We were both terrified to tell our parents. I remember sitting in his truck in my driveway on that cool April afternoon, the pregnancy test still damp with urine, both of us crying. He took my hand and his brown eyes locked with mine and he said, "God planned it this way, Elle. We are supposed to be together forever."

Nathan was with me every step of the pregnancy. I remembered the tears of joy he cried when Vaiden was born on Christmas day. He moved into my home for a few months and slept in the guest bedroom upstairs, a baby monitor next to the twin bed. If ever Vaiden woke in the night, he rushed to my room to help me take care of her. So many nights I rested because he stayed up and cared for our baby.

We'd made plans to marry once we both finished college. It was going to be a September wedding at his parent's farm overlooking the lake. The cotton bolls would be in bloom, and the pictures would turn out beautifully.

I wondered if Nathan was married now. Did he have sole custody of Vaiden or did she still live with my parents? Did his new wife treat our daughter like her own?

I wept for hours, until I was out of tears. I knew it was time to learn all of the answers to my questions. I knew it was time to go home.

TEN

I paid Clarence another week's rent on the following morning. I headed into town to use the payphone that I had spotted in the pharmacy parking lot the week before. I pulled my car close to the decrepit phone box, and I was relieved to hear a dial tone when I lifted the receiver to my ear through the rolled down window. I dumped a ton of change into the machine, and I dialed the familiar number.

The phone rang several times as my heart pounded. Why wasn't anyone answering? Sure, my parents could simply be at the grocery store, but then other thoughts-scary thoughts flooded my mind. Were there people tapping the line, either the police or some thugs who worked for Jonathan? Were police standing in the living room, tracing the call, telling my mother not to answer yet? Were Jonathan's cronies holding my family hostage in the storage shed behind the house? Had Ernesto failed to contact them?

I became frantic at these thoughts as my heart skipped and sweat broke on my brow. I felt nauseated as I threw the receiver into the phone box and sped out of the sleepy fishing town.

I arrived in Nashville nearly two hours later, amazed at the changes that had taken place since I had been gone, amazed that my familiar hometown seemed so new. I gawked at different buildings and freeways, but I took the old route to my neighborhood, miles away from bustling downtown.

I drove down streets where I had ridden my bike so many years before. Mr. Pritchard's rose bushes were still the size of mammoths, spilling onto the sidewalk. So many times I had been scratched by them while rollerblading by his house.

I couldn't drive this car past my home. It was too obvious. The missing wife of the owner of the most successful Land Rover dealership in Houston was, in fact, driving a Land Rover. I knew it was silly to still be in this brand of vehicle, but it's all I could do.

Before I escaped Texas the week before, I had left my Jaguar parked in the garage of our River Oaks home. I'd dressed in black, kept my head down and walked nearly three miles to the dealership. I sneaked to the back of the building and used my key. I carefully rummaged through the paperwork on Jonathan's desk until I found the documentation of the Land Rover that I was now driving.

Jonathan had sealed the after-hours deal earlier that evening. It was still in the maintenance department, not yet ready to go onto the lot. I got the keys and drove away. No one knew that car existed at Jonathan's dealership except for Jonathan and the previous owner. It was as simple as that.

After I drove the Range Rover off the lot and parked it out of the way, I went back into the office and erased the security camera footage. I managed to sneak by the cameras on the way out since I had studied for years where they were placed. No one would know that I had been at the dealership that night. No one knew what I was driving.

However, it still seemed risky to drive directly past my home. I pulled into the cove adjacent to Pine Hills where I could peek through the Magnolia trees of the Barkley's yard and view the property.

Everything still looked the same. Ivy still grew along the north side of the house, digging into the white mortar and red bricks. The same large oaks shaded the yard, and ferns lined the front porch. It was as if time had stood still.

I saw a strange SUV parked in the driveway, but it could have easily belonged to my mom or dad. Surely they had traded vehicles in the last ten years. Besides that, there were no police cars, no pickup trucks like the ones Jonathan's men usually drove.

I sat there tapping my fingers on the steering wheel, praying for a glimpse of Vaiden. I needed to see her. I needed to see that she was okay.

Hours passed as I sat quietly in the cove across from my home. I was worried that someone would think it suspicious that I had been there for so long. I knew it was time to either drive back to the river or pull into my driveway, only 100 yards away.

Was I ready? This was the moment that I had been waiting for since September 4, 2001. I had longed to see my home and run through the kitchen door for almost ten years. As deeply as I had yearned for this moment for so many days, hours, months and years, now that it was finally upon me, I was scared.

As I mentally prepared to pull in the driveway, something happened. In the two hours that I had sat there, no one came or went from my home. The split second before I started my ignition, a police car stopped in front of the house.

My heart was pounding as I watched the young officer walk past the mailbox and up the steep and shady driveway. He entered the garage and was out of sight.

"Ernesto, what's going on?" I whispered to myself as I sped out of the cove and headed for the camper.

My mind and my car raced. Who was that police officer? Why was he there? Had someone seen me on the news? Had someone called the police and told them that I wasn't Claire Marsh? Had someone told them that I was, in fact, Elle Holley, and my parents resided at 542 Pine Hills in Nashville, Tennessee? Had the Houston police figured it all out? Even worse, had something happened to my family? Were the police coming back to investigate a crime scene? I was confused and nervous. I knew now that I couldn't call home any time soon. I knew now that home was still out of my reach.

I also knew that I could retrieve some kind of information if I could just get to a computer. Jonathan had put spy ware on all of our computers and my cell phone. He constantly checked the internet history and would know if I searched for my family online. He said he would kill me if he found out that I tried to contact them in any way. So many times I wanted to see if my sister or even my daughter had a social networking page. I wanted to

Google their names to see if I could catch a glimpse of them or learn some small facet of their lives.

I'd lived in fear for so long. Just when I thought I had conceived an idea to reach them, an idea that would really work, Jonathan would stifle that idea with his threats. I couldn't call because of the phone taps. He constantly reminded me that he had people in Nashville stationed close to my parent's home, even Nathan's home, keeping an eye on them, checking their mail for any sign of correspondence from me. He watched me like a hawk, monitored my internet usage and tracked my vehicle. I wasn't allowed to go anywhere with computer access, not even the library. He knew my every move for so many years, and even now that I was away from him, I still lived in fear.

Before driving over the bridge, I pulled into the library on slow Main Street. I raced inside, eager to search for answers.

I first searched my alias, Claire Marsh. I read my story in *Houston Chronicle*. According to the article, there were no clues to the tragedy that had taken place in my River Oaks home a week earlier. I was relieved.

I searched Elle Holley, and surprisingly, nothing appeared. There weren't even any articles about my disappearance ten years ago. There was nothing.

I searched Vaiden's name. No social network page, no mention of her name in Nashville newspapers. There was nothing.

I searched my sister's name. A link to the birth announcement section in the Pine Hills Baptist Church online newsletter flashed upon the screen.

Chad Hilton and Emma Holley Hilton are pleased to announce the birth of their baby boy, Martin Knox Hilton, born on November 12, 2010. Knox weighed 8 pounds, 3 ounces and was 20 inches long. Baby and mother are doing fine.

My sister was a mother. My baby sister, who was nearly a baby the last time I saw her, was now a mother. My eyes glazed over with happy tears, and I smiled. I couldn't wait to see her baby, my nephew named after his grandfather, and hold him close to me, breathing in the smell of his hair and his soft skin. I had another reason to hurry home.

After digesting the fact that my baby sister was no longer a baby, I searched for any information about Nathan. There was another hit. My heart broke, my hands shook, my stomach turned as I clicked on the wedding announcement in *The Tennessean*.

Sarah Beth Daley, daughter of Mr. and Mrs. William Daley of Franklin, TN and Nathan Bingham, son of Mr. and Mrs. Gregory Bingham of Nashville, TN are pleased to announce their engagement and forthcoming marriage to take place on September 19, 2009.

I didn't know I was crying until the salty tears dripped down my nose onto the computer keyboard. Nathan had married. He had married my best friend.

I tried to pull myself together. I searched for the positive side. Sarah Beth and I had been inseparable since we were five. She knew everything about me. She was the best friend that I had ever known. There was no doubt that she was a wonderful mother to my child.

However, it still hurt. The thought of Nathan and my best friend sharing secrets in the dark, the thought of him kissing the nape of her neck, the thought of *their* September wedding, the thought of Sarah Beth taking my place hurt me terribly. What had happened? Were they consoling one another after my disappearance? Had one thing lead to another? The entire clichéd idea was sickening.

I shook it off. I literally shook my head and my shoulders, and I pushed the sadness deep down into my gut. I could mourn this loss later. Right now I needed to focus on searching for my parents.

I doubted they even owned a computer. They had always been old school, shunning cell phones and CD players, preferring the days of rotary phones and rear projection televisions and Hank Williams eight tracks. They probably had no clue what the internet even was.

I searched my mother's name first and, not surprisingly, there was nothing. I sighed loudly and typed my father's name in the search bar. What showed on the screen left me paralyzed-literally unable to move, unable to breathe.

ELEVEN

I'd been held captive for six days. I'd experienced six days of debilitating fear, sadness and anger. Jonathan decided to pump me full of Prozac, but unfortunately, the medicine wouldn't build up for at least two weeks. Even then I knew it wouldn't help.

"This will make you happy," he said every time he handed me the small green capsule.

"You think an anti-depressant is going to make me forget my family?" I scoffed.

"Well, hell no, Claire, but it can't hurt," he shoved the pill into my hand. I grabbed a bottle of water off of the kitchen counter and swallowed.

He put the bottle of pills in his back pocket. You couldn't find so much as a Tylenol in the house. He kept everything that could harm me in any way- razors, NSAIDs, butcher knives, shoe laces, guns, all locked away in a secret place. My legs would soon be due for another waxing, and I couldn't even slice an apple without his supervision.

"Come here," he called me over to the kitchen table where he was going through mail. "I want you to see something."

I slowly shuffled to him, uninterested in anything he had to show me.

"Look at this," he laughed and handed me a newspaper clipping.

"What is it?" I examined the paper.

"It's an article from *The Tennessean*. Read it," he grinned. "One of my associates in Nashville sent it to me."

My eyes darted across the article.
"Questioning…disappearance...Elle Marie Holley," I mumbled.

"Do you see who they are questioning in your disappearance?" he smirked.

"Michael Kee?" I asked.

"Damn right!" Jonathan slapped his knee, laughing hysterically.

"I don't understand. Who is that? Who is Michael Kee? What does this mean?" I begged him for answers.

"My Lord, Claire, is your memory *that* bad?" he rolled his eyes at me and walked to the refrigerator.

"That's the name I gave my father," I remembered.

"Can you believe there is actually a Michael Kee in Chicago? Could that be any more perfect?" he rummaged through the Sub-Zero and popped grapes into his mouth.

I began to re-read the article.

"I guess I should have checked to see if there really was a Michael Kee in Chicago. I swear I pulled that name, that city, out of thin air. I must have some kind of psychic powers or something, right?" he passed by me and playfully nudged me with his elbow.

"They will eventually let him go. They have nothing on him."

"Maybe so, but this has bought some time. There's no way in hell they think you are in Texas," he headed for the stairs. "They will search for you another week or two, maybe a month, and then write you off as a runaway or something. My contacts in Nashville say the police visits to your house have ceased dramatically. No one is coming to Texas for you."

He was right.

Ernesto woke me the next morning as he usually did. My sleep was never sound, but the sleeping pills that Jonathan gave me seemed to help. Of course he kept them locked away so I wouldn't swallow the entire bottle.

"Miss Claire, come downstairs," Ernesto somberly called from the doorway.

I groggily nodded and sat up in the bed, surrounded by fleece blankets and heavy down comforters.

"Hurry," he quickly left the room.

I knew something was wrong. My first thought was that Jonathan had died. He had some kind of freak accident while weight lifting that morning. Hope emerged. I was going home.

I raced down the stairs and through the living room to see him sitting at the kitchen bar, his head in his hands. The television on the kitchen wall showed smoke, buildings falling, airplanes. I was terribly confused by it all.

"Claire?" Jonathan looked to me, his eyes red, and tears streaming down the stubble on his cheeks.

"What happened?" I pulled my heavy bathrobe closed over my flannel pajamas, the house seeming colder than usual.

"The world is coming to an end," he sniffled and wiped his face.

I watched the television screen in awe. I thought the images that I was seeing had something to do with me- with my disappearance. My vanishing was surely the most important and tragic thing to be happening in this world. Surely the chaos on television had something to do with me.

I sat beside him, Ernesto hovering over the both of us, and we all silently watched in horror. I began to piece together what was happening. This was an attack on our country. The world could quite possibly be coming to an end.

"I had friends in that building," tears fell from his eyes. "They are dead, Claire. They must be dead."

I looked at him and the hurt covering his face as he sobbed. I had the urge to reach out and touch him, to comfort him in some way. I didn't know where this compassion came from, but I pushed it away. I kept my hands in my lap, and I let him cry.

Ernesto and I were glued to the screen as Jonathan paced the house making phone calls. My eavesdropping informed me that Thomas Marsh was a personal friend of the President. My future father-in-law had the President of the United States' phone number. The President could help me, a kidnapped girl, couldn't he? He could help me get home. He could protect my family.

The thought was absurd. There was no way I would be able to contact the President. It wasn't like Thomas Marsh had his number stuck to the refrigerator; easily accessible while I helped Mrs. Caroline put away the dishes at our next family get-together.

Besides, America had suddenly turned into a scary place, a place under attack. My lavish kidnapping was not a top priority.

I wanted to know that my family was safe. I wanted them to know that I was safe. It was a scary day. I needed to know that everyone was okay.

"I need to call my family today. Please let me call them," I begged Jonathan as he paced the living room and mumbled to himself.

He stopped pacing, stared at me and surprisingly, he nodded.

"Take her to a payphone in Galveston, Ernesto. I know there are a couple of them down by the shore," Jonathan instructed as we walked to Ernesto's truck parked in the circle driveway. "If she tries to run, kill her."

I swallowed the knot in my throat.

"Yes, sir," Ernesto nodded and climbed into his tall truck.

"Claire, I'm serious. Don't cause any trouble. Call your parents, tell them what we discussed and get back home. The police may be standing there when you call, but I have surveillance on their house, as well. Do you understand?"

"I understand," I said.

"If Ernesto has to kill you, I will send orders to the Santo brothers to see that your family has the same fate,' he said firmly.

"Who are the Santo brothers?" I asked as I opened the truck door.

"They are only two of the twenty men that I have in Nashville watching everyone you love. They are no saints, either," he turned to walk into the house.

"Santo means saint in Spanish," Ernesto clarified as I climbed into the truck and we headed for Galveston.

My eyes searched for payphones, and we found one at a Valero gas station only a few blocks from the sea.

"Don't do anything stupid, Miss Claire. Say exactly what we rehearsed in the car. Say what Mr. Jonathan told you to say. Nothing else," he strictly demanded as he pushed me to the phone.

Ernesto stood close to me, the sleeve of his shirt touching my back, as I inserted the money and dialed the number.

"Hello?" my father practically shouted.

"Daddy! Daddy, is everyone okay? Vaiden?" I asked.

"Elle, my God in Heaven! We are fine. Are *you* okay?"

"I'm fine, Daddy. I just had to make sure everyone is safe. Have you seen the news?" I began to cry into the receiver.

"Of course I've seen it! Where are you, Elle? Where are you?" my daddy's voice cracked.

"Michael and I are in Galveston. We are headed for New Orleans and then Miami," I repeated what Jonathan had instructed me to say.

"Elle, the police have Michael Kee in custody! They are searching all of Chicago for you!" he shouted.

"They must have the wrong Michael. I'm with Michael, Daddy," I repeated. "We are fine."

Ernesto motioned for me to hang up the phone.

"Come home, Elle, baby, please come home," he cried. I heard my mother in the background hysterically begging to speak to me.

"Mama?" I shouted.

Ernesto snatched the phone from my hands and hung it up.

"Good job, Miss Claire. Let's go."

TWELVE

When Ernesto and I arrived at the house, we found Jonathan standing in his closet, frantically throwing clothes into his suitcase.

"Where are you going?" I asked him.

"I have to go," he replied, searching for something in the chest of drawers.

"Go where?" I asked again.

"My father and I are going to Washington with some friends. I don't know how long I will be gone," he replied, anxiously matching socks.

This was my chance. He would be gone. I would escape.

"I'm one of the richest men in the whole damn city and here I am matching my own socks!" he yelled, marching past Ernesto and me to his bathroom where he started throwing toiletries into a black leather bag.

"The phone call went well?" he looked at Ernesto.

"She did exactly as she was told," he nodded.

"Good girl, Claire," he never looked to me.

"You don't know how long you'll be gone?"

"I said I don't know, but I hope you will continue to be a good girl," he paced the bathroom, tossing things into the bag.

"I will," I said. "Thank you for letting me call home."

Again I wanted to be in his good graces. And I *was* thankful that he let me make the phone call.

"Claire, go up to your room. I need to discuss some things with Ernesto," he instructed me as if I were a child.

I turned to leave the bathroom and do as I was told.

"Wait," he called as I turned around to face him.

He walked to me and took me into his arms. My arms continued to hang to my side. He didn't say anything, but I heard him sniffle in my ear. I was certain that he was crying again. I didn't know if he was crying for our country or crying because he thought I might try to escape while he was gone and Ernesto would have to kill me. Or maybe he was simply crying because he would miss me.

He let me go, quickly turning so I wouldn't see his wet face, and I walked up to my room.

All flights had been cancelled, but a car arrived for him at around seven that evening. Mr. Marsh was waiting in the back of the dark Suburban when it pulled up the drive.

"You are going to have to kiss me," Jonathan instructed as we walked down the stairs with his luggage.

"Why?" I asked, trying to keep up his steady pace.

"Because my father will be watching us say goodbye. Dammit, Claire, the country is under attack and your fiancé is leaving. You need to look a little distressed considering the circumstances."

I understood his point, but it wasn't like he was going off to single-handedly catch the monsters that had killed thousands of people that day. He was riding comfortably with his father and some other retired politicians en route to nose around Washington and contribute their two cents on the whole situation.

"I've given Ernesto strict orders concerning you. Promise me that you won't do anything to jeopardize this, to jeopardize your family's safety. Promise me," he stopped at the coat closet to put on a light running jacket over his t-shirt.

"I promise," I said quietly.

"Give me a good send off," he nodded and opened the front door.

The driver took Jonathan's suitcase and opened the back door of the Suburban. Mr. Marsh motioned for me to walk closer to the car.

"Thanks for letting him come along, Claire. I really need his company right now," Mr. Marsh said, distress in his voice

"Yes, sir," I glanced at all of the powerful looking men in the back of the SUV.

"I'm sure Caroline will be in touch with you while we are gone. We will be back as soon as we can," his loud voice boomed.

"Yes sir,' I nodded. "Have a safe trip."

I backed away from the car knowing the men were looking at Jonathan and me through the dark tinted windows. I knew what he wanted me to do. I knew he wanted me to show his father how much I really loved him.

I sighed and put my arms around his neck. I pulled him close and my mouth covered his. It wasn't comparable to the little peck that we had shared in the garden after he proposed. It was a real kiss, the same way that I would bid my Nathan farewell.

I felt one of his arms reach around the small of my back and the other at my neck. Finally Mr. Marsh interrupted us, his strident voice booming from the car, "Come on, lovebirds. We've got to go!"

We let go, staring into one another's eyes. I knew he was amazed, surprised at what had just happened. I found it pretty astonishing that I had stood there and kissed him for so long. I interrupted our gaze by clearing my throat and looking past him to the beautiful orange sunset.

"I love you, Claire," he entered the dark vehicle.

Soon they were out of sight. If Ernesto hadn't been standing behind me, I would have taken off running right then.

"Don't do it, Miss Claire," Ernesto warned me as we entered the house.

"Do what?" I asked him.

"Don't think of running. By the time you go to sleep this evening, you and I won't be the only ones in this house," he locked the door and set the security system.

"Why, Ernesto. Are you saying that I'm too much for you to handle? You have to call for back-up?" I smirked.

"That's exactly what I am saying," he left me standing alone in the foyer and he went upstairs to his room.

My eyes began to scan the house for a means of escape. I could stab Ernesto, plain and simple, if only there had been sharper weapons in the kitchen besides the butter knives. But what if I actually did kill Ernesto? What if I made my break? I still had my family to consider. I didn't think that Jonathan was bluffing in any way when he threatened harm to them. Maybe I really had been defeated. Maybe I should put the thoughts of escaping out of my mind.

As I sat in my room contemplating what to do, I heard voices downstairs-Spanish speaking voices, at least three of them. I knew that the other bodyguards had arrived. I knew I should probably just go to sleep before I ended up getting myself or my family killed.

Three days passed. The other men, two Hispanics and a brawny white guy with star tattoos on his knuckles, were all well-dressed. They looked more like secret service men than thugs. They lounged around the house watching my every move.

Jonathan had called to check in with Ernesto several times a day. He requested to speak to me on the telephone twice. As we sat on the line, I knew he wanted me to tell him that I loved him, that I missed him and that I wanted him to come home. I wouldn't dare say such things to him.

One of the men, Marco, was an excellent cook. He slaved in the kitchen, preparing our meals, more than he eyed me. I ate in silence while the men, even the white guy, all spoke in Spanish. I had no clue what they were saying, but they seemed to look at me and laugh quite often.

Mrs. Caroline arrived unannounced that evening. Ernesto greeted her at the door, and I heard him explaining that Jonathan had sent the other men over to keep a close watch on me during this unsure time in our country.

"Mr. Jonathan is just so worried that there may be an attack on Houston. He wants to make sure Miss Claire is protected," I heard him say as I walked down the stairs.

"Claire, darling," Mrs. Caroline rushed to me, her familiar perfume surrounding me, "I'm just so frightened."

"I know," I said as I wrapped my arms around her.

"I don't know what Thomas thinks he can do. He's no longer in office. I think he's just grieving the loss of so many friends in New York and Washington. He just feels like he has to do something," she reasoned.

"I'm sure they are fine. They will be home soon," I said.

She nodded at me and watched the thugs as they passed through the living room.

"He has you secured like Fort Knox in here, doesn't he?" she whispered.

"Yes, he does."

"Would you like to go to dinner? Let's get our minds off this mess for a little while," she suggested.

My eyes lit up.

"That's an excellent idea."

Mrs. Caroline argued with Ernesto about my leaving.

"She isn't a child, Ernesto. Jonathan won't mind if she has dinner with her mother-in- law," she said.

"I know, Mrs. Caroline, but I was given strict orders not to let her leave the house. At least let one of the men come with you. Mr. Jonathan is scared that-" Ernesto quarreled with her.

"That's enough, Ernesto. Nothing is going to happen. We are big girls. Come on, Claire," she pulled me out the front door.

We were riding in Mrs. Caroline's Jaguar for a mere ten minutes when Jonathan called her cell phone.   "We are fine, son. Claire needs to get out of that house and breathe. Quit your worrying," she said.

Jonathan asked to speak to me.

"Don't do anything stupid, Claire. Do you understand? When we hang up, tell me you love me."

"I understand. I love you," I hung up the phone.

"Jonathan said you lost your mobile phone on the trip from Oklahoma City. When will you be getting a new one, dear?" Mrs. Caroline asked me over the clicking of her blinker.

"Soon I hope," I said.

We were seated at a beautiful table in a dimly lit Italian restaurant. Mrs. Caroline ordered the alfredo, and I feasted on a plate of spaghetti. She talked mostly about the events of the last several days and then apologized for ruining our nice dinner with such morbid conversation.

"No more talk of airplanes and burning buildings," she instructed. "Let's talk about you."

"You know all there is to know, Mrs. Caroline," I lied while scooping marinara sauce onto the breadstick.

"I'm so glad Jon found you," she stated, drinking her wine, her diamond jewelry sparkling. "I have to admit that I was concerned when he told me how young you were. But when he explained the way you feel about one another, my mind was put at ease."

"What did he say?" I asked curiously as I spotted Marco sitting in the front of the restaurant.

"I'm sure you know that Jon has had plenty of women over the years. He's such a handsome and sweet boy, but let's face it, most of the women he's brought around were simply gold diggers."

"You don't think I'm a gold digger?" I asked, remembering our fake love story about asking him to buy me a British car.

"I don't, Claire," she said firmly.

It started to make some sort of sense. I mean, the kidnapping was a horrid experience, a ridiculous plan, but I began to sort of understand why he had taken me. He'd been heartbroken so many times. He was handsome enough, but women mostly came around for his money. Somehow in his sick and twisted mind, he thought kidnapping me would lead to real love.

"Your age didn't bother me once he told me some of the things you've said to him," she dabbed the napkin at her lips and brushed a crumb off the lapel of her royal blue jacket.

"Like what?" I asked, confused, still eyeing the bodyguard.

"Oh, that conversation between the two of you about how you've always felt lost, out of place, with the death of your parents and the foster care. Claire, he nearly cried when he told me what you said about finally feeling at home with him. He says your words are genuine. He says that he's learned how to spot the gold digging liars, and you aren't one of those," she reached across the table and patted my hand.

I didn't know what to say.

"He's only ever felt this way one other time," she said.

"Suzanne?"

She nodded. "God, he loved that girl. I know he loves you, but I don't think he will ever get over her death."

Death? I inhaled sharply. He had simply told me that Suzanne and Grant sleeping together had ended the relationship.

"How long ago did she pass?" I asked, fishing for answers.

"Her car accident was in 95. It was such a freak tragedy, too. Her brakes just suddenly going ka-put like that? Jonathan was devastated," she shook her head.

1995? Jonathan said Suzanne and Grant had their affair in 1995. I trembled at the thought of him tampering with her brakes and causing her death because she had cheated on him. I knew it was entirely possible.

When we arrived at the house, Mrs. Caroline kissed me goodbye, drove away and left me standing on the massive front porch. Was now my chance? Couldn't I just take off running, across the yard, down the street?

"Get inside, Miss Claire," a broken English accent called to me from the side of the house. It was Marco, who had been following us all night.

I did as I was told. The man walked in behind me, locked the doors and armed the security system.

"Have a nice dinner?" Ernesto called from the living room as I walked up the stairway.

"Lovely," I answered.

I knew there were cameras in my room and probably more hidden throughout the home. If only I could find and tamper with them. I wanted to snoop through Jonathan's office and the drawers in his bedroom. I didn't know what I would be looking for, but I wanted to find something. I had to find something that explained Suzanne's death.

THIRTEEN

Three more days passed. I was kept inside, serving my sentence. I was going crazy formulating escape plans only to back out because of fear. Jonathan continued to call, Marco continued to cook and the others continued to watch my every move.

"Mr. Jonathan set up an appointment for you with Miss Camilla," Ernesto said as we sat around the kitchen table feasting on Marco's omelet.

"Why?" I asked as the men stared at me.

"He thought you might enjoy some pampering today," he replied.

"That's so nice of him," I said wryly.

Ernesto and the white guy drove me across town to the boutique. Again we were greeted by Camilla, this time her pixie cut was an unsightly shade of purple. She drooled over my ring and then pulled me to the back of the empty salon where she drew a privacy curtain. Ernesto and Roger sat in the chairs at the front, softly speaking in Spanish and looking at women's magazines.

"How is Jonathan?" Camilla asked as she heated the wax for my legs.

"He's okay."

"He sounded terrible when he called me yesterday. This attack has really taken a toll on him," she nodded at me. I reclined on the table as she put the scorching wax on my legs and ripped the hair from them.

"I'm sure you are missing him."

"Very much," I said, tears welling in my eyes from the pain of the waxing.

"He was so sweet to arrange this for you. He said this was stressful for you on top of so many other changes you've been through recently."

I suppose it was kind to arrange for me to have hot wax poured on my legs followed by ripping the hair from their follicles. I missed shaving with a regular old Bic and my dad's Barbasol.

"I will fill in your nails and give you a massage," she smiled at me.

"Thank you," I quietly spoke and watched the ceiling tile.

When she was done with my legs, I peered through the curtain to see the chairs where Ernesto and Roger had been sitting were empty. My eyes searched the small boutique for them, but they were nowhere to be found. Finally I eyed Ernesto outside on his phone. They were both standing beneath the shop's awning as Roger lit a cigarette.

"Camilla?" I asked as she rubbed moisturizer on my legs. "Can I use your telephone?"

"Sure," she said, leaving me alone for only a second and returning with a cordless receiver.

I remained reclined on the table as she cleaned spilled wax from the vanity. I frantically dialed my parent's number. I didn't know what I would say. I didn't care that Camilla heard. I wasn't thinking of the risks associated with making this call- the risks to myself or to my loved ones. I just saw an opportunity and took it.

The phone rang four, five, six times. I became infuriated that my parents were living in 2001 without an answering machine or caller ID, especially now that their daughter was missing. I wanted to curse my father for still being stuck in the 1950s.

Why weren't the police there to monitor calls? I had only been missing for twelve days. Why had they already given up on finding me? The police should have been the ones tapping my home phone, not Jonathan Marsh. Someone should have been home to answer the phone. This was my only chance to be saved, and my family probably couldn't hear the telephone over Bob Barker on the deafening television.

I ended the call, and I began to dial Nathan's home. I would call as many numbers as I could, next would be 911, until I reached a comforting voice on the other line.

The call to Nathan's house didn't even have a chance to ring before Ernesto came inside the boutique. I quickly hung up the phone and handed it to Camilla.

"No answer?" she asked. I shook my head quickly and tried to change the subject.

"My legs feel smooth as a baby's butt now, Camilla. Thank you," I sat up and followed her through the curtain to the manicure table.

Ernesto watched us move to the opposite side of the salon. I had a seat at the table, my heart pounding. He didn't know I had tried to contact my family. I was still safe.

Camilla sat before me and spread all of the nail tools in front of her. "Whoops, forgot the phone," she stood. "If I don't keep it on the charger, it won't last ten minutes."

My eyes shifted to Ernesto. He had heard what she said. However, this didn't mean that he knew I'd used the phone.

"The static on this thing is terrible, too. I'm surprised you could even hear a dial tone," Camilla said, returning the old cordless phone to its cradle and sitting back in front of me.

I closed my eyes. I tightly closed my eyes, gulped, and waited on Ernesto to say something.

"Who did you call, Miss Claire?" he asked. His tone was kind.

My heart palpitated as Camilla dug under my cuticles.

"I called my fiancé," I lied.

Ernesto knew this was a fib. I didn't even know Jonathan's mobile number.

"No answer?" Ernesto quizzed me.

"No," I shook my head and glanced at him.

The look on his face terrified me.

~ 83 ~

I said little as Camilla polished my nails. I didn't want the massage, this pampering, to end because I knew I was about to be punished. I knew that my life and my families' lives were in grave danger. The only place I would be safe was here, in this salon, with a purple-headed girl rubbing my tense shoulders with oil.

But the time had come to leave. Camilla thanked us, and I followed Ernesto out of the shop. Roger followed closely behind me. As I was sitting in the middle of the truck bench seat, Ernesto driving and Roger to my right, I was shaking.

"Tsk, tsk, Miss Claire. Why did you do that?" Ernesto asked. Roger was staring at me, the hot breath from his nostrils landing on my neck.

"I don't know," I replied honestly.

"Who did you call? Tell me the truth," Ernesto demanded.

"No one answered," I looked to my hands.

"Who did you call!" he exclaimed. Roger was still peering at me.

"I called home!" I shouted back to him.

"Mr. Jonathan is not going to be happy. Not at all."

Roger tightly grabbed my arm and escorted me to my room. I was locked inside for hours. I sat on the bed, crying, shaking, and I vomited twice. What was taking so long? Was someone harming my child at that moment? The thought was too much to bear.

Ernesto woke me after I fell asleep from fear. He handed me the telephone.

"Hello?" I sat up, my eyes fixated on all of the frightening men surrounding my bed.

"What did you do, Claire?" Jonathan shouted.

"I'm sorry," I cried. "I wasn't thinking. I'm so sorry."

"No, you weren't thinking! You are going to be punished. You understand?" he screamed to me.

"Yes, but please don't hurt my child. Please don't hurt Vaiden. I am begging you," I sobbed into the phone, snot dripping from my nose.

The phone clicked, and all was silent.

"I hate to do this, Miss Claire. I certainly hate to do this," Ernesto said as he took the phone from my hand and then struck my cheek with his fist.

I was certain that my head had fallen off of my shoulders. I was certain that the stinging and swelling of my eye would leave me blind for the rest of my life.

One by one, the men beat my body. Ernesto only struck me in the face once, but Roger and Louis threw his heavy fists into my stomach and my back. Marco stood to the side, watching, smirking and eating an enchilada.

I lay motionless on the floor, my body aching. My smooth legs were covered in bruises, my manicured nails broken from the fight. I felt heat rising from my purple stomach, the taste of blood was in my mouth. I was motionless on the floor for hours, tears stinging my broken eye, wishing that death would come.

I finally limped to the bathroom to survey the damage. I stared at my broken and bruised body in the mirror and remembered the men's words.

"Let's rape her," Roger had casually suggested.

My blood was covering one of the star tattoos on his knuckle.

"No!" Ernesto exclaimed. "Do you want Mr. Jonathan to kill you?"

"But she's pretty," Roger shrugged.

"That's out of the question, Roger. We would all end up dead," Ernesto shouted and shook his head.

"She's had enough," Marco said, leaning against the doorway, arms crossed, as if he were now bored with it all.

"Let her rest," Ernesto said. "She needs to heal. Mrs. Caroline or someone could show up for another unexpected visit."

I stepped into the shower and washed the sweat from my hair. The cool water stung my body, yet relieved my wounds. I stood under the waterfall, praying that Vaiden was safe. I'd learned my lesson. I would never attempt to reach my family again.

FOURTEEN

I don't know how many days I was locked in the room, without food. I drank from the bathroom tap. I nursed my wounds with a tube of Neosporin that I found in the vanity drawer. I sat in the marble tub of cold water, hoping to relieve the swelling and pain.

As the days passed, I watched my contusions slowly change from purple to light green. I sat on the bed, starving, hurting, and wishing to see someone. As absurd as it sounded, I wished Ernesto would visit me. I knew he would kill me if instructed to do so, and he had nearly knocked my head off with his powerful blow, but he didn't let the men rape me. I'm sure he did that out of fear for his own life, but I also believed that he cared about me in some way.

The exhaustion of it all forced me to sleep. Surprisingly, I slept soundly. I wanted to sleep as much as possible. It was the only way that I could escape this nightmare.

While Jonathan was gone, the house hadn't been as cold. I even heard the thugs complain about the freezing temperatures in the home, thankful that they could set the thermostat to any number above 60 while Jonathan was away.

So when I woke one night, shivering from the cold, I knew Jonathan had returned. I opened my sleepy eyes and shifted them around the dark room. I saw the clock on the bedside table, the bright green numbers displaying 9:14 PM. I felt something move, and I caught his silhouette sitting at the foot of the bed.

I turned over, prepared to battle with him, prepared for more punishment, when his shadow turned to face me in the dark.

"How are you feeling?" he asked. His voice was low.

"Fine," I lied.

"I'm sorry this had to happen," he sounded remorseful.

"Is my family okay?" I asked, frightened to know the answer.

He paused for a few moments and my eyes filled with tears, my soul filled with dread.

"They are fine," he said.

"You're telling the truth? They are really fine?" the hope rose in my voice.

"They're fine, Claire," he stated. "But I promise that I won't be so kind next time. Consider this a warning."

"Thank you," I said, relieved.

"You're welcome," he answered. "Are you sure you're alright? Have your bruises healed?"

"I will be fine. As long as my daughter is okay," I said.

"Your daughter is fine. I will have my contacts send some pictures of her just so you know I'm telling the truth," he offered.

"I'd love to see a photo of her. Thank you."

I'd thanked him twice in the same minute. He'd stolen my life and my happiness. He instructed men to beat me within an inch of my life, and yet, I thanked him. The words were bitter when they rolled off my tongue, but I knew I would continue to thank him when he spared the lives of those I loved. I knew I had to show him more compassion. I knew he was a dangerous man, and I knew the only way to keep myself and my family alive was to show him kindness.

"My mother called for you several times while you were locked up here. Ernesto told her that you were battling the flu. Mother is persistent, so she showed up with a pot of homemade chicken noodle soup this morning."

"That was nice," I said quietly.

"Besides being persistent, she's terribly afraid of vomit. The only thing that kept her from barging up here to check on you was Ernesto telling her that you've been puking your guts up for two days," he explained. "Anyway, I can warm some and bring it up to you if you'd like."

"I'd like that," I confessed. I was starving.

After taking a hot shower and changing into clean pajamas, I exited the bathroom to find all of the lamps in the room lit and

Jonathan lying on the bed, one foot crossed over the other. He was wearing a navy Astros sweatshirt and blue jeans. Nathan owned the same pair of pants-light blue, boot cut, Levis 517 Red Tabs, with a small fray on the left knee. I had no idea old men wore the same style jeans as twenty-year-old kids. I looked past him to the tray of soup and crackers that was sitting on the right side of the bed where I slept.

"You'll need to wash your sheets tomorrow," he said. "You've been lying in them for six days."

"Six days!" I exclaimed, famished and nearly running to the food on my side of the bed. "I had no idea I was in here that long. What is today?"

"September 23rd. It's Sunday," he answered. "I guess you need a television in here, too."

"That would be nice. Thanks," I slurped the delicious soup, warmth filling my body.

"Your face has healed nicely," he reached over and grazed my cheek with his hand. I didn't pull away from him. His touch made me quiver, but I kept calm and composed.

"I'm feeling much better," I glanced at him as he rested his head on the pink pillow and stared at me regretfully.

"I'm so sorry, Claire. I hate this had to happen. You know I'd never want to hurt you."

"I know," I nodded and ate a cracker. I believed that he was repentant. He was a mad lunatic, but I knew that he didn't want this to happen. "How was your trip?"

He looked at me for a moment, pleasantly surprised that I would even care to ask. Then he stared across the room, his face overcome with sadness.

"The world seems so different now. We visited New York for two days. I was shocked at the mayhem and the chaos there. I was also shocked at how people are coming together across the country," he spoke earnestly. "This tragedy is going to bring us all together. I just know it."

"I'm sorry your friends died, Jonathan," I said before I swallowed the warm soup.

He was quietly lying beside me, and I could feel his head turn towards me on the pillow. I could feel his aqua eyes watching me.

"What did you say?" he quietly asked.

"I'm sorry your friends died," I repeated.

He continued to soundlessly stare at me.

"What?" I looked at him, wondering why he wasn't speaking.

"You said my name," he replied.

"What?" I ruffled my brow with confusion.

"You said my name. You've never spoken my name," he glowed.

He was right. I'd never spoken his name out loud to Camilla, Ernesto, the thugs. I'd always said "him" or "he". His name had seemed too blasphemous to even speak aloud.

"You said my name," he said again, expecting me to reply.

I remained silent and continued to slurp the warm soup.

FIFTEEN

As the weeks passed, we fell into our own dysfunctional routine. Ernesto was left in charge when Jonathan went to work. We stayed in the house watching television or playing Yahtzee while the security system stayed armed-not to keep anyone out but to keep me in.

I wasn't yet allowed to leave the house as part of my punishment for attempting to call Nashville. I was told that with good behavior I would be allowed to go outside again. Jonathan even said that I could drive once enough time had passed.

Ernesto and I formed a friendship of sorts. I laughed at his corny jokes, and he listened to my stories about Vaiden's first steps and first words. I could see the sympathy in his eyes when mine would fill with tears at memories of my little girl.

We played a game of pool now and again and threw darts in the game room. At first I viewed the pool stick and the sharp darts as weapons, but I was reminded of the bruises, the blood, the warnings from Jonathan, and I quickly put those thoughts out of my mind.

When Ernesto ran errands or left the house for one reason or another, Roger would arrive to babysit me. Every time I looked at him, I could still hear his casual suggestion to molest me. I was terribly afraid of him. He would stare at me, mumbling vulgar comments, winking at me as he chewed on a toothpick.

"There are cameras everywhere in this house. If you touch me, he will see," I said as he walked closer to me in the living room.

"The only cameras on this property are outside and in your bedroom," he looked around. "And we aren't in either of those places are we?"

This was news to me. I thought that I had been watched everywhere I went throughout the home. And at that moment, I wished the cameras had actually been there.

"I will tell him," I backed away from Roger as he came closer to me.

"I've known Jonathan a long time. He won't believe you over me. He'll think you are just up to causing trouble again."

I continued to back up until I reached the foyer stairway. Then I turned and ran as fast as I could up the stairs to the safety of the cameras. Roger stomped behind me as I ran, but he never gave full pursuit. I heard him laughing once I was protected in my room.

I joined Jonathan in the dining room for dinner every night. He wanted so badly for ours to be a normal relationship as he told me about his day at work and discussed the government and the country since the attack. He asked my opinion on what tie he should wear to meetings or what I would like to have for dinner on the following nights. I remained elusive and gave quick answers to his questions.

On the rare occasion that I fell out of my vague routine and gave him an in-depth reply to his questions or spoke his name, his face would light up with hope that I was learning to love him.

I wasn't.

"Here," he slid an envelope across the dining table to me. I put down my fork and opened it.

Inside was a photo of my family. Vaiden, Nathan, my mother and Emma were all standing in my driveway. October had officially arrived, and bright orange and yellow oak leaves covered the yard. Vaiden appeared to be riding her tricycle while my mother and Nathan spoke. Emma stood to the side, arms crossed, as her foot kicked at a pebble or something on the drive.

"They are okay," I sighed in relief.

By the angle of the photo, I could tell that it was taken from down the street, possibly in front of the Barkley's home. He did have surveillance on my house after all.

"I told you," Jonathan poured himself another glass of wine.

"Oh, thank God," I studied the photo. My mother's face looked sad and weary from my disappearance. Vaiden's hair seemed longer. Nathan's tall truck was as muddy as usual as he stood beside it in his camouflage cap and green jacket.

Jonathan remained silent while I studied the picture. I finally put it down and resumed eating the pot roast.

"Before you came along, I had a maid and a chef," he stated.

"Yeah?"

"I was thinking maybe you are ready to start performing some housewife duties. You know, keeping the house clean, maybe learning to cook. I thought you could ask my mom to share some of her recipes with you?" he suggested.

"I guess," I shrugged.

I was bored being cooped up in the house all day. Cooking and cleaning would at least help the hours to pass, to keep my mind off missing my family. Besides, if Roger was right, and there weren't cameras placed throughout the house, maybe I could snoop around while cleaning and find out some more information about my fiancé.

"I let the help go when you came because it would be too complicated. Who's to say you wouldn't go blabbing to Dorothy about your family while she dusted the lamps?"

"I wouldn't do that," I lied.

"Sure," he said sarcastically.

"Jonathan?"

His head shot up at the sound of my voice speaking his name, and his eyes were beaming.

"Roger scares me," I confided in him. "I know he and Ernesto are meant to intimidate me, but I'm really uncomfortable around him."

"They aren't meant to intimidate you unless you need to be intimidated. If you are playing by the rules and doing as you're told, there's no reason to be afraid of them."

"I have been doing as I'm told, and Roger still frightens me," I looked down at my empty plate.

"Why? What has he done?" Jonathan's tone became concerned.

"He's always saying disgusting things to me. I don't like the way he looks at me, either," I confessed.

"What has he said?" Jonathan pushed his plate away while staring at me, looking worried.

"Have you seen the footage of the beating?" I asked him.

He shook his head. "I couldn't watch it."

"I think you should. Then you'll know what I'm talking about," I urged him.

He immediately stood up from the table and told me to follow him. In all of the hours, days, weeks that I'd spent in the house, I'd never been down the hallway past his bedroom.

At the end of the hallway, there was a door with a keypad. I was instructed to look away as he typed in the numbers. When the door opened, there was a stairway that led down to the basement.

The basement wasn't damp or dreary. Rows of fluorescent lighting made the room bright. A shelf of monitors and computers lined one of the walls. There I could see the outside surveillance and the observation in my bedroom. Roger had been right. There weren't any more cameras in the house.

Jonathan rummaged through some digital tapes and found the one of the beating. I could tell from the angle that the camera must have been concealed in the smoke detector on my ceiling. It gave a bird's eye view of the entire room.

After a few minutes, the tape began to play. Jonathan looked away, turning the volume low so that he couldn't hear the sounds of the men's fists hitting my flesh. I watched the recording without flinching.

"Turn it up."

He looked to the monitor and increased the volume, and he heard Roger's callous words.

"That son of a bitch," he muttered, rewinding the video and listening again. And again.

"He scares me, Jonathan," I said his name just to get my point across.

He looked to me.

"You won't have to worry about Roger anymore."

And I knew I wouldn't.

"Are you nervous?" he asked as we merged onto the freeway that night, heading to a charity event for the Humane Society.

"I don't know," I said, watching the cars of happy families pass us on the busy expressway. They were happy families on the way to dinner, the movies. They were happy families living a normal life. Mothers were within reach of their children.

"You'll do fine," he reassured me as I pulled the cardigan sweater close to my body.

"Does it have to be so cold in here? It's October now. It's colder in this car than it is outside," I murmured.

"I'm hot natured. You know that," he adjusted the Jaguar's thermostat from five blue bars to four.

"Where's he been keeping you hidden?" Mrs. Caroline wrapped her arms around me, her familiar and comforting scent engulfing me. "I haven't seen you in weeks."

"We've been busy, Mother," Jonathan answered her question.

She gave him a kiss on the cheek, and we followed her through the civic center and into the grand ballroom as she spoke to several people who worked for the Humane Society and introduced me along the way.

I stood in the corner, sipping my water, wishing I could drink liquor like the grownups. I'd only drunk alcohol a handful of times in my life, the episode always ending in a vomiting spell and a hard scolding from my father. But I remember the looseness that I felt when I had consumed a couple of wine coolers or beers. I felt invincible. I felt carefree. I needed to feel those things now.

I met one person after another, and I could barely keep the names and faces straight. As ridiculous as it sounded, I wished Ernesto was there. He could have easily killed me at any moment, but he was the only friend that I had.

"Claire?" a sweet voice approached me.

I turned to see a woman only a few years older than me. She had long, strawberry blonde hair. She was tall and thin, nearly the same height as me. Her smile, the freckles on her cheeks, her green eyes all seemed warm and inviting.

"Yes?" I turned to her.

"We're neighbors," she extended her hand. "Cybil Baker."

I shook her manicured hand and eyed the chocolate diamond ring on her finger. I had to think for a moment to make sure that I gave the correct name.

"Claire Harper," I said.

"I'm sorry I haven't been over to introduce myself sooner. My husband and I have been in New York for the last couple of weeks," she took a drink of her cocktail, her black ball gown sparkling under the colossal chandeliers.

"Oh," I said. "Is your husband a politician?"

"Oh, no," she laughed loudly. "Andrew is in real estate. My parents live in New York. We went up to visit with them for a few weeks after the attack."

"Is everyone well?" I asked.

"Yes, they are all fine. Nervous, but they are fine," she stated. "I'm so glad to finally meet you. Jonathan told us all about you before you came down to Houston."

"I'm glad to be here," I lied.

"I live two houses down from you. The white brick with the columns?" she asked.

"Oh, your home is beautiful. I've admired it many times," I said. "The Magnolia trees are breathtaking."

"Thank you," she smiled. "Some girls and I get together for Grub and Gab every Wednesday. We grub and we gab. We are meeting at my house next week. I would love for you to come."

Her invitation was sincere.

"I would love that," I confessed.

"Great!" she exclaimed, looking around the room of elite animal lovers. "These events bore me to tears."

I giggled. "I'm still new to all of this."

"I grew up in Memphis. My father sold cars, and not Land Rovers or Jaguars, but used Chryslers with transmission problems," she laughed.

Memphis, Tennessee. Oh, I so wanted to talk about Memphis, Tennessee with her. I wanted to talk about the barbeque, the Pink Palace Museum, all of the places I visited when I stayed there with my aunt before she had died.

"How did you end up here?" I asked as I watched Jonathan laugh loudly with a group of men.

My mother always wanted to live in New York. We all moved up there after I graduated high school. I met Andrew in New York. He's from Houston so when we married, we ended up here," she explained.

"I'm still in culture shock," I said.

"So you weren't born with a silver spoon in your mouth, either?" she nudged me.

"No," I laughed as I struggled to remember my fake past. "I was raised in foster care in Oklahoma City. This is all new to me."

"Well, you can stick with me. I'm not like these other upper-crust bitches," she grabbed another cocktail from the bar behind us. "Cheers!"

I tapped my glass of water against her pink drink.

I liked Cybil.

"It's out of the question, Claire," Jonathan argued with me as we drove home in the pouring rain that evening.

"You want me to fit in don't you? Do you expect me to never have any friends?" I pleaded with him.

"Of course I want you to fit in and have friends, but-" he began, his eyes focused on the wet road.

"I've learned my lesson. I'm not going to call home again. I'm not going to blab our little secret," I yelled at him. "I'm coming to terms with the realization that I'm never leaving. At least let me have a damn friend!"

He sighed loudly and looked at me.

"I guess that beating is just what you needed then?" he asked.

"It's exactly what I needed, Mr. Marsh. You win," I crossed my arms.

"Watch that pretty little mouth, Claire."

I rolled my eyes and stared at the rain pouring onto the glass, wondering if it was raining at home. Vaiden hated thunder. If it was storming at home, she was surely snuggled in my parent's king sized bed, one leg in my father's back, the other in my mother's abdomen. She was the wildest sleeper I'd ever seen. I missed her sweet little foot buried in my armpit.

"Okay," he conceded. "You can go."

"Well, thank you."

"But if you screw this up in any way or if you go blabbing the truth to these bitches, then that last ass whipping will be mild in comparison. Do you hear me?" he banged the steering wheel with his palm.

"I hear you," I groaned.

Cybil called the landline on Wednesday morning and asked me to bring a dish for the Mexican themed Grub and Gab. I agreed, thanked her again for the invitation and hung up the phone.

"The theme tonight is Mexican. I need to take something," I looked around the kitchen, wondering where to begin.

Ernesto sat silently at the bar while reading the newspaper and sipping his coffee.

"What about you, Ernesto?" I interrupted his reading.

"What?" he looked up to me.

"It's Mexican night. Can I take you?" I grinned at him.

"Very funny, Miss Claire," he smirked. "Can't you make a queso dip or something?"

"No, but I could buy something. Will you take me to the grocery?" I asked.

~ 98 ~

"Mr. Jonathan doesn't want you leaving the house yet. You're still on punishment," Ernesto shook his head.

I sighed loudly. "Can you go for me?"

"There's no one to stay with you."

"What happened to Roger?" I wondered aloud.

Ernesto clicked his tongue and shook his head. "You don't want to know, Miss Claire."

Ernesto made some phone calls, and Marco showed up at the house with a sack of groceries. I was standing in the kitchen with a fearsome criminal teaching me how to make homemade salsa and stuffed Jalapenos.

Jonathan walked me to the door that evening, the Pyrex dishes of appetizers in my hands.

"Marco will be following you, Claire," he said as I exited the front door.

"Do you really think I'm going to take off running with all of this?" I held up the dishes.

"Have a good time," he shut the door and left me alone on the front steps.

Of course I had thought of running. The thought of running was always in the front of my mind. I'd been missing for six weeks, and my longing became deeper, my heart more broken every day that I was away from Vaiden, my parents, Emma and Nathan. But I was too terrified to run. I knew that living in bondage was my destiny. I fervently tried to replace the thoughts of escaping with thoughts of contentment at this entire absurd situation.

I walked to the house with the columns, aware that Marco was only a few steps behind. I stepped onto Cybil's massive porch, admiring her beautiful fall wreaths, as Marco concealed himself in the landscaping.

The doorbell rang, and Cybil greeted me.

"I'm so glad you could come, Claire," she smiled at me, margarita in her hand. I thanked her and entered her home.

"Your home is beautiful," I eyed the flowers in the vases, the knick knacks on shelves. Her home had a woman's touch. Jonathan's home was decorated beautifully, but it lacked something. It lacked *my* touch.

She thanked me, and we entered her elegant kitchen crowded with ladies. Cybil introduced me to them all. They were all dressed casually, but they exuded wealth. Still, none of their diamonds compared with the one that I donned on my left hand.

I was familiar with my past at that point. The story easily rolled of my tongue- foster care, Marion, meeting Jonathan in the Bordeaux club. The women contently listened, smiling at the tale of how I had met the love of my life.

"Rags to riches," a short fat girl with highlighted hair crooned over her tequila cocktail.

All of the women seemed to think highly of Jonathan. They praised his looks, his personality and his generosity to numerous charities. They praised him for taking in a sad and broken girl.

"He saved you," another woman, her neck covered in an orange scarf, grinned at me.

If only they knew.

All of the women, except Cybil, had children. They talked about their kids' education, their play dates, their boutique clothing and potty training attempts. They passed pictures of their little ones around the room, smiling and laughing at recent stories of the cute things they had done.

"Do you want children, Claire?" the lady with the scarf asked me.

The question nearly rocked me to my core. My knees buckled, and my heart skipped a beat.

"I love children," I answered truthfully. The pain of missing my own child was unbearable at that moment.

When the serving dishes of quesadillas and bean dips were empty, the ladies began filing out the door, thanking Cybil for a wonderful evening and saying how nice it was to meet me. Cybil asked me to stay a little while longer. I knew Marco was still hidden outside, but I was unsure if I had a curfew.

I followed Cybil onto her back porch, the crisp October wind blowing the large magnolias surrounding her house as she lit a cigarette and offered me one.

"I don't smoke," I shook my head.

"And why not?"

"I don't know," I shrugged. "I just never took it up."

"I'd go stark raving mad without my nicotine," she confessed, the smoke rolling out of her nose, her royal blue sweater shining under the porch light.

I giggled softly and wondered if I was even allowed to smoke. Would Jonathan approve if I were to take up any bad habits?

"So you don't drink. You don't smoke. What do you do?" she sang the Adam Ant song.

"I don't know. Nothing I guess," I replied, feeling like a prude.

"I keep forgetting you are just a baby, not even drinking age yet! When is your birthday?" she asked me.

Elle Holley would turn twenty one on June 3rd. At that moment I couldn't remember when Claire Harper turned twenty one. I struggled to remember the date, but it just wouldn't come to me.

"Not for a while," I said, hoping that would satisfy Cybil's question.

"We should have a huge party for your birthday. Will you already be married by then?"

March. My fake birthday was in March.

"My birthday is in March!" I nearly shouted, thankful that I had remembered. "We haven't set a date for the wedding."

"Well, you have a lot of work cut out for you, girl. Jonathan Marsh's wedding will be *the* social event of the season,"

Cybil flicked her cigarette to the yard. I secretly hoped it had found Marco hiding in the bushes.

SIXTEEN

The days became shorter, the Gulf of Mexico wind became cooler, and the yard was covered in leaves. Fall had always been my favorite time of the year. My father and I managed to squeeze in a Knoxville trip to see a Vols football game each year, and I would get up before dawn and tag along with Nathan on a couple of hunts. I favored my wool sweaters and cowboy boots. I'd been looking forward to autumn for months.

I never imagined that I would be spending the change of seasons in Houston, Texas. I'd missed taking Vaiden trick or treating. I'd missed the exciting fall carnival at our church. I was missing so many events back home and missing so many people.

My mother's birthday was on November 3rd. She weighed heavily on my mind as I spent the day cleaning the house. I scrubbed Jonathan's toilet and yearned to hear her voice. I missed her hands, her nails always freshly painted in pink polish. I missed the smell of her Liz Claiborne perfume. I ached at my mother's absence.

Nathan's twenty first birthday was four days later on November 7th. Again, I tried to keep busy vacuuming and folding Jonathan's boxer shorts, but memories of the love of my life wouldn't let me be. Nathan had been planning for months to have a party at his parent's house to celebrate his twenty first. I wondered if he'd gone through with it, if he was playing beer pong and partying around a bonfire or if he was too distraught with my absence to celebrate.

I have to admit that the thought of Nathan being too bereaved to live a normal life was somewhat reassuring. I knew how selfish that sounded, and the thought made me feel terrible, but if the tables were turned and Nathan just vanished, I don't think I'd be in the mood to celebrate anything-even my birthday-for years after his disappearance.

Two months after I had attempted to call home, my punishment was still in full effect. I wasn't allowed to go anywhere except to the salon with the supervision of Ernesto. I still went to the weekly Grub and Gab with one of my chaperones hiding outside in the bushes, behind a tree or in a sandbox. Cybil had invited me over often just for a cup of coffee or to talk, but Jonathan refused to let me go. I was growing tired of feeding lies and excuses to Cybil as to why I couldn't come and hang out for the afternoon.

We visited Jonathan's parents regularly. We attended several family gatherings at his brother's home. Our weekends were always busy with a charity event or social function. I was learning to fit in with the other women, feeding them my rags to riches fairytale, smiling and nodding as much as possible.

On Thanksgiving evening, I was overcome with depression. I missed the Thanksgiving breakfast that we shared at Nathan's house. I missed sitting next to his grandfather at the dining table as he told stories about growing up a poor farm boy in the hills of East Tennessee. I missed the wonderful smells that filled my home on Thanksgiving evening-the turkey, the casseroles and the pumpkin pie. I missed dressing Vaiden in an adorable outfit and posing her next to the pumpkins and gourds on the front porch. I missed telling my sister to get her elbows off the table while we shared stories of why we were thankful.

As I sat at the Marsh family table that evening, surrounded by an elegant spread, beautiful china and the largest turkey that I had ever seen, I was on the verge of an anxiety attack. I wanted the Prozac to kick in and relieve me of the unease that I felt. I wanted to scream to the chandeliers that I didn't belong there. I wanted to blab our secret to all of Jonathan's relatives and beg them to convince him to let me go home; beg them to convince him to let me and my family alone.

But I didn't. Even if his mother pleaded forgiveness on her son's behalf and persuaded him to set me free, Jonathan was liable to hunt me down years later and destroy everything that was precious to me. If I revealed the truth now, I would still live in fear for the rest of my life.

I tried to remain calm, nudging my fork at the cranberry sauce, when it was my turn to tell everyone why I was thankful. Jonathan and I had rehearsed my answer in the car.

"I'm so incredibly thankful that Jonathan loves me and that he rescued me. I'm grateful that I will soon be a part of your family," I said as realistically as possible as his mother gave me a genuine smile.

Jonathan reached over and kissed my cheek as I shuddered inside but managed to cover my weariness with a smile.

"I'm thankful that Claire came into my life," he stated.

I knew he meant it.

"So," Mrs. Caroline's eyes examined us both, "when can we start planning the wedding?"

I looked to Jonathan as he chewed his food.

"Jonathan?" I asked him.

His face went all aglow, as usual, at the sound of his name rolling off my lips.

"Well, we were thinking after Claire's birthday in March. Claire thinks an April wedding would be nice," he gave the conversation to me.

"I've always dreamt of a spring wedding," I lied.

"I think April would be lovely," Mrs. Caroline agreed and nudged Mr. Marsh.

"Yes, lovely," he said, not really caring to get involved in a womanly wedding conversation.

"Have you picked a venue? The country club?" Adrienne asked, no doubt jealous that she'd been engaged to Casey for years and hadn't yet married.

"Well, actually, we were thinking maybe here, I mean if it isn't too much trouble?" Jonathan asked his parents.

"Oh!" Aunt Junie gasped. "That would be gorgeous!"

Mrs. Caroline and Aunt Junie passed excited glances.

"It sounds absurd, but I don't really want a wedding planner. I'd like to try to do everything myself. But, would you ladies consider helping me plan it?" I looked at them both, asking them exactly what they wanted to hear. Jonathan looked pleased as he gently squeezed my knee under the table.

"Claire!" Mrs. Caroline shrieked. "I would be honored."

"I would, too, dear!" Aunt Junie squealed.

Mr. Marsh nodded gladly as Casey's bloodshot eyes stared at his mashed potatoes.

Adrienne gave me a harsh look. I felt bad for her. I'd only known these people for a few months, and here I was stealing a wedding right out from under her. She'd invested most of her life with this family. I knew it wasn't fair.

We continued to discuss the wedding plans, the dress, the colors, while the men retired to the living room to drink whiskey and nap on the couch.

"Adrienne?" I asked while Mrs. Caroline went upstairs to find her old wedding album and Aunt Junie followed.

"Yeah?" she glared at me as she filed her fingernails in the keeping room.

"I know I've just waltzed in here and made everything about me, I mean, the engagement and the wedding. I want to apologize for that," I sat down beside her.

"Well I appreciate that, Claire," her face softened. "You know, I've waited a long time. I just feel like I should be the one planning a wedding right now."

"I know you do," I nodded at her, her olive face smooth and her long bangs hanging in her green eyes. "Would you like for us to hold off the wedding?"

Her mouth opened in shock, and she shook her head. "No, I can't ask you to do that. I've been begging Casey to set a date for years. He's just not ready."

"I would be glad to do that. I feel terrible stealing your spotlight," I bit my lip.

"That's sweet of you, Claire. I really appreciate the fact that you even asked," she reached out and patted my hand.

"Well, would you consider being my bridesmaid?" I asked her.

She grinned widely, "I'd be honored."

"Thank you, Adrienne. I really hope that we can be friends," I spoke the truth.

She reached out to hug me.

"Always a bridesmaid. Never a bride."

"You're very believable," Jonathan said as he drove us home that evening.

"I'm getting better then?" I asked, the frigid air conditioner causing me to shiver beneath my sage sweater dress, heavy pea coat and scarf.

"I don't think you're getting better at lying. I think you're getting better at telling the truth," he replied.

"That doesn't even make sense," I scoffed at him.

"I think you are embracing this life, this wedding and the idea of our marriage."

"You're wrong," I corrected him.

"You aren't excited about the wedding?" he merged off of the freeway.

"I was excited to marry Nathan Bingham. Not you," I said harshly.

"Well, then, you *are* getting better at lying," he stared at the dark road.

***

"I won't go," I demanded as I sat on my bed on Christmas morning.

"Claire, you have to go!" Jonathan shouted to me and walked to my closet to pick out my clothes.

"It's my child's third birthday! I can't spend the day *not* acknowledging that!" I screamed through tears and buried my head in the warmth of the bed.

~ 107 ~

"It's also Christmas. Christmas is a pretty huge deal," he called from the closet.

"My baby's birthday is a huge deal! You have to let me call her today, Jonathan! You have to!" the tears soaked my face as my stomach became more nauseated.

He remained silent, still hidden in my closet.

"It's my baby's birthday," I sobbed quietly into the down comforter.

He returned to the bedside, a pink chenille turtleneck and black pants in his arms.

"You're killing me," I continued to moan. "You are sucking the life right out of me."

He sat down at my feet and watched me gasp through my tears. He sighed loudly and looked to the ceiling.

"If I let you call, will you willingly come to Christmas dinner?" he asked.

I didn't say anything. I wanted to call my daughter, but I didn't want to go to Christmas dinner with his family.

"Claire!" he shouted angrily. "If I let you call, will you *willingly* come to Christmas dinner?"

"Yes," I sniffled.

"I should have found someone without a child," he mumbled to himself and left me alone in my room.

"Find someone else and let me go home!" I shouted to him.

We got in his car at nine that morning and we arrived in New Orleans after 3 PM. The ride was mostly silent as he flipped through the radio stations and called several distant relatives and friends to wish them a merry Christmas.

I sat in a ball, the seat heat of the Land Rover turned on high, still freezing from the air conditioning, freezing from the depression of missing my child's birthday.

"You're supposed to be in Miami with Michael Kee. It would make more sense if you called home from a Miami phone number," he thought aloud as we pulled up to a payphone in an abandoned parking lot on the west side of town. "Better yet, this is it. This is the last damn time you call home! Ever. Period."

"Thank you for letting me call her," I whispered through my scratchy throat, a throat sore from sobbing all day.

He walked me to the old dusty payphone. He dug the change out of his coat pocket, and he dialed the number. He held it to his ear for a moment, and then he passed it to me.

"Hello?" my mother spoke in a low, sad tone.

"Mama," I sighed into the phone, relieved to hear her voice.

"Elle!" she shouted.

"Mama, I called to speak to Vaiden. Will you put her on the phone?" I asked. Of course I wanted to have a lengthy conversation with every member of my family, but I had to say exactly what I was instructed to say.

"Where are you, Elle?" she cried into the receiver.

"I'm in New Orleans with Michael, Mama. We haven't made it to Miami yet."

"Baby, please come home. We are all so worried. We need you home with us, Elle. Are you in trouble?" her cries were frantic.

"Mama, I'm fine," I lied. "I need to speak to Vaiden."

The phone rustled for a moment, and I heard my sweet child's voice come over the line. It was the same adorable tone, only three months older and more pronounced.

"Mama?" Vaiden asked as my knees buckled, my eyes watered, and I couldn't form the words to speak.

"Baby," I gasped through my tears and listened to her breathe on the other end of the line. "Baby, Mama loves you. Happy birthday."

"I'm three, Mama," she said proudly.

I chuckled, tears blinding my eyes. "You're a big girl, Vaiden. Mama misses you so much. I miss you so much, baby."

Jonathan nudged me, bored with it all.

"Miss you, Mama."

Rustling came over the line again.

"The police gave up, Elle. They said you'd just run away. There's no crime in running away. They say there's nothing they can do. You can bring this Michael with you, but please come home," she continued to beg.

I held the receiver tightly, wanting to scream to my mother for help.

"Can I speak to Daddy?" I asked. Jonathan jerked the phone from my hands and slammed it into the box.

"Talking to Daddy wasn't part of the plan," he ushered me back to the car. "You spoke to your kid. That's the end of it."

When we arrived extremely late to Christmas dinner at his parent's house, Jonathan fabricated a lie about the two of us wanting to spend the afternoon together.

"She's having a rough time today, missing Marion and all," I overheard him say to his mother.

"Bless her heart," she replied.

They all assumed my blank stares and quiet demeanor stemmed from missing my English foster mother. No one pressed me with questions or forced me to join the conversation. They all knew it was a sad day for me, but they couldn't fathom the heartache I was experiencing as I stared at the tree. I felt empty and dead inside.

That night, Jonathan and I lugged all of my presents up to my room. Jonathan's parents had given me gorgeous clothes and scarves and gloves and a couple of early wedding presents- crystal picture frames, a wedding planning book. Jonathan gave me beautiful diamond earrings and matching necklace. My face was blank when he fastened the chain around my neck.

"Merry Christmas," he said before slamming my bedroom door behind him.

He was aggravated with the entire day, with the six hour drive to New Orleans for a one minute phone call. He was growing tired of me missing my family. In his psychotic mind, he had assumed I would be over them by now. He thought three months was plenty of time. Jonathan Marsh was a fool.

SEVENTEEN

A constant chill took to the air, and I craved the warmth of my mother's words, of my father's hugs, of Vaiden's smile, of Emma's sarcasm, of Nathan's love. I craved *any* kind of warmth in the freezing house.

"This is ridiculous," I marched to the thermostat and pressed the up button until it reached 77.

"Mr. Jonathan won't like-" Ernesto began.

"I don't give a damn what Mr. Jonathan won't like, Ernesto," I snapped at him and then stomped into Jonathan's bedroom to change the sheets on his bed.

I'd grown comfortable enough with my new "family" to express my frustrations. Jonathan *was* a powerful man, and I feared him to an extent. I knew he would have no problem putting a bullet through my head if I was to run down the street screaming for help, but I also knew that he would take most of my complaining without any retaliation.

We'd rung in the New Year the night before, and Jonathan was sleeping off a hangover. The heavy drapes were pulled tight as he slept soundly in his plush bed, drool dripping from his lip and stubble covering his cheeks.

"Rise and shine, sweetheart," I called loudly and sarcastically as I pulled back the burgundy curtains.

He mumbled and hid his head beneath the pillow.

"You shouldn't have had so much to drink," I scolded him as I walked around his large room and retrieved last night's clothes from the floor. "Get up. I need to wash your sheets."

He incoherently protested, his face still muffled by the pillow.

I watched him with anger and hate for what he'd put me through the night before.

"I guess you're still upset about last night? He sat up in the bed and yawned.

I said nothing.

"I guess I'll just have to get you drunk so you'll sleep with me, then?"

"There's not enough vodka in the world," I continued to clean.

"You know you're going to have to have sex with me eventually, Claire. That's what happens in a marriage!" he shouted, still irritated at me for refusing his advances the night before.

"We aren't married yet."

"Oh? You're going to happily sleep with me once we're married?" he smirked.

I remained silent.

"You had a baby at seventeen, Claire. You aren't *that* wholesome," he got out of the bed and walked to the bathroom. "Oh, and you aren't supposed to do laundry on the first day of the New Year. Don't you know that?"

I sat down on his bed and sighed. He'd tried to put his hands on me all night at the party. The more he drank, the more he insisted on kissing and groping me. Once we arrived home, he barged into my bedroom and pulled me into his arms. I slapped his jaw and he became irate, but he didn't force himself on me. Instead he stormed out of my room and slammed the door.

I knew the time would come when I would be required to have sex with Jonathan Marsh. I didn't care how handsome he was. The mere thought of being with him in that way, in *any* way, made me want to vomit.

I wondered how Nathan was handling the sexual part of his life. He was a twenty one-year-old man after all. Surely he wasn't going without, waiting on me to return. The thought of him with another woman in that way, in *any* way, also made me want to vomit.

I ripped the sheets from the huge bed, the smell of cologne and liquor permeating from them, and I left the bedroom, angry and nauseated.

"I'm going to Cybil's," I stated that afternoon.

"You are?" Jonathan asked, wearing only his boxer shorts, eating popcorn and watching television on the couch.

"She's invited me over to her house so many times, Jonathan. I can't keep making excuses not to go. We are supposed to be friends, and I haven't even invited her here. I told her at the party last night that we would get together today," I stood over him as his bloodshot eyes scanned the T.V.

"Invite her here then," he suggested.

"I don't want her in here seeing you lying around half naked, running to puke every ten minutes," I stated.

"You don't want her to see my body. Is that it?" he flexed his arms to show off his muscles.

"You make me sick," I rolled my eyes.

He quickly stood and darted over to me. "You better start showing me some respect, Claire. I get why you have a bad attitude now and then. I get that I've made your life a living hell. I get all of that, but you've gotten too comfortable with the way you speak to me. You need to have a little reverence and fear towards me, do you understand? I can make your life much worse than it is right now!"

~ 113 ~

At that moment, I was frightened. He'd yelled at me before, and he threatened my loved ones' lives on a daily basis, but his extreme lividness made me very afraid.

"I'm sorry," I looked to my feet, scared that he was going to hit me.

"Don't touch my thermostat again, either," he snapped, walking towards his bedroom. "If you want to hang out with Cybil, invite her over here. I will stay out of your way."

His bedroom door slammed.

I did call Cybil to come over that afternoon. She was nursing her own hangover, and she showed up with a bottle of Bloody Mary mix and circles under her eyes.

"I feel terrible," she confessed when she entered the kitchen and immediately mixed a drink.

"You drink too much," I said as she nodded.

"I know I do. I've turned into one of those rich lushes. Terrible, isn't it?" she grimaced.

"Why *do* you drink so much?" I pulled out a stool and watched her take over my kitchen.

"I drink because I hate my life. I hate my husband. I hate Houston, Texas," she replied bluntly.

Maybe I should start drinking, I thought.

"So you've got a nice place here," she looked around my home. "It was so nice of you to finally invite me over."

There was sarcasm in her tone.

"I'm sorry, Cybil."

"Where's stud?" she peeked around the corner at the living room, the television still blaring.

"He's got his own hangover. He's in the bedroom," I nodded towards the hallway that led to his room.

"And where is Ponch?" she looked around for Ernesto.

"Ponch has the day off. He's with a lady friend," I replied.

"What exactly does Ernesto do?"

"He's Jonathan's assistant," I said. "And mine."

Cybil shrugged and took a seat beside me.

"So," I turned to her, "did you have a good time last night?"

She nodded.

"It was okay. That Mary Margaret Wilcox is a talker, isn't she?"

I laughed.

"I thought she'd never shut up."

"Claire, I swear I heard her voice in my sleep. I woke up with the cold sweats," she cringed. "Oh, Cybil, your dress is *to die for!*"

I laughed at Cybil's Mary Margaret Wilcox high-pitched impersonation.

"Yeah, she's an annoying old hag," I agreed.

"So, I saw you and Jon get in a little tiff," she said, sipping the red mix.

"He just had too much to drink," I took up for him.

"He was awful handsy last night, wasn't he?"

I didn't want Jonathan to overhear Cybil talking badly about his behavior. She might end up with the same fate as Suzanne Simmons.

"He just had too much to drink," I repeated. "Everything is fine today."

"They all turn into horn balls when they've had too much sauce. I, on the other hand, am the complete opposite. I don't care for sex when I'm sober, and I certainly don't care for it when I'm drunk," she confessed.

I became embarrassed at the conversation. I certainly didn't know much about sex. Although I had a child so young, I wasn't experienced. I'd only been with Nathan a handful of times. He urged me to be with him more often, but fear of the birth control not working and having another child before we were married scared me to death. My strict Baptist upbringing also left me feeling pangs of guilt at the mere idea of sex before marriage.

"How is it with big J?" she motioned towards his room. "I bet a strapping thing like that can go all night, right?"

I sighed, wishing I could avoid the question, but she asked me again.

"I don't know," I admitted.

"What!" she exclaimed and slammed the red glass to the granite countertop.

"Shhh," I told her.

"You haven't slept with Jonathan, Claire?" she looked at me, stunned.

I shook my head.

"You don't drink, you don't smoke and you don't sleep with your fiancé?" she sang the Adam Ant song again.

"What is it with you and Adam Ant?" I glared at her.

"This is unbelievable," she shook her head.

"It isn't *that* unbelievable, Cybil. I haven't even known the man that long," I defended myself.

"But you are engaged to him, and you live with him. *You live with him.* What does he do? Surely he can't watch a pretty young thing like you walk around here and not have urges!" she stared at me like I was a prude.

I shrugged.

"He must really love you," she clicked her tongue.

"He does."

"Are you a virgin?" her questions kept coming.

"There was a boy in high school. My first love," I thought of Nathan.

"I just can't believe it," Cybil shook her head, her long pony tail resting on the shoulder of her NYU sweatshirt.

We were interrupted by the sound of Jonathan shuffling down the hardwood hallway. I hoped he hadn't heard the conversation. I didn't want him to know how comfortable Cybil and I were around one another. I didn't want him to know that I'd revealed such personal information to Cybil about our relationship. I didn't want him to know that I was thinking of Nathan when questioned about sex.

"Hey, Cybil," he replied as he entered the kitchen in his frayed jeans and gray sweatshirt.

"Jon," she smiled at him. "Well look at you all casual. I don't think I've ever seen you when you weren't in a three piece suit."

He laughed at her and kissed the top of my head, my blonde hair hanging loosely over my shoulders.

"What are you girls gabbing about?" he opened the refrigerator.

"Sex," Cybil replied very matter of fact.

He looked to us, my face turning a shade of crimson.

"Oh yeah?" he asked, eyeing Cybil's drink as he took a swig of orange juice.

My heart began to pound. I feared that Cybil would let Jonathan know that we had been discussing him. I feared that I would be punished for running my mouth.

"My sex life, not yours," she shook her head. "In fact, Claire won't tell me a thing about your sex life. Seems you've got a pretty classy dame here. She doesn't kiss and tell."

I sighed in relief as Jonathan walked over to me.

"Seems I do," he said.

Jonathan talked with us for the next hour. We spoke about the party the night before and Andrew's real estate slump. After Cybil ran to the bathroom and vomited up the Bloody Mary, she grabbed her bottle and went home.

"Are you telling her our business?" Jonathan gripped my arm once the door shut behind Cybil.

"No," I shook my head. "You heard her. I didn't tell her a thing."

"If you make me look bad to her, I will beat the hell out of you. I can just see her now, going home and telling that prick Andrew Baker all of our business. He runs his mouth like a damn woman. I won't have him smearing my name," his tone was livid, his grip on my arm was constricted.

"I didn't say anything! In the beginning you told me that you wanted me to portray myself as a classy woman who values her privacy. That's exactly what I'm doing. She asked about our sex life, our relationship. I didn't tell her anything," I fibbed.

He let go of my arm and sighed.

"Well, speaking of, I'm going crazy, Claire! A man can't go this long without sex! I'm short tempered with you because I'm going crazy!" he shouted again and returned to his room.

I rubbed my sore arm, and I knew the time was coming. The nausea returned.

EIGHTEEN

The wedding would take place at the Marsh estate on Sunday, April 14th, my father's birthday. I was firmly against the date because I couldn't bear to walk down an aisle without him, especially on the day he was born. But Jonathan's busy schedule interfered with every other weekend that month, and he was persistent that we marry in April.

By March, the wedding preparations were in full swing. The colors, the cake and so many other decisions had been made. I had been allowed to go on numerous unsupervised shopping trips with Mrs. Caroline and Aunt Junie, and I'd been given a mobile phone for Valentine's Day, complete with spy ware to monitor my location and every call that I made or received. I would hold the phone in my hand, my fingers skimming over the numbers that would reach my parents, Nathan, the police. Sometimes the temptation to call home was so strong that I would throw the phone across the room.

I was also allowed to drive a few days each week. Jonathan made sure that I knew the car was also equipped with a tracking device.

"I can monitor your location at all times. If you make one wrong turn or leave this city, I can detonate the vehicle," he looked at me seriously.

I laughed aloud.

"You're telling me that you can blow up the car, McGyver?" I said sarcastically.

I knew he was powerful and dangerous, and I didn't doubt that he was capable of heinous things, but threatening to "detonate" anything seemed a bit much.

"That's what I'm telling you, Claire," he retorted in a severe tone.

"Okay," I nodded, still not believing him. "Just don't blow it up while I'm hauling your mother and aunt around town."

"Yeah, well, you just play by the rules!" he exclaimed.

I shook my head at him and reversed out of the garage.

As I drove to his mother's house on that March afternoon, I passed exits that would take me to Nashville. I quickly looked away, shunned the idea, and followed the direct route to Mrs. Caroline.

My heart sank at the thought of meeting Jonathan at the end of the aisle in only a few weeks. Nathan Bingham should have been waiting for me there. My life wasn't supposed to turn out this way-ripped away from my family and destined to spend the rest of my days with a mad stranger.

As I stood in front of the mirror in the dress shop that afternoon and eyed myself in the elegant A-line wedding gown, I nearly fainted. Mrs. Caroline and Adrienne ran to my side, sure that I was lightheaded from the excitement of it all.

"I need my mother," I whimpered into Mrs. Caroline's chest as she rubbed my head and tried to comfort me. They assumed I meant my deceased mother, Ann Harper, or my deceased foster mother, Marion Stewart, but I meant my alive and well mother, Judith Holley, who was 800 miles away.

They brought me to my feet, the weight of the gown pulling at my hips, and Adrienne gave me a sip from her water bottle. I put my head in my hands and fought the tears. I was so tired of emotion bubbling from my eyes.

"I can't marry him," I sighed.

"Darling, you've just got cold feet. Everything will turn out fine," Mrs. Caroline patted my back and pulled me close.

"You don't understand," I couldn't hold the tears any longer. The sales lady watched the dark mascara leak from my lashes and became extremely nervous that it would stain the stunning white gown.

"Shhh," Mrs. Caroline whispered in my ear.

I was fully prepared to divulge our story to Mrs. Caroline. I didn't care that I would be killed. Surely his family would stop him before he harmed my family. The words were on the tip of my tongue.

"Therefore what God has joined together, let no one separate," she rocked me in her arms.

Like a faucet that had been turned off, the tears immediately ceased. I sat up, my face red and my makeup streaked. I wanted to tell Caroline that the devil had brought Jonathan and I together, not the Lord. The devil was responsible for the evil motives that lurked in Jonathan's mind. The devil was responsible for my kidnapping, my heartache, my family's heartache.

Jonathan had separated me from Nathan. Jonathan had torn apart something that God had brought together. And he would be punished for it.

"Amen," I said.

Once Mrs. Caroline purchased the costly dress, I thanked her and dropped them off at home so I could make it to my hair appointment with Camilla. As I pulled into the crowded salon parking lot, my cell phone rang. It was Jonathan.

"You're getting your hair done?" he asked, already knowing my location.

"Yes," I watched the busy street in my rear view mirror.

"Did you find a dress?"

"Yes," I sharply stated.

"I will expect you home by five," he hung up the phone.

I entered the crowded beauty shop. It was the first time Jonathan hadn't scheduled a private session with Camilla.

Camilla met me at the door, her hair now longer and a dastardly shade of blue. I immediately noticed that her demeanor was far different than usual. She spoke softly and didn't smile. I followed her to the chair at the back of the room.

"Busy day?" I looked around at the other women setting under dryers, the smell of hair dye and acetone crowding the small building. Camilla's co-workers frantically ran around tending to the other customers.

She nodded quietly and began removing the ratty extensions from my hair.

"Your hair has grown quite a bit," she examined my natural hair which was now almost to my shoulders.

"I'm glad to be rid of these extensions. They make my head itch," I watched her face in the mirror.

"It shouldn't take too long to get them out. We will freshen up your color, too," she said quietly.

"What's wrong?" I asked her, sensing her unhappiness.

"Nothing," she shook her head and continued to remove the fake hair.

"Camilla, something is wrong. You aren't your usual bubbly self," I noted as the heavy extensions fell to the floor.

Tears filled her eyes, but she never made eye contact with me in the mirror.

"Nothing," she shook her head.

"Camilla?"

She removed her hands from my hair and looked down at her dirty Converse. Then she slowly rolled a stool next to my chair and sat beside me, never looking me in the eye, keeping her head and shoulders hung low.

"I don't think I can do your hair today. Maybe Allison can do it once she's done with that pedicure," she sniffled.

"What?" I asked, baffled. "Why?"

She wiped the tears with the back of her hand and finally looked at me.

"I've done something terrible, Claire. I thought I could do your hair today, but when I saw you come through the door, I knew I couldn't face you," she spoke quietly over the whirring of hair dryers while looking around the salon to make sure no one was eaves dropping.

"Just tell me," I became annoyed.

She sighed loudly as she worked up the nerve to tell me her news.

"I slept with him," she said almost in a whisper, looking back to the stained sneakers.

"What?" I asked.

At that moment, I was confused about who she had slept with or why it was such distressing news.

"I slept with Jonathan," she finally looked to me, remorse heavily covering her face.

I stared at her blue eyeliner, unsure of what to say. I didn't love Jonathan. I didn't care who he slept with, and yet a strange feeling began to rise inside of me. Surely it wasn't jealousy, but the feeling scared me. I tried to ignore it and push it away.

"I- we- did after his appointment last week. I'm so sorry, Claire," she smeared her face again, the heavy mascara leaving smudges on her cheeks.

I still had no idea what to say.

"I didn't mean for it to happen. He was flirting with me. He said I had a cute nose. I mean, how lame is that? How lame is it that I was actually flattered that he told me my nose was cute? And then, I don't know. I mean, one thing just led to another," she explained.

A cute nose? Her nose seemed rather large to me.

"Camilla, I-" I tried to form words, but they wouldn't come. The strange feeling kept trying to rise, whether it was anger or jealousy I didn't know, but I continued to reject it.

"I thought I could keep it a secret. I thought that I could cope with it, but I just can't. I know I've done something terrible. The guilt is killing me. He's practically your husband. I'm so sorry," she said again.

"Camilla, I, I really don't know what to say," I stuttered.

"He told me I could tell you if it helped clear my conscience. He said the two of you could work through it," she sniffled and picked at her green fingernails.

He wanted me to know. He wanted these feelings to surface. He wanted me to feel angry and jealous. He wanted me to feel something, *anything*.

"Finish my hair, Camilla," I looked away from her and focused on my haphazard mane in the mirror.

We barely spoke as she worked. She apologized to me many times, tears randomly forming in her eyes. I firmly told her that I forgave her. I didn't care so much about her regret as I did about my bizarre feelings.

I ran my fingers through my natural hair, still blonde, but the extensions removed, as I walked through the garage door and found Jonathan and Ernesto talking at the kitchen table.

"Your hair looks good," he said. "It's grown."

I nodded and sat the package containing my wedding shoes on the counter.

"Ernesto, may I speak with Mr. Marsh in private?" I looked at Ernesto as he gathered his newspaper and left us alone.

"What is it?"

I sat across from him at the kitchen table, unsure of what to say. If this had been Nathan, and I had learned that he'd cheated on me, my heart would be broken, and tears would fall from my eyes as I asked him to explain to me why he'd done it.

"Camilla told me," I mumbled while avoiding contact with his aqua eyes.

"She did?" he fidgeted in his chair.

I nodded.

"Are you trying to make me jealous?"

He laughed.

"Claire, I didn't think you'd mind, actually. You hate me, remember? You won't come within ten feet of me. I'm a man. I had to get it somewhere."

"But, Camilla? She's my friend. You've made me look like a fool!" I exclaimed as our eyes finally locked.

He said nothing as he moved his gaze from me to the kitchen window, the tension thick.

"You're right."

"You could have *anyone*. Why the grungy girl with the purple hair?" I wondered aloud.

"I want you, Claire," he looked back to me. "I didn't want Camilla. I don't want anyone but you."

"Are there others?" I asked, picking at my fingernails, looking at my reflection in the glass table.

"My God, you *are* jealous, aren't you?" he grinned and leaned forward in his chair.

"No I'm not!" I yelled loudly.

I stormed up the stairs and sprawled out on my bed, continuing to fight my emotions. I told myself that I wasn't jealous. I wasn't. I told myself that I wasn't angry, either. I hated Jonathan Marsh. He could sleep with whoever he damn well pleased and I wouldn't care. I didn't love him. I loved Nathan.

But the feelings kept surfacing, begging to be acknowledged. I had a vision of Jonathan and Camilla on the waxing table where so many of the follicles had been ripped from my legs. I envisioned him pressing her naked body close to his, biting her grotesque lip piercing. I envisioned his large hands holding her by the back of her neon hair, and there was that awful feeling again.

I'd never hated myself more than I did at that moment. It *was* jealousy.

NINETEEN

My fake birthday arrived. I dressed in a silky green top, my shoulders exposed, and I threw on a pair of dressy jeans. I applied my makeup and fixed my hair in a loose bun, stray hairs framing my face.

As I sat on the bed, mentally preparing for the party, I heard the doorbell chime several times and voices began to fill the house.

"Are you coming?" Jonathan opened the door and stood before me in his striped shirt and jeans.

I nodded and stood.

"Happy birthday," he walked to me and pulled me into his arms. His fragrance was different. I was relieved that his scent, his cologne, didn't remind me of Nathan as it usually did.

He kissed my cheek, complimented my looks, and we walked down the stairs to the party.

Mr. and Mrs. Marsh greeted me, followed by Cybil and her husband. I scanned the living room to see familiar faces with names that I couldn't recollect. Then I spotted Camilla in the corner of the room, looking out of place with her black clothing and dyed hair as she sipped a turquoise drink.

"You invited her?" I looked to Jonathan as he shrugged.

I made my way around the room, mingling and grabbing a glass of champagne from the server's tray. When Camilla saw me approaching, she looked nervous.

"Camilla?" I asked.

"Your hair looks nice," she glanced at my bun.

"Camilla, I forgive you. Jonathan and I have worked it out," I said, the champagne burning my throat.

A look of relief came across her face.

"I wasn't going to come tonight, Claire. I just, I really value our friendship. You and I have grown close in our conversations at the salon. I don't want my stupid actions to ruin that," she confessed, running her fingers along the rim of her glass.

"It's forgotten," I gave her a small smile.

"I will never betray you again."

She sighed in relief and her posture immediately became more relaxed.

"I'd like to propose a toast to my beautiful fiancé on her birthday," Jonathan lifted his glass as the room quieted and all eyes were on me. "Claire, I want to thank you for making me a happy old man."

Everyone chuckled and raised their glasses as my face became flushed and the three servings of champagne began to make me feel a little woozy.

"Ernesto?" Jonathan turned to Ernesto in the foyer as he stood next to a large white sheet covering my present.

Ernesto lifted the sheet to reveal a beautiful black Steinway baby grand piano. The guests gasped and my face was covered with an authentic smile.

"Claire, you play?" Mrs. Caroline asked.

I nodded.

"I took lessons for eleven years."

I didn't know how Jonathan had known about my love of the piano. He'd known so many other things about me, down to my shoe size, so it wasn't really a surprise. But we'd never discussed the piano. I assumed he had seen me rapping my fingers to the radio as we rode in the car.

"Play for us, Claire," Jonathan extended his hand.

"I haven't played in so long. I couldn't," I shook my head and felt embarrassed.

"Claire, please?" Cybil asked.

"Bang one out for us, Clairee," Casey slurred, his eyes their usual glassy shade of red.

I sighed and walked over to the beautiful instrument. I'd never played anything so elegant. I was accustomed to the old brown upright that sat in our family den, but I pulled out the bench and sat down.

I stared at the 88 keys, a feeling of peace overcoming me. Throughout my life, I'd played the piano to relieve stress. This was exactly what I needed.

I placed my fingers on the ivory, and my mind was flooded with notes, with chords, and my fingers began to move. I closed my eyes, taking in the acoustics of "Clair de Lune" reverberating from the tall ceiling.

I pictured Vaiden as she usually ran around the piano while I played. She'd interrupt my piece by banging on the low keys, proud because she thought she'd contributed something beautiful to the song.

I didn't miss a note. My hands moved effortlessly across the keyboard. I could hear Mrs. Melba, my old piano teacher, telling me to slow it down, speed it up. *Gently, softly, Elle. That's right. Gently, softly.*

The guests stood around the piano as Mrs. Caroline swayed to the beautiful sounds and Casey steadied himself against the doorframe. I blocked them out, though, focusing only on the music.

All of my hurt and my mourning poured through my fingers onto the keys. The piano shouted my story, my tears, my anguish, my longing, my heartache.

Once I was done playing, I opened my eyes, not realizing that they were wet with tears. I quickly wiped them as everyone clapped. Mrs. Caroline leaned down and kissed the top of my head.

"Beautiful *and* talented," she boasted.

I thanked her and stood from the piano. My eyes caught Jonathan's, and I gave him an appreciative smile.

"Thank you," I silently mouthed to him.

He nodded.

"That was some fine playing in there," Cybil said as we shared a cigarette on the back patio.

"Thank you," the smoke exited my nose and complimented the taste of champagne.

"Does your stud know that we are secret smokers?" she asked.

I shook my head.

"He's got me eating healthy and exercising with him before work in the mornings. The body is a temple, Claire," I mimicked him.

"How does it feel to be a twenty one-year-old temple?" she asked, smoke surrounding her long strawberry blonde hair.

I shrugged. I didn't quite know since I wasn't technically twenty one for three more months.

"Well how do you fancy your liquor?" she nodded at the fifth glass of champagne in my hand.

"It's okay," I burped.

My feet were unsteady, my head starting to spin, although I did feel more comfortable than I had in months.

"I wonder if you'll be like a man when you drink," she cocked her head. "You know, a horn ball?"

"For someone who hates sex so much, you sure do talk about it a lot," I passed the cigarette back to her.

"Tonight might be the night, my dear," she winked at me.

"The night for what?" I frowned.

"You know, you and Jonathan," she made a crude gesture with her hands.

"You're gross," I discarded the idea.

I thought I had been somewhat jealous when I learned about Camilla and Jonathan, but that was absurd, wasn't it? It couldn't have been jealousy. The mere thought was ludicrous. I told myself that it couldn't have been jealousy. It was just confusion, and maybe a little shock. That's what it was.

When the last glass of champagne had been drunk and Ernesto, Jonathan and I were left alone in the house, I sat back at the piano and played. Ernesto retired to his room as Jonathan sat in an oversized chair and watched me. Although I possessed a buzz from the alcohol, my fingers found the correct keys.

I scaled down the keyboard, finishing the classical piece on a G chord, and I looked at him. Adoration filled his eyes.

"Thank you," I spoke. "Thank you for the piano."

"You're welcome," he said softly.

My eyes locked with his, and a new feeling surfaced. It was the same compassion that I had felt for him when he sobbed in his hands on September 11th. I knew this was surely an effect of the alcohol, for how could I have compassion for a man who had stolen everything that was precious to me? I didn't know how I could view him as anything more than a monster, but at that moment, I felt compassion for him.

He could see the kindness in my eyes, the thankfulness for receiving the piano. He stood and slowly walked to me. I thought he may kiss me, possibly lead me to his bedroom, and at that point, I didn't care. I was too drunk to care. I knew it would have to happen eventually. I may as well get it over with.

I closed my eyes, preparing for him to lean down to me on the piano bench and cover my mouth with his, but instead I felt a soft peck on my forehead.

"Good night, Claire," he whispered to me and left me alone in the foyer with my birthday present. "Happy birthday."

I rubbed my eyes, shunning of the feelings of compassion, and I began to play again.

TWENTY

When I'd first been captured, the days dragged on slowly as I mourned every second, every moment away from my loved ones and my familiarity. But somehow, with time, the days began to fly by. I kept busy with wedding preparations, cleaning the house, experimenting with new recipes and playing the piano. Between filling his belly with slop and his ears with countless hours of Debussy and Beethoven, Ernesto was somewhat annoyed with me.

"Carlos Santana, Miss Claire? Do you know any Carlos Santana?" he would shout over the classical music.

I finally found a way to merge "Chopin's Ballade No. 1" into "Black Magic Woman". Ernesto and I shared a laugh, and he didn't mind my piano playing so much anymore.

As Jonathan drove us to our engagement party that April evening, the mere idea of marrying him was so surreal, so unbelievable, that my heart would palpitate and a knot would form in my throat.

What did my parents think I was doing at that moment? Did they think I was in Miami being abused or tortured by Michael Kee? Did they think I was happily in love with the stranger from Chicago, content with my decision to abandon my child? Whatever they thought, they had no idea that I was about to marry one of the wealthiest and debonair men in Houston, Texas. They had no idea that I was en route to a mansion filled with new friends, new family and caviar. They had no idea I was celebrating my engagement.

It had been seven months since I had smelled my daughter's strawberry scented hair. It had been seven months since I laughed at my father's corny jokes and kissed my mother on the cheek. It had been so long since my sister and I argued over the remote control or I held Nathan's hand in the movie theater. My heart was still heavy with memories of my past life.

But I knew that if I continued to dwell in my sadness, my life would be miserable. I just couldn't bear the depression that hovered over me like a dark cloud; so somehow, I made the decision to practice being content with this new life. I knew I wasn't going to escape. I knew I might as well accept it and try to function somewhat normally.

Thoughts of Vaiden being well taken care of by Nathan, my parents and his parents gave me comfort. Thoughts that possibly one day, in the far off future, I would be able to see her and hold her again kept the hope alive within me. I couldn't meditate on the sadness. I just focused on that comfort and that hope.

My long pink dress dragged the hardwood floor as I mingled with our guests at the engagement party. I headed to the bar for another glass of champagne. I'd grown accustomed to the taste and the feeling that the bubbly provided.

"You look beautiful tonight, Claire," a deep voice breathed from behind me as I stood at the bar at the back of Uncle Jim and Aunt Junie's great room. Before I even turned around, I knew it was Grant.

"Thank you," I replied while retrieving my glass from the bartender and turning to face him.

"So, the big day is fast approaching?" Grant grinned at me with straight teeth, gleaming white. I wondered how long he had worn braces to achieve such a perfect smile.

"Yep," I gulped the champagne, eager to walk away. I watched Jonathan laughing with a group of fraternity brothers across the room.

"I've known Jon my entire life. He's always had a pretty girl on his arm, but none as pretty as you," his tone was flirtatious as he confidently leaned against the bar.

"Thank you," I gave a small nod.

We stood there in awkward silence for a moment. I began to walk away when he spoke quickly.

"I'd like to speak to you in private."

His statement caught me off guard.

"Why?" I asked, feeling uncomfortable.

He swirled the glass in his hand, the ice cubes clinking together.

"I think you should know a few things," he watched Jonathan.

"What?" I asked, watching Jonathan, too. I was hoping he wouldn't witness this conversation.

"We'll talk later," he winked at me and walked away.

I went back to Jonathan, pondering the confusing conversation, both curiosity and fear rising within me.

Throughout the night, Kevin, one of Jonathan's fraternity brothers, had been pumping Jonathan full of liquor. He was an annoying guy, longing for his twenties and a full head of hair, demanding that Jonathan take shots, encouraging him to relive the glory days.

A few hours later, when I noticed Jonathan on the floral settee, eyes closed, I knew he was inebriated enough that I could slip away for a few minutes. Most of the guests had gone, and only a few friends and family members remained, including Grant.

I saw him standing in the kitchen with Uncle Jim, and I bobbed my head towards the back door. He nonchalantly nodded at me and continued listening to Uncle Jim's story about Mesothelioma lawsuits.

Cybil had put a cigarette in my purse before she left, so I snuck behind the pool house. I inhaled the smoke and thought about Grant's words and tried to imagine what he was going to tell me.

"Thinking about me?" his voice interrupted my thoughts as I nearly screamed and dropped the cigarette.

"What is wrong with you creeping up like that? You scared me to death!" I shouted at him and peeked around the pool house to make sure no one could see us.

"I thought you wanted me to follow you?"

"You said you wanted to talk to me," I stated.

"Did he tell you what happened to Suzanne?" he bluntly asked me as he took the cigarette from my hand and put it in his mouth.

"Yes. She had a car accident."

"I don't think it was an accident," he confessed and handed the cigarette back to me.

"What do you mean?" I seemed oblivious.

"Suzanne broke off the engagement. She was in love with me," he looked into my wide eyes.

"I didn't know," I shook my head.

"He found out about us and she died three days later, Claire. I don't think it was an accident," he gulped the remainder of his whiskey.

"What are you saying?" I asked, completely aware of what he was implying.

"I think it's probably dangerous for you to be speaking to me. That's what I'm saying."

"You said you wanted to talk to me. I didn't approach you!" I quietly exclaimed.

"I just wanted to warn you," he said casually.

"You think he killed her? You think he caused the accident?"

"Well," he sighed. "I think it's a pretty big coincidence."

"Why didn't you tell the police?"

He laughed.

"Only the three of us knew about the affair and the broken engagement. His parents *still* don't know. No one knows his motive but me."

I didn't know what to say as the cigarette burned to my fingers.

"There have been others," he said.

"Others?" I asked.

"There was Marcie Carter in high school. Jonathan really liked her, but she asked me to a dance one year. She had this dog, Muffin. It was a teacup something or another. She loved that stupid dog. Someone went into her backyard and gave it antifreeze," he said, staring at the vast acreage beside us, the moon shading everything white, "while she was at the dance with me."

"So you think he killed the dog?" I smirked.

"He dated Angela, oh what was her last name? Anyway, he dated her the summer after high school graduation. She was really flirting with me one night at a party. I mean, she was throwing it on thick in front of everyone. A few days later, a car hit her and sped off while she was crossing the road to go to her mailbox. She's still in a wheelchair," he said as I gasped.

"Laura Leighton dated Jonathan before he met Suzanne. She broke up with him and asked me out. A few weeks later, she was jogging and some mysterious guy in a ski mask pulled her off the running trail and punched her in the face. He didn't rob her or rape her or anything like that. He just punched her in the face a few times and ran off. Her nose is still an ungodly sight," he winced.

"You are saying Jonathan is responsible for all of this?" I peeked around the house again. The coast was still clear.

"I think so," he nodded.

"Why didn't you warn these women instead of undressing them with your eyes and telling them how beautiful they are? You are just as much to blame!" I shouted angrily.

"Undress them with my eyes?" he laughed.

"That's what you do to me," I stated.

"I didn't come on to a single one of those girls. And I must admit that I thought it was all coincidence, too. I even thought that Suzanne's death was an accident. But after stewing on it, it just didn't add up. If I had pieced it all together before, I wouldn't have slept with Suzanne. I would have warned her. That's why I am telling you this," he shouted to me.

"Why doesn't he just kill *you*? Wouldn't that solve the problem?" I threw the cigarette to the damp ground.

"I'm like a brother to Jonathan. He couldn't bear to see my mother mourn my loss. He has no problem hurting some chick, but he wouldn't hurt me. I'm like family. He couldn't hurt his family," he shook his head. "I think Suzanne ended up dead because that was the worst hurt. He really loved her. I also know how much he loves you. I don't think you'd end up with a dead dog or in a wheelchair or with a broken nose if you betrayed him. I think you'd end up dead, too."

His words sent a shiver down my spine as I stared at him in the moonlight, a small bug crawling on the collar of his white dress shirt. I wanted to confess everything to him. I wanted him to help me concoct a plan to get home. I wanted him to know that Jonathan wasn't only a murderer but a kidnapper, too. I wanted Grant to know that I was stolen.

I shook my head. "Have you confronted him with this?" He nodded.

"He says it is all happenstance. He laughs and says his girlfriends must be cursed. He has a way of making me doubt the entire thing for a few days. Jonathan's a very convincing liar."

This was true.

"I wasn't in love with Suzanne. I should have never slept with her. I shouldn't have let her call off the engagement. I told Jonathan how sorry I was. He said he forgave me. He just couldn't forgive her."

"What would he do if he knew you told me this?" my heart pounded.

Grant shrugged.

"It wouldn't be pretty, I suppose."

"That's it? You tell me all of this and I'm just supposed to be warned and not do anything about it? I'm supposed to live in fear? What can I do?"

"Don't fall in love with me," he said, and he walked back to the house.

Jonathan drunkenly slouched in the passenger seat of my Land Rover as I drove us home that night, Grant's information swimming in my head. I glanced over at him, drool dripping down his chin, a random whiskey hiccup escaping his lips every now and then. I realized how easy it would be to take an exit to Nashville, or better yet, drive straight to the police station and tell them everything.

I'd often thought of killing Jonathan. He was so drunk in the car that night that I could have effortlessly murdered him. He wouldn't have seen it coming. There would be no struggle.

As I thought about slitting his throat and shoving him out of the Land Rover, I was reminded of one night as we ate dinner, and my eyes caught the steak knife on the table. I mentally prepared myself to grab it and lunge it into his chest. But, of course, Jonathan always seemed to read my thoughts.

"You know, if you were to stab me, and I was to die, my associates would immediately move in on your loved ones," he said without removing his eyes from his New York strip.

"I wouldn't-" I stuttered.

"Didn't I tell you that?" he asked, still watching his food.

"Tell me what?" I breathed heavily.

"All of my associates have been instructed that if anything was to happen to me that they are to assume you are responsible. You would be punished."

"What if something happened to you that wasn't my fault? What about a-a-a random car accident or a robbery or-or something that has absolutely nothing to do with me?" I worried aloud.

"Doesn't matter," he shrugged, slicing the sharp knife through the meat. "If something happens to me then something happens to you and your family. It's that simple."

"You won't live forever," I replied. "What if you keel over from a heart attack?"

"Well, then no more complaining about being forced to exercise with me in the mornings. You better hope I stay healthy and alive as long as possible. So thrusting that steak knife into my heart isn't the smart thing to do," he replied and chewed the red meat.

It seemed that he'd thought of everything. I couldn't run, I couldn't kill myself, I couldn't cheat, I couldn't blab and he couldn't die. So I drove us home and asked Ernesto to help me walk his drunk and limp body into the house.

TWENTY ONE

April 14th, 2002. It was my father's 59th birthday. It was also my wedding day.

I stood alone in the guest room of Mr. and Mrs. Marsh's home and examined myself in the full length mirror. My eyes scanned the Swarovski crystals donning the beautiful A-line gown, the veil and tiara placed carefully on top of the French twist in my hair. I forced myself to hold back the tears that would ruin the elegant makeup that Camilla had applied.

My mind and my heart both raced as I watched the clock. I would become Claire Marsh in eight minutes. I didn't recognize the name or the girl in the mirror's reflection. I didn't recognize my own life. I wasn't me anymore. I wasn't Martin and Judith's daughter. I wasn't Vaiden's mother, Nathan's future wife. I wasn't Emma's big sister. I wasn't a student at Tennessee State aspiring to someday own my own business, probably a tanning salon or clothing boutique. I would never find myself sitting on a front porch with Nathan, watching our daughter and future children play together in the soft Tennessee grass. I wasn't living the life that I'd always envisioned. Instead I was about to participate in a real marriage, with a fake name, to a murdering kidnapper.

The knock on the door startled me as Mrs. Caroline entered in a beautiful cornflower blue suit. She immediately gasped at my appearance and placed her hands over her mouth.

"You're just gorgeous, darling," she panted.

I couldn't respond. I couldn't form words for fear that they would be words that explained to Mrs. Caroline how wrong this wedding really was.

"I have something for you," she walked to me while dabbing the tears from the corner of her eyes.

She took my hand and placed a gorgeous sapphire bracelet around my wrist.

"Mrs. Caroline," I looked at the stunning piece of jewelry.

"This was my mother's bracelet. It is your something blue," she fixed the clasp and admired the sparkling blue stones against my tan skin.

"I can't take this, Mrs. Caroline," I shook my head.

"Nonsense. My mother gave it to me on my wedding day. Now I'm giving it to you," she smiled warmly.

"I can't," I stuttered. "Adrienne should have this. She's been part of this family longer than-"

"Oh, hush. I'm liable to be dead by the time Adrienne and Casey are married. Jonathan is my first born. This bracelet belongs to his wife."

I knew I couldn't argue with her. I looked at my wrist, in awe that I owned something so graceful.

"Thank you," I looked at her.

"Thank *you*, Claire," she said. "Thank you for making my son so happy."

I knew I had made him happy. The women before me-Suzanne, the other cheaters, the gold diggers-they all broke his heart. The other women- the free women- did as they pleased, and they all hurt him in some way. I wasn't free, but he knew my fear would prohibit me from cheating on him or leaving him. I made him happy because he knew I was too scared to ever wound him. Jonathan just didn't want to be hurt anymore.

"Are you ready?" she gave my hand a squeeze and examined my dress again.

"As ready as I'll ever be," I answered, exhaling deeply and following Mrs. Caroline out of the guest room.

I stood behind the large French doors at the back of the house. The wedding coordinator, a plump woman named Francine, ran around instructing the wedding party. My bridesmaids, Adrienne and Cybil, stood before me in long, flowing peach dresses.

The Marsh ladies had insisted that I invite my old friends in Oklahoma City to be a part of the bridal party, or at least come to the wedding, but I gave them a detailed story (that Jonathan had written) of how I chose to leave everyone in Oklahoma behind and start new with him.

I heard the violinist begin "Canon in D" as the doors opened, and Mr. Thomas and Mrs. Caroline proceeded down the aisle. 250 guests sat in white chairs on the manicured lawn, smiling at Mrs. Caroline in the attractive blue suit, her diamonds sparkling.

The lake was glistening beyond the beautiful white columned altar. My eyes watched the water ripple softly and the mighty oaks blow in the April afternoon wind when I saw Jonathan, Casey and Grant take their places.

My heart was pounding so much that a loud gasp slipped from my mouth. Adrienne and Cybil turned to me.

"You're fine," Cybil whispered as Adrienne nodded. "You're going to be fine."

I nodded back to them, breathing loudly.

Francine straightened Adrienne and Cybil's dresses and instructed them to smile and walk slowly. I was left there with the ring bearer and flower girl, Caleb and Anna, two of Aunt Junie's relatives.

I gazed at the flowers in Anna's hair. They were placed beautifully among her blonde ringlets, hair that resembled my Vaiden's. I quickly looked away so that I wouldn't break into sobs at the thought of my daughter.

The guests were smiling as the pretty children walked down the aisle and left peach petals for me to walk on. I looked away from the ceremony to the porch door to my right. I had the powerful instinct to run. I felt the same impulse when Jonathan had entered my car seven months earlier- to run, to scream, to cause as much attention as possible, create a diversion. The first rule of survival- never drive and never walk down the aisle to join lives with a monster.

I stood there alone, waiting on my queue from Francine to move. I held the bouquet tightly, wishing my father were there to keep me steady. He should have been on my arm. He should have been giving me away to Nathan.

I heard the "Wedding March", my heart about to leap from my chest, tears the size of quarters about to stream down my cheeks. My legs were shaking, and the overwhelming urge to urinate was upon me. I didn't think I would make it to the end of the aisle without fainting or peeing on the wedding gown.

"Go, dear," Francine whispered, the smell of her Dentyne gum surrounding me, "and smile."

I felt her straightening the long train as I took the first step. I watched the crowd stand, their heads cocked, their smiles wide, their complimentary whispers drowned out by the sound of the orchestra playing Mendelssohn. I wanted to look to my feet, but I kept my chin up, my posture straight, my hands tightly gripped around the bouquet of white miniature carnations and Gerbera daisies and peach roses. I was sure my palms would pour blood from the firm grip.

I didn't want to see Jonathan, but as I got closer to him, I couldn't help but to look at him. As our eyes locked, I realized that only he and I knew (and Ernesto)- out of 250 people there watching us- only we knew that this wasn't supposed to be happening. We were the only ones among all of these people that knew this romance and this wedding was a lie. This wasn't the life that I was supposed to be living.

I couldn't help but notice the tears in his eyes. They were genuine tears. They weren't tears because he was remorseful for stealing me. He was crying because this was the moment he'd coveted for so many years. He'd been waiting to marry a woman who would be true to him, if not out of love then out of fear.

I finally took my place beside him, still unsteady on my feet. I handed my bouquet to Adrienne, and Jonathan wrapped my hands with his. He studied my face and my eyes.

Reverend Hill began speaking, but I didn't listen. My mind was crowded with voices telling me to run and to scream and to get home. The voices belonged to my family.

"Jonathan means 'God is gracious'. The meaning of the name Claire is 'bright'. May your future be one that is bright and manifested in God's grace," the reverend smiled upon us as the sky spun above me, and I tightened my bladder so that I wouldn't pee on the altar.

It seemed we stood there for an hour as Reverend Hill blessed our marriage. Finally Jonathan slipped the heavy diamond-studded band onto my finger and said, "I do." I held his platinum band in my hand. I stared at him blankly, holding back vomit and tears, picturing Nathan's deep brown eyes. Those eyes should have been looking upon me as I said the words.

"I do," I whispered, slipping the ring onto his finger. When Reverend Hill pronounced us man and wife and Jonathan lifted my veil and pressed his lips against mine, the tears that I had held back began to pour.

Jonathan pulled me up the winding staircase and into the guest bedroom while the guests made their way to the reception downstairs. I was still in such shock from all of the events that had taken place, from the kidnapping in the mall parking lot seven months ago to exchanging vows three minutes earlier. I looked at him, not believing that I was bound to this man by law and by the band on my finger.

"I can't believe this," I thought out loud.

His expression was that of an overjoyed groom, ecstatic at the thought of the future with his beautiful bride. He walked to me and wrapped his arms around me.

"Oh, Claire, I love you so much," he breathed into my ear, his grip around me tight.

I hugged him, burying my face into the arm of his black suit. I just wanted to cry and be held by someone, anyone, even if it was him.

We walked down the stairway hand in hand, everyone smiling and applauding. The living room had been cleared of all the furniture and beautifully decorated tables and chairs had been brought in. The lighting was dim as servers rushed around to make sure everyone had food and drink.

We took our place in the center of the vast room and began dancing to Etta James. At last, Jonathan's love had come along.

We posed for photographs. We looked into one another's eyes as the photographer captured our smiles, the beginning of our lives together. Jonathan adamantly declared that none of the photos be featured in Houston's VIP magazine.

"I have a refined woman here that really values her privacy. Please respect our wishes," he patted the photographer on the shoulder and slipped several green bills into his coat pocket.

I'd heard how gorgeous the wedding was numerous times. I gave my usual smile, my usual nod, my usual soft giggle. I held Jonathan's hand and repressed my sadness. I drank as much champagne as possible, hoping it would kill the misery that was dwelling inside of me.

Grant seemed to disappear shortly after the reception began, but not before quickly giving Jonathan a hug and innocently kissing my hand. He did not undress me with his eyes.

I didn't know what time it was when the white limousine dropped us off at the house. My head was swimming from the alcohol and although I had changed into a white pant suit after dinner, my hips were still hurting from the weight of wearing the heavy gown. I vaguely felt Jonathan pull me from the car and pick me up off the ground.

"It was a beautiful ceremony," I heard Ernesto's voice as we entered the house and my body began to freeze.

"Thank you, Ernesto," Jonathan replied. "Miss Claire has had too much to drink this evening. I need to get her to bed."

"Wouldn't that be *Mrs*. Claire?" Ernesto playfully laughed.

"Yes, it would," I could tell by Jonathan's voice that he was grinning as I rested my drunken head on his shoulder, my legs wrapped around his waist. He was holding me as if I was a sleeping toddler.

He carried me as I dozed in and out of consciousness, knowing that puking would be the only solution to end my drunkenness. I awakened when he put me in the soft bed, and I felt the heels being removed from my feet.

"I'm going to be sick," I mumbled.

He laughed.

"Well, I would think so. No one should drink that much champagne, Claire. You're going to have to find another alcoholic beverage of choice."

I groaned and swallowed to keep the champagne in my stomach.

"Just try to go to sleep," he pulled off my white jacket, and I was left in a camisole and white pants. Then he covered me with a heavy blanket.

"You're not going to strip me naked?" I burped.

"Not unless you want me to," his voice trailed into another room.

I hadn't realized that I was in his room until I opened my groggy eyes. I was surprised that he had such a heavy quilt on his bed. Then I noticed that it was the pink feather down comforter that I slept with nightly. He had brought it downstairs and put it on his bed.

"This is my comforter?" I asked.

"I know you get cold," he walked out of the bathroom in his boxer shorts, and he crawled into the king sized bed.

"I have to sleep with you?" I asked as my uneasy stomach churned.

"Yep," he reached towards his nightstand and turned off the dim lamp. "We are married now."

I lay there motionless, wondering if he was going to attempt to consummate our union. As always, he could read my thoughts.

"I'm not going to bother you, Claire. You don't have to lie there so rigid. Relax and go to sleep," he said from the opposite side of the bed.

So I did.

TWENTY TWO

The cruise ship left Galveston at four the next afternoon. I was still feeling the effects of my hangover as Ernesto pulled into the port. The drive had been mostly silent except for the pounding in my head and Jonathan and Ernesto's quiet conversation in the front seat.

"I'll never drink again," I rubbed my pounding temples and exited the back of the car.

"That's highly unlikely," he laughed and retrieved our bags from the trunk. "Thanks for driving us, Ernesto."

"No problem. Have a wonderful honeymoon," Ernesto smiled at us before getting into the Jaguar and driving back to Houston.

As we were walking through the underground parking garage, the ship finally came into view.

"Oh my God," I gasped, mesmerized at the ship's size.

"Now *that's* a boat," he said over the sound of his suitcase rolling on the pavement.

I had to stop and stare at the vessel. I felt like an ant standing before a skyscraper. I'd never seen anything so huge or so exciting.

"Mam?" Jonathan called to an older woman in a straw hat, "would you mind taking our picture?"

"Of course," she smiled and took the camera from Jonathan as we posed in front of the colossal boat. "Say cheese!"

I felt an authentic smile cover my face. I'd always wanted to take a cruise. I'd studied ports and islands and nautical things for hours in the library at school. I'd always yearned to travel the open sea.

"Newlyweds?" she asked and handed him the camera.

"Yes mam," he nodded.

"How exciting. Your life is just beginning," she winked at me and walked away.

Once we'd gone through all of the clearances and finally boarded the boat, I noticed Jonathan nodding to several of the ship's employees. He even addressed one of them by name.

"You've been on this cruise before?" I asked.

"No," he replied.

"How do you know so many people?"

"Associates, Claire. They are all associates," he said as we stopped in front of our cabin door.

"There are eyes on me all of the time, aren't there?" I asked.

"Yes mam," he opened the door to reveal a beautiful and spacious cabin.

"Wow," was the only word I could muster, my eyes scanning the beautiful blue and white nautical furnishings, the gorgeous ocean view beyond the balcony.

When I saw the terrace, I immediately thought of pushing him overboard. I waited on him to read my thoughts and warn against it, but he didn't. Instead I warned myself.

"Wow," I repeated, setting my luggage in an oversized chair, taking it all in. Jonathan stared at me the same way I stared at Vaiden on Christmas when she was so excited to receive a new toy.

"You want to walk around?" he asked.

"I want to stand on the deck when we leave the port," I looked at him, excitement in my eyes.

"Of course," he smiled.

"Hurry, hurry!" I began to run down the hallway when I heard the horn blow and the ship began to move.

"I'm coming!" he shouted from behind me.

He finally caught up with me, and he grabbed my hand. And there we were, sprinting hand in hand, like excited school children.

"It's amazing," I leaned against the railing on the ship's deck as the port grew smaller in the distance. The wind was blowing my hair into a mess.

We silently stood there as the waves splashed against the boat, seagulls flew into the sunset and Galveston, Texas became just a speck.

Night had fallen when we sat down in the dining room that overlooked the dark ocean. Our dinner plates were stacked with seafood.

"Try this crab cake," Jonathan insisted.

Without hesitating, I put my fork onto his plate and took a bite. Nathan and I always shared food, picked from the other's plate. I'd always viewed it as a romantic gesture, and Jonathan was my husband now. I guess he expected a romantic gesture once in a while.

"Superb," I chewed slowly and savored the taste.

"I have a surprise for you," he said.

"Yeah?" I looked to the black vastness on the other side of the window.

"It's amateur night at one of the bars downstairs," he replied.

"What does that mean?"

"It means that you are going to play the piano," he stated.

"No, Jonathan," I shook my head. "Don't make me do that."

"Claire, you haven't even given me a wedding present. I gave you a ring, a honeymoon cruise and you haven't given me a thing," he complained.

I ran my fingers across my wedding present- the diamond dinner ring on my right hand.

"Playing the piano is what you want for a wedding present? I play the piano at home all of the time," I took the last bite of shrimp.

"I know, but I want you to play one of my favorites for me. Here, tonight," he also finished his food. He pushed his plate aside and drank his water.

"What is it? Maybe I can't even play it," I argued with him.

""Maybe I'm Amazed"," he put his glass down on the bar.

"Paul McCartney?" I asked as he nodded.

I knew the song well. It was my father's favorite.

"My daddy loves that song, too" I smiled and remembered aloud. "I can see him now. He would sing the chorus as my mother washed the dishes. She would laugh and turn to kiss him. Emma and I were always so disgusted at their displays of affection. We would make gagging noises and leave the room. But I miss it now. What I wouldn't give to see my mama and daddy dancing in the living room one more time."

This was the first time I'd ever shared any kind of memory with Jonathan. I could tell by his attentiveness that he'd enjoyed my story. No, he didn't feel at all guilty for physically taking me away from those memories, but for the first time, he seemed interested in my past.

"Can you play it?"

"I can play it."

I'd made a vow earlier to never drink again. I broke that vow once we reached the party below deck. It was a beautifully decorated ballroom with a large baby grand piano, drum set and other instruments on a bulky stage. A mahogany bar wrapped around two of the walls. People talked and threw drinks down their throats as we sailed across the Gulf of Mexico.

Jonathan handed me a fruity pink glass. I couldn't taste the alcohol. Instead I tasted cherry Kool-Aid, and I was immediately reminded of ruining our white carpet with the bright sugary concoction when I was eight-years-old.

"I think you're next," Jonathan called over a girl attempting to sing a Pat Benatar tune.

"Everyone has been singing karaoke. No one wants to hear the piano," I shouted over the pitchy-ness of her voice.

"That one guy played drums," he nodded to a guy dressed in all black with long hair who had done a fourteen minute Alex Van Halen solo.

"I don't think anyone enjoyed it, either!" I exclaimed.

"Just play it. For me," he pouted.

The DJ called my name and I finished the pink drink and walked to the piano.

"Now we have Mrs. Claire Marsh, who will be performing her husband's favorite song on the piano, 'Maybe I'm Amazed' by Paul McCartney and Wings!" he shouted as he read my information from an index card like he was hyping the crowd for an actual appearance by Sir Paul.

There were several shouts and applause filled the room. A cowboy in the corner howled his approval. I didn't know so many people cared for Wings.

I sat down at the beautiful piano while Jonathan moved from the back of the bar to a table on the front row. I was nervous playing in front of so many people. I felt the way I did as a child before piano recitals. I kept thinking of Mrs. Melba's advice. *Just breathe, Elle. Don't be nervous.*

My fingers found the chords, and I envisioned my father. He'd taught me the song when I was just a child. He would drag a kitchen barstool into the living room and back me on the guitar while I played the piano.

When I made it to the chorus line, the crowd began to sing the words. I felt like a rock star. No one started singing words when I played "Ode to Joy" at piano recitals. The louder they sang, the harder I played. Suddenly I saw Jonathan on the stage grabbing a microphone.

His voice wasn't too terrible as he kept in tune with my chords, but I couldn't help but laugh at his awful dance moves. When the song was through, the crowd clapped and the drunken cowboy shouted "Do another'n!" I felt my face blush beneath the stage's lights as Jonathan grabbed my hand and we took a bow.

I ordered another drink while strangers approached me and asked if I would play their favorites. I declined, but Motley Crue's

"Home Sweet Home" was requested twice. We sat at a table at the back of the room, and I found that I was enjoying myself.

When I was aware of my cheerfulness, I immediately felt guilty. I felt guilty for laughing at Jonathan's jokes about the large lady doing the electric slide. I felt terrible for smiling without effort. I felt like an awful mother and daughter for enjoying myself when I should have been focusing on getting home.

I ordered another drink, and another, until my head was swimming as badly as the night before. I rubbed my eyes, annoyed at the terrible Peaches and Herb duet, and I rested my head on Jonathan's shoulder.

"I need to go to bed," I mumbled into his ear.

Jonathan combed his fingers through my hair and said, "Let's go."

I didn't know if it was just my head or if we had sailed straight into a hurricane, but I swayed back and forth until I finally plowed into the wall.

"Whoa," Jonathan reached down to pick me up. He held me like a toddler once again.

"I have to quit drinking. This is embarrassing," I closed my eyes and craved sleep.

Somehow I made it into the bathroom and removed my clothes, but not before tripping over my own pants and falling into the shower.

"I'm okay!" I called to Jonathan knocking on the door. "Be right out."

I put on my pink flannel pajama pants and white sweatshirt. I looked at myself in the mirror and laughed.

"Mighty sexy, I must say. Mighty sexy honeymoon lingerie," I whispered to myself, examining my tired face and glassy eyes.

I threw open the bathroom door.

"Ta-da!" I said as I put one hand on my hip and the other on the door frame and attempted to look seductive.

He sat on the edge of the bed in navy blue pajama pants, his chest bare. His hair was messy and his teeth were gleaming white as he laughed.

"Beautiful, Claire. Just beautiful," he winked at me.

"Maybe not beautiful, but I'll be warm," I hiccupped and steadied myself as I walked to the large bed.

I crawled under the heavy blankets as Jonathan tossed them off of him and shut off the light. The air conditioner was humming, but I could still hear the sound of the massive boat slicing through the water.

"I had fun with you tonight, Claire," he spoke into the dark.

"I had fun, too," I replied without hesitating.

"I think we might work, don't you?" I could feel him turn over and face me.

"Maybe," I thought out loud, "But you know I'll never forget them, Jonathan."

"I know."

"I'm trying to be content with this, and I will play along, but I can't forget them," I confessed, my head still spinning.

"I'm sorry, Elle," he said softly.

I turned my woozy head towards him. I could smell the fresh mint toothpaste on his breath. I could make out the whites of his eyes from the bright moon shining through the window.

"Elle?" I asked. "You called me Elle."

"I'm speaking to the girl who I took seven months ago. I'm sorry I've caused you so much pain."

I was surprised, and pleased, that he would confess this.

"Why did you do it?" I asked him.

"I didn't want to be hurt anymore," he admitted to me. "I played by the rules for so long. I treated all of those women like queens, and they all betrayed me. Even Suzanne."

"Someone would have come along, Jonathan. I mean, aside from being a kidnapper, you seem like a decent person. You are attractive. You are smart. Someone would have come along," I spoke quietly.

"I don't think so," he stated.

~ 152 ~

"Did you kill her?"

The words left my mouth before I even realized it.

"What? Who?" he sounded confused.

"Your mother told me about Suzanne's car accident. You didn't do that?" I turned on my side to face him.

"Why would you think that?"

"I don't know. You said she slept with Grant. I thought maybe you were so angry that-" I began.

"I'm not a murderer. A kidnapper maybe, but I'm not a murderer."

Grant was right. He was convincing. I actually believed him in that moment, although he'd threatened to murder, to harm, me and my family on numerous occasions.

"Do you see why I took you?"

"I sort of understand."

"Will you ever forgive me? You think you'll ever love me?" he wished aloud.

"I don't know," I said, our faces close together in the darkness.

"I hope you will, Claire. You could have such a wonderful life with me if you'd just be open to it. I promise that I will give you everything that you want if you just love me."

"I want my daughter," I begged. "I will stay married to you. I won't tell my family about the kidnapping. I won't leave you for Nathan. I think my family would actually like you, Jonathan. I could be me, you could be you, and we could still be married. I could have Vaiden."

He said nothing. My heart was pounding, hope emerging. He was going to agree to it. He was going to let me go home. I would stay married to Jonathan if it meant I could go home. I would long for Nathan from afar for the rest of my life if it meant I was reunited with my child. It was a superb plan. I didn't know why I hadn't thought of it earlier.

"You'd stay with me? You wouldn't betray me? You wouldn't run back to Nathan?" he asked.

"No!" I exclaimed. "I won't hurt you, Jonathan. I promise."

"You're saying that I could have you? I could really have you without all of the threats, the lies?" he seemed amazed.

"Yes," I said softly.

He reached for me in the dark, his arms pulling my drunken body close to him. He kissed me gently.

"I love you," he whispered.

"I think, I think I might love you, too," I lied, knowing it would be the only way that I'd ever see my family again.

He kissed me again, and as Cybil had said, one thing led to another.

Jonathan wasn't rough or cruel. He held me softly, he was patient, and he repeatedly asked if I was okay. Surprisingly, I didn't feel guilty. I didn't feel as if I was cheating on Nathan. I felt as if this was what I was supposed to do with my husband. It was what I was supposed to do in order to go home.

Of course it was different than the handful of times that I'd been with Nathan. It wasn't familiar, but it was somewhat exciting. It was something new. I shunned the thoughts of Suzanne's demise, of the threats to those I held closest to my heart. I forgot all of that, and I made love to my husband.

TWENTY THREE

When my eyes opened the next morning, I shot up in the bed. I felt something I hadn't felt in so long. I felt joy.

"Jonathan?" I called his name as he stepped out of the bathroom wearing fresh clothes. His hair was still wet, his face was clean shaven. He looked so handsome.

"Good morning," he smiled at me.

"Are we going home after the cruise? Can I go home? Can we go home to Nashville?" I was beaming and my heart was pounding.

I didn't like the look that replaced his smile. He'd thought it over. He thought it was a terrible idea.

"I don't know, Claire," he sighed and sat on the bed. "What would I tell my family? How can I tell them that I've lied to them for so long?

I crawled close to him and put my arms around his neck.

"We would think of something," I kissed his cheek. "Please, Jonathan. You thought it was a wonderful idea last night. We could make it work."

"Quit begging, Claire. I'm no fool," he stood up, walked to the dresser and fastened his watch on his wrist.

"What?" I asked.

"I'm no fool. You'd leave me for Nathan. You'd tell your family. Something would go wrong. I'm not falling for this," he shook his head and left me alone in the cabin.

I began beating my fists into the satin sheets, too angry and disappointed to cry. Instead I buried my head in a feather pillow and screamed as loudly as I could.

We were at sea all day. He left me alone in the cabin the entire time. I didn't know where he was or what he was doing. I sat on the balcony smoking cigarettes and staring at the open water. I contemplated jumping, hurling myself into the ocean, ending this nightmare.

My mind raced as I thought of multiple ways to convince him that going to Nashville was a wonderful idea. I would introduce him to my family and then gladly bring Vaiden back to Houston with us, if Nathan would ever permit it. However, I was nervous at the thought of Vaiden growing up with such a dangerous man. I didn't know what he was capable of doing. Would he harm her for spilling Kool-Aid on the carpet? If I was reunited with Vaiden, would I still spend the rest of my life not only fearing for my safety but also fearing for hers?

It was a terrible notion. Vaiden belonged with Nathan and my family in Nashville. Jonathan was no idiot. He'd never let my family know where I was. It was just a ridiculous, drunken idea.

"Where have you been?" I asked when Jonathan entered the room late that night.

"Gambling," he quickly answered.

"You left me here all day."

"Shut up," he snapped.

I looked at him silently.

"I had to think. I just had to get away and think. Am I allowed to be alone, Claire?" he rolled his eyes.

I didn't know what to say. He'd been so kind and compassionate lately. Now he was reverting to the Jonathan, the monster, that I loathed.

"I'm sorry for my suggestion last night. I know I belong in Houston with you," I looked to my hands and tugged at a hangnail.

He emptied his pockets onto the night stand.

"It's alright," he mumbled.

"It's just that you know how much I miss them. I was thinking I could have you both-you and my family. You know, the best of both worlds," I muttered.

Of course it wouldn't be the best of both worlds. If it were my choice, I would have nothing to do with Jonathan Marsh.

"Best of both worlds?" he smirked.

"Yeah," I shrugged, wondering again how he always read my mind.

"You expect me to believe that you *want* to be with me?" he laughed out loud.

I sighed, still picking at the stubborn nail.

"I do want to be with you," I lied.

"Bullshit, Claire," he walked into the bathroom while I sat on the bed.

This man, my life, was driving me insane. I had been kidnapped and then forced to marry my kidnapper. I was sailing across the Gulf knowing that I needed to convince my kidnapper husband that I loved him. Convincing him that I loved him was the only way that I'd ever earn his trust and be permitted to go home.

I'd been taught the art of lying for the last seven months. I'd practiced lies in the mirror, spoken them to my parents over payphones, told them to every person I'd met in Houston. Jonathan had molded me into a liar. He'd molded me into a *really* great liar. He had been my lying instructor. It was time that I used my new skill on my teacher.

"I love you, Jonathan. Don't you see that?" I called from the bed, waiting on him to exit the bathroom, waiting on him to look at me and ask me to repeat myself.

"What?" he asked right on queue.

"I love you," I looked at him with dramatic eyes. "I've tried to fight it, but I've fallen in love with you. After I played the piano and our eyes met at my birthday party, I knew it was true."

He walked closer to me.

"You've taken so much from me, but you've given me so much in return. Having you and Vaiden *would* be the best of both worlds," I managed to muster up a few tears. "I want to be with you, Jonathan."

I paused for dramatic effect, crying at the thought of my daughter.

"I was jealous when I found out about Camilla. I really was," I shook my head, tears still streaming. "That jealousy scared me. You were nothing but a monster until I felt that jealousy. And then the piano and my birthday and the wedding and-"

He pulled me into his arms and passionately kissed me, and I knew that he had believed my confession. The father of all lies had believed mine.

We spent the next three days in Nassau, lying on the beach, shopping in the market. I bought knick knacks and beaded jewelry and had my hair braided by a large, loud, native woman who cussed a lot and thought my husband was beautiful.

I posed next to palm trees and shops on the busy streets while Jonathan snapped my picture. I laughed at his jokes and held his hand. I repeated the words when he told me he loved me.

When we retired to the ship after a long day on the island, we dressed in our best and danced in the ballroom. We kissed on the deck as the moon shone down on us. I gave an award-winning performance that I was in love. Either he was giving an award-winning performance, too, or he actually believed me.

And when we returned home, our skin tanned and our waistlines expanded from eating like royalty for nearly a week, the performance continued.

I pulled him into the bedroom when he arrived home from work. I took his hand while we watched television on the couch. I imagined he was Nathan, and I played the giddy girl who was in love.

"You love him, don't you, Mrs. Claire?" Ernesto grinned as he helped me prepare breakfast one morning.

"I do," I looked at him squeezing oranges while I scrambled the eggs.

"See? I told you, Mrs. Claire. I told you that you would be happy here."

"Ernesto knows best," I put the eggs on a plate as Jonathan walked into the kitchen, sweaty from his morning workout.

"Good morning, my love," he put his arms around my waist and kissed me.

"Good morning."

"This is just wonderful, Mr. Jonathan. I told you, too. I told you both," Ernesto put the pitcher of orange juice on the breakfast table.

"Told us what?" Jonathan sat at the table.

"I told you that she would come around. I told Mrs. Claire that she would be happy. I just had a feeling about it. I knew it would work," he nodded his head at his own words.

"Well, you're always right, Ernesto. You know that," Jonathan paused and began laughing. "Remember Phoenix? You were definitely right then, my friend."

Ernesto laughed too, as he put bacon on his plate and sat next to Jonathan.

"What happened in Phoenix? What's so funny?" I asked, joining them at the table.

Their smiles both faded.

"Nothing," Jonathan shook his head.

"Oh, come on, "I said. "What?"

"Dammit, Claire, drop it. Know your place," Jonathan shouted.

I sat quietly and stared at my plate as they looked to one another.

"Mrs. Claire," Ernesto began.

"I shouldn't have said anything," Jonathan interrupted him. "I'm sorry, Claire. I forgot you were standing there. That's no one's business but mine and Ernesto's. That's the past. I'm sorry."

"Okay," I said, still watching my plate.

"Hey," he said as I looked to him. "I'm sorry, okay?"

"Okay," I repeated.

"Ernesto, I'm sorry for bringing it up. I shouldn't have brought it up in front of Claire."

Ernesto bobbed as my curiosity about Phoenix escalated.

"Anyway, Claire," Jonathan interrupted my thoughts. "I thought we could send one of the wedding photos to your family."

"What? Really?" I asked.

"Of course it would be one of just you. I thought you'd like them to know that you are doing okay. You could write something on the back about marrying Michael Kee. I'm sure they'd be relieved to know that you aren't being locked in a basement or something."

"That would be wonderful, Jonathan. Thank you," I beamed.

"I will have to send it to one of my associates in Miami and have them mail it to your family from there. It will need a Miami postmark. It'll all have to be handled very carefully, but that's the least I can do to ease their minds. I'm sure they are still worried sick about their Elle," he drank his juice.

He'd never cared about my parent's feelings. I knew my open display of love was softening his heart. I might get home yet.

"That means so much to me. Thank you," I said again.

"That's nice, Mr. Jonathan," Ernesto chimed in.

"Well, I'm just a nice guy," he smiled and scooped eggs onto a piece of wheat toast. "Also, Claire, we have a lot of things to settle now that we are married."

"Like what?"

"I have to change my will, my life insurance policy, my tax returns. There is so much to do."

He trusted me enough to do these things? I'd only "loved" him for a little over a week, and he was already concerned with my parent's feelings and trusting me enough to make me his beneficiary?

"You'd get it all, Claire. If I died, you'd get it all. Of course that means that you probably shouldn't kill me soon after your name is put on everything. That would just look, well, bad. Really bad," he chuckled.

He laughed as if he was kidding, but I knew that he was serious. He was willing everything to me just to show others how much he trusted me. He knew I wouldn't do anything to him if he gave me an obvious motive for killing him.

I could face a lifetime in prison, and I'd still be glad to slit his throat. The only thing that kept him safe was his threats to my family if I hurt him.

"Don't start talking like that," I seemed annoyed. "You know I love you. I don't appreciate you talking like that anymore."

I pouted and finished eating my breakfast.

"Baby, I was kidding," he reached across the table and touched my hand. "Tell her I was kidding, Ernesto."

"He's joking, Mrs. Claire. You know that," Ernesto took his empty plate to the kitchen sink.

"I know you are too smart to kill me for millions of dollars," he said. "That money could never buy back your family's lives, could it?"

I looked at him grinning at me, evil in his blue eyes. He could be so caring and compassionate, but his words reminded me that the monster inside of him was still alive and well.

TWENTY FOUR

"Happy birthday, Elle," Jonathan whispered before kissing my forehead.

I opened my eyes to see him leaving the bedroom in his suit and tie. I yawned and stretched my arms across the bed, and my hand brushed against a small white envelope lying next to me on the sheet. I sat up in the bed and opened it.

A picture of Vaiden fell to my lap. She wore a white smocked dress that I'd never seen, and a purple wicker basket hung on her arm as she knelt beside the largest oak in our front yard and reached for a bright yellow egg. The photo was crisp and clear, zoomed in so much that I could see the pink fingernail polish that she wore.

I wondered who had taken this photo of my child. I was relieved to see that she was living a somewhat normal life while I was gone, but I was nervous at the fact that some stranger was close enough to her to take such a clear shot. Where had they been concealed while taking the photo? Did my mother not notice some creep in a cable van snapping pictures of Vaiden as she hunted eggs? Or was the photo taken by someone that my parents trusted? Had someone infiltrated their lives and posed as a decent, good person, only to be one of Jonathan's associates?

"Happy birthday," Ernesto called to me as I walked up the stairs, cleaning supplies in my arms.

"Thanks, Ernesto," I said as I rounded the hallway and entered Jonathan's office.

I sprayed some Pledge on the large desk, and I listened for the sound of Ernesto's shoes shuffling on the hardwood downstairs. When I was certain that he was on the lower level, I began rummaging through the drawers.

I didn't find anything of importance. There was an electric bill and a credit card statement stuffed in a binder, and two of the drawers were completely empty except for a broken rubber band and a paper clip.

I turned on the computer, but I couldn't access any information. Everything was password protected. I tried several different words and gave up before the entire system was locked at the failed password attempts.

I ran my hand across the bookshelf, admiring all of the literary works displayed there. It was a random collection, from Virginia Woolf to Hunter S. Thompson and Don Quixote. There was a wedding photo of Jonathan's parents setting on one of the shelves next to our own wedding portrait. I observed the emptiness in my eyes as Jonathan and I leaned against a tree growing alongside his parent's pond.

He had let me send a wedding photograph to my parents a few weeks earlier. I had picked one of me posing beside the same tree. I'd written a short note on the back stating that Michael and I were happy. I told Vaiden that I loved and missed her. I told them not to worry about me and that I was doing fine.

I dusted a large framed painting, *Fox Hunt.* My rag scattered the inch of dust that rested on the dark frame throughout the room. I dusted it again, and it swayed against the wall, revealing the safe behind it.

I couldn't help but chuckle quietly at the fact that Jonathan had a hidden safe behind a picture. It was so cliché. All of the information that I needed could probably be found there. Information about Suzanne and the associates watching my family could be found within the fireproof box. I knew that things of great importance to me could were probably concealed in that hidden safe behind the photo of an 1840's hunter riding his horse in pursuit of the fox.

I checked to make sure that Ernesto was still downstairs, and I removed the heavy painting to examine the safe. It had a digital keypad. I tried several numbers, and to no avail, I hung the dust-free picture back on the wall.

I went downstairs and sat across from Ernesto at the kitchen bar. I rested my head in my hands and sighed loudly.

"Bored?" Ernesto asked.

"Yeah."

"Are you done cleaning?" he peered over his newspaper.

"Yeah."

"Do you want to go do something for your birthday?" he raised his eyebrows.

"Yeah," I grinned like an excited child.

The humidity tugged at my hair, leaving the blonde strands around my face in corkscrew curls. I sat on the bench overlooking the park and the still pond while sweat suffocated my armpits, and I frantically licked the rapidly melting ice cream cone.

"Should have gotten a cup," Ernesto nodded at the streaks of melted vanilla on my hands.

"You're always right, aren't you, Ernie?" I glanced at his neat Styrofoam cup of chocolate swirl.

"Yes," he stated.

"Why can't you tell me about Phoenix? How you were right then, too?" I shifted my eyes and watched his rugged face.

"Some things aren't your business, Mrs. Claire," he took a bite.

I quietly looked at the pond as the ice cream continued to melt down my hands. I tossed the half-eaten cone to the garbage can beside the bench.

"I feel like you're my friend," I spoke into the hot still air as Ernesto remained quiet. "You know what I've been through. You know my entire story. You know that I don't really belong here."

He scraped the bottom of the Styrofoam cup with his white plastic spoon.

~ 164 ~

"Will I ever get home?" I looked at him.

He took the last bite of chocolate and tossed the cup across me and into the garbage bin.

"I don't think so," he confessed while wiping his mouth with a napkin.

"I love him," I lied, "but I need to get home. How can I make that happen?"

"We shouldn't be discussing this," he looked at me. "You aren't going home. We all know that. When Mr. Jonathan makes up his mind to keep a woman, she stays kept."

"What?" I asked.

"You heard me. You aren't going home. You shouldn't be discussing this with me," he began.

"You said keep *a* woman. Has he kept another woman? Has he, Ernesto? I'm not the first that he's kidnapped?" I kept my voice low as a couple walked by pushing their sweaty and crying baby in a stroller.

Ernesto's silence had answered the question. I wasn't the first one. I wasn't the first woman that Jonathan had taken.

"Ernesto, tell me!" I demanded.

He remained silent.

"I can't believe I didn't think of this before. I thought I was the first one. I know about the other women. I know he killed Suzanne and punished the other girls for leaving him, but I didn't know he'd taken anyone else. As absurd as it sounds, I thought I was special in that way. I thought he'd chosen only me," I quietly thought aloud.

"What did you say?" Ernesto gawked at me.

I shrugged.

"He told me about Suzanne."

"He told you he killed Miss Suzanne?" confusion covered his face.

"No," I shook my head. "I assumed he did. He told me about Suzanne and Grant. It's no coincidence is it, Ernesto?"

"I'm not going to sit here and tell you that Mr. Jonathan killed anyone. I'm not going to do that," his tone became aggravated. "That's simply not true. If you're silly enough to fish for these kinds of answers, then ask Grant Mallory about Miss Suzanne's death. Don't ask me!"

We sat there without a sound, looking in opposite directions.

"Look, I will tell you some things, but you can't mention this to Mr. Jonathan. If you tell him this, we will both end up dead. Do you want that?" he interrupted the silence.

"Of course I won't say anything."

"I know Mr. Jonathan has wronged you. I am not a wicked man, Mrs. Claire. I know right from wrong. I see you hurting. I know that taking you away from your child is wrong, but I also know that Mr. Jonathan isn't an evil man. He didn't hurt those girls long ago, and he didn't kill Miss Suzanne," he paused. "It is true that Grant stole those women. He promised them things and lied to them about Mr. Jonathan. He scared them into leaving Mr. Jonathan for him. And then he hurt them. He beat them and raped them and he even killed Miss Suzanne. He did all of this because he is evil, Mrs. Claire. He did it to hurt Mr. Jonathan, but he's also simply evil. I won't deny that Mr. Jonathan has done wrong by taking you, but he is no murderer. He's never hurt a woman the way Grant has."

I tried to process Ernesto's words, skeptical that they were sincere.

"I wouldn't be surprised if he doesn't try to woo you. I wouldn't be surprised if he doesn't approach you with lies about Mr. Jonathan, in hopes of taking you for himself. You are a pretty one, Mrs. Claire. Grant likes the pretty ones. You have to stay away from him. He's dangerous."

"Ernesto, if this was true, then why did Jonathan ask him to be in the wedding? Why is he still friends with-" I argued.

"Mr. Jonathan can't prove these things. Grant says it is all coincidence. He's very convincing," Ernesto spoke the same words about Grant that Grant had spoken about Jonathan. "But I'd kill him myself if Mr. Jonathan would allow it. I cared for Miss

Suzanne. She was a good girl. I'd kill Grant for what he did to her *and* Mr. Jonathan."

"I don't know what to believe," I peered at the mossy trees above my head.

"I will tell you about Phoenix, too," he said softly and turned to me on the bench. "You are the first woman that he's kept, but there was another years ago. Mr. Jonathan spotted her at a restaurant in Phoenix. When he arrived home, he told me what a beautiful woman she was. He told me that she looked like she'd make a wonderful wife. I told him to take her. Don't waste the time getting to know her or dating her, just take her, I said. It was *my* idea. And we found her and studied her for months. We had a plan, a perfect plan, and I disguised myself and grew a beard and went to Phoenix to get her. I waited on her outside the clothing store where she worked. I told her that her sister, a prostitute, was in trouble. I gave her a spill about how I knew her sister and we had to go help her. She was a naïve one. She didn't hesitate to hop into the car. We drove a few miles out and I quickly injected her with a sedative. She was sleeping in the passenger seat as I started the drive back to Houston, but I noticed that he looked sickly. She didn't look right. She had these sores on her mouth, Mrs. Claire," he remembered aloud.

I listened carefully, my ears transfixed on his words.

"I pulled over on a secluded road in Catalina Foothills, and I inspected her. She was still sedated, and I stripped her naked and gave her a thorough examination. She was sick. I called Mr. Jonathan and told him what I'd discovered. I left her there on the side of the road. She had these sores," he grimaced. "I saved him from a dirty whore."

"Oh my God," I whispered and shook my head.

"We made sure to check all of your medical records before he took you. Lesson learned," he added.

I sat there, speechless, my mind trying to digest the information. Had Grant lied to me about Jonathan? Was Ernesto telling the truth? Had the poor Herpes-infested girl found her way back to Phoenix?

"You are special to him. He researched other women, and they never came up to par. *You* were good enough for him."

I chewed on my lip and looked at the sticky sugar on my hands.

"Why wouldn't he tell me this? Why wouldn't Jonathan tell me that Grant killed Suzanne so that I wouldn't suspect him? It seems like he would tell me the truth about Grant, even if just to scare me into staying away from him," I reasoned.

"I don't know. He has his reasons," Ernesto shrugged.

"After he spotted you in the airport, and we planned to bring you here, he told Grant that he'd met a beautiful girl. He told him that you were untouchable. Miss Suzanne and the other ladies were in the past, but he said he wouldn't hesitate to kill Grant if he tried to take you. You are special to him, Mrs. Claire. You're more special than any other."

I didn't know I was about to confess what Grant had said to me until my mouth opened.

"Grant told me about the other women. He told me that Jonathan killed Suzanne. Grant told me that if I wanted to stay alive, then I shouldn't fall in love with him. Why did he say that? If he *wanted* me to fall in love with him, then why would he tell me *not* to?"

Ernesto sighed.

"Reverse psychology, Mrs. Claire. Of course he wants you to fall in love with him. Don't you see that? He *wants* you to run from Mr. Jonathan straight into his arms. He *wants* you to think he can save you."

I tried to replay past conversations in my head. I remembered the way Grant had undressed me with his eyes, and then casually warned me about Jonathan's evil ways. I remembered Jonathan threatening to slit my mother's throat if I ran away with Grant Mallory. I remembered the first night I heard his name as we studied, and Jonathan's warnings that he was dangerous. Who was the dangerous one, or was it both of them? I didn't know what or who to believe.

I pulled Vaiden's Easter photograph from my purse and handed it to Ernesto.

"She's beautiful, Mrs. Claire," he grinned and examined the picture.

"Can you see her fingernail polish?" I looked over his shoulder at the photo.

"Pink," he nodded.

"Who took this photograph? Who was close enough to my baby girl to capture her fingernail polish?" I fished for more answers.

His smile vanished and he handed me the picture.

"I've said enough today, Mrs. Claire."

Ernesto changed the subject to the weather, and we left the park. We talked about baseball and the swimming pools' pH level on the ride home. As we pulled into the driveway on my 21st birthday, Ernesto looked at me.

"Not a word about today, Mrs. Claire. I won't mention your inquiries or what Grant said to you, and you won't mention what I said to you. Do you understand?"

I nodded.

"Thank you, Ernesto."

"Consider this information your birthday present and don't put me in this position again."

TWENTY FIVE

"Did you enjoy your birthday? I mean, your *real* birthday?" Jonathan asked when he arrived home from work that evening.

"I did," I answered. "Ernesto and I went to the park. Ice cream melted all over my hands."

Jonathan smiled and tucked a strand of hair behind my ear as we sat together on the couch.

"Thank you for the photograph of Vaiden. I've been looking at it all day. You've no idea how happy it made me to see her," I smiled at him.

"I know you miss her. She's doing fine. Nothing for you to worry about," he stood from the couch. "Do you want to go out to dinner?"

I shook my head.

"I thought we could order a pizza or something? I'd like to hang out on the patio with a bottle of wine. Maybe we could swim?" I suggested.

"That sounds great," he walked towards the bedroom. "I will change clothes."

Once the large pizza had been eaten and the bottle of wine was gone, Jonathan and I were wrapped in beach towels and swinging in the hammock, watching the water flow from the fountain and into the pool. Jonathan was nearly asleep, his eyes half closed, as the wine coursed through his veins.

"Baby?" I asked.

Jonathan was still pleased at the the sound of his name rolling off of my lips, but if I used a term of endearment when addressing him, love overtook his face.

"Yes," he enveloped his arms around my body as we swayed in the hammock.

"Can you tell me who took the photo of Vaiden?" I glanced at him.

"An associate," he replied, his eyes still sleepy.

"I know that, but how did they get such a good photo? It's so clear, as if the person taking it was only a few feet away from her," I thought out loud.

"Great camera, Claire," he explained.

"But her fingernail polish, I could see it so clearly, even where it was chipped on her thumb."

"I don't know what to tell you," he became annoyed. "It was taken with a good camera. Zoom. That's all I know."

I knew it was best to leave the subject alone.

"Okay," I sighed.

"I'm so tired. I have to get some sleep," Jonathan yawned.

"You can go on to bed. I will be there in a few minutes," I rested my head on his chest. I could hear the slow sound of his heartbeat.

"Come with me," he began to stand as the hammock rocked.

I nodded and followed him to bed.

Despite Jonathan being so drowsy and inebriated, the sex that night was the longest that I'd ever experienced. I was bored within the first three minutes, and I was anxious for him to go to sleep. Once we were done, though, he was out. A freight train hitting a nuclear power plant wouldn't have woken him.

I rummaged through his suit pants that were lying on the floor, and I found his wallet. It was beautiful, expensive, chocolate leather. I'd never held it in my hands, much less looked through it.

His driver's license picture was handsome although he had a cheesy grin, as if he were posing for a school photo. I rummaged through the wallet's compartments as he quietly snored a few feet away in the bed.

I found his social security card. I grabbed a pen from the night stand, and I wrote the numbers on my palm by the closet light. Then I crept out of the bedroom, shot up the kitchen stairway and down the hallway to the office.

Ernesto was visiting a lady friend that evening, so I was alone upstairs. I pulled the picture off of the wall, and I keyed in the last four digits of Jonathan's social security number. I had no idea if it would work, but while mulling over potential passwords all day, I knew I had to try a number sequence that only he would know. I'd tried his birthday, his parent's birthdays, my birthday-the

~ 171 ~

real one and the fake one, but I knew I had to try his social security number.

It worked. By God, it worked. I wanted to jump up and down and squeal with glee, but instead I quickly opened the safe and removed the thick binders that were hidden inside. When I opened the first green folder, I saw a photograph of me.

I was at Tennessee State, crossing a familiar and narrow street on campus, backpack hanging from my shoulder. I had no idea when it was taken, but I was reminded of how short and brown my hair once was.

There were more pictures. There were photos of Vaiden, photos of my parents in the grocery store, and there was even a photograph of Nathan, Vaiden and his parents sitting on the bleachers at a high-school football game. I couldn't believe that these pictures had been taken to no one's knowledge.

Nothing was handwritten, everything was typed. My birthdate and social security number were there, along with my clothing and shoe sizes. My love of the piano was documented, next to Mrs. Melba's name. I wanted to read through all of the notes and lists, but I knew I had to be quick.

I saw a paper that listed the names of Jonathan's associates. I recognized the first four names. Ernesto Mendoza, Marco Reyes, a line scratched through Roger Watson's name, and Louis Caballero. The list was long, at least thirty or forty names, including The Santos brothers, Saul and Lino. They were mostly Hispanic names, but some weren't. They were all followed by three digit numbers. I didn't know what the numbers meant. It must have been some kind of code that I'd never crack.

I scanned the rest of the papers, looking for any clues as to who was watching my home in Nashville, who could have taken the photograph of Vaiden on Easter Sunday, but there was nothing.

At the back of the folder rested my squeaky clean medical records from Dr. Matheny's office. How he had obtained all of this information, I didn't know.

In a separate binder, there was Suzanne's obituary. She was strikingly beautiful, with big blonde hair and dimples in her cheeks. The obit even mentioned Jonathan as her fiancé, along with the other survivors: her parents and three sisters.

There were photos of Suzanne and Grant, taken from a distance as they embraced one another outside of a beautiful home, another in a parking lot. I could only imagine the hurt that Jonathan had felt when he first viewed this infidelity in black and white.

I scattered through the papers, checking the doorway every few seconds, and then I came upon an envelope addressed to Jonathan. I yanked the folded letter from inside.

Jonathan,

You won't answer my calls, and this was the only way I knew to get through to you.

I can't imagine the hurt that I've caused you. I know you are in pain. I know you are angry. I know you can never forgive me, but for what it is worth, I am sorry.

I know that you don't owe me any favors, but I need your help. I don't know what Grant is capable of doing, but you do. Please call me.

I will always love you.

LL

I expected to see Suzanne's name signed at the bottom of the crisp paper, but there were hearts doodled around two L's. Who was LL? I tried to remember the names of the women that Grant had given me that night behind the pool house, but my mind was blank.

I neatly stuffed all of the papers back into their folders. I closed the safe, and I carefully placed the fox hunt painting back on the wall. I tiptoed down the stairs and slipped into the bed next to Jonathan before wiping the social security number off of my palm with a glob of spit.

I stared at the ceiling fan whirring above my head, Jonathan's loud breathing echoing throughout the room, and I asked myself a million questions.

Had Ernesto been right? The letter from LL stated that she was afraid of Grant. Was Grant Mallory the callous and malicious one? Had he really injured those girls and killed Suzanne because *he* was the monster? Jonathan had stolen me, yes, but he hadn't killed anyone, had he? Maybe he wasn't the most evil villain that I'd come across since I'd been in Houston, Texas. He wasn't a murderer.

My screams sliced through the night like the ceiling fan blades.

"Baby! Wake up!" Jonathan reached over and shook my shoulder. I sat up and gasped for air before burying my head in his chest.

"Are you okay?" he comforted me and stroked my hair.

"I had a terrible nightmare," I breathed loudly.

"What was it?"

"Grant," I replied, as his hands paused on my head. "I dreamt that Grant tried to kill me, Jonathan."

"Why would you dream *that*? Has Grant said anything to you?"

"No," I gazed up at him.

"You're psychic then?" he offered.

"Psychic?" I asked.

"You must be," he switched off the bedside lamp and turned away from me.

"It was just a dream, Jonathan. It was a terrifying and strange dream, but it was just a dream," I replied.

"A probable dream," he mumbled as he kicked the heavy comforter off of his feet.

"Hey," I touched his arm. "Tell me what's going on. I had a

terrible nightmare, and you're mad at me? Do you think I can control what I dream?"

He turned towards me.

"You're right. I'm sorry."

"You've warned me about Grant many times, Jonathan. That's what caused this dream. Why should I fear him?"

"Because he's dangerous," he sighed.

"But what does that mean?" I exclaimed.

He reached for me in the dark and pulled me close to his body.

"He's seduced nearly every girlfriend that I've ever had, even my fiancée. He told them terrible lies about me and then convinced them that he was the better man. And once he got them, he turned on them. I mean, he really hurt these women. And Suzanne, well, you know what happened to Suzanne, don't you?"

"You're saying Grant killed Suzanne?" I asked in the most shocked tone that I could muster.

"That's what I'm saying," he said.

"Why would he kill her?"

"She had an affair with him for months, but two days after she called off our engagement, she begged my forgiveness. She told me some of the terrible things that he'd done in those two short days. In forty eight hours, he'd turned into a completely different man. He threatened to kill her. I didn't believe her until after the car accident. And then I pieced it all together. Angela Marbury, Laura Leighton, Stephanie Reid, they all left me for Grant. And they all suffered some kind of accident. They all four came back to me, begging my forgiveness, telling me how evil Grant really is. They were terrified of him. They still are. They were too scared to go to the police, but they came to me. I never believed them. I really never believed that he was capable of such things until Suzanne died."

LL. Laura Leighton. Was that the one who was beaten? Grant had said her nose was still an ungodly sight. Had Grant been the cause of her disfigurement?

"Why haven't you taken care of him? I mean, the way Roger was taken care of, you know?" I questioned.

"It's crossed my mind plenty, Claire. Grant Mallory will get what's coming to him. It takes time."

"What about the police? Why haven't you told them?"

"And tell them what?" he asked. "I can't prove anything, Claire. It's all circumstantial. Angela tried to prove that Grant had been involved in her hit and run, but nothing could be verified. They called him in. They asked him questions. Nothing could be proved."

"At the very least, why continue to be his friend? He was in our wedding."

"Because it's expected. Look, our parents are close friends. We grew up together. What? Am I going to tell my mother, 'Grant isn't going to be my best man because I think he killed Suzanne and broke Laura Leighton's nose?'" He laughed. "That sounds absurd."

I couldn't believe that I'd been ripped from a normal life and thrown into one that involved kidnapping and betrayal. Murder.

Jonathan didn't seem to hear my thoughts, as he continued to talk.

"I've told you that the others were gold diggers, and they weren't true to me. They dated me for my money, and then they weren't true to me because they all left me for Grant. And they all ran back to me once they realized how despicable he really is. But, you know what's ironic? I've always been a rule follower, a good guy, and women dumped on me for so long. Now I'm the bad guy, and it seems to have paid off. You aren't going anywhere, are you?"

"No."

"And not just because you fear for your life and your family's lives, but because you've fallen in love with me, right?" he hoped aloud.

"Yes," I lied.

"You don't have to worry about Grant Mallory, Claire. He will get what he deserves. And if he ever, *ever* says or does anything inappropriate to you, you will tell me, right? You will tell me?

"Of course I will tell you," I said.

"Good girl," he kissed my neck. "I'm glad you know all of this now. It's like a weight has been lifted off my shoulders. I should have told you this sooner."

"Why didn't you?"

"I don't know. There was no need in telling you, I guess. You weren't going to run to Grant Mallory, not because you feared *him*, but because you feared *me*."

He reveled in being the bad guy. He was proud of himself for getting away with the kidnapping and making me fall in love with him. He wanted to be the *only* man that I feared.

I was proud of myself, too. I was proud that I'd become an outstanding liar and actor. I was so good at deception that I almost believed that I'd had a nightmare about Grant Mallory.

TWENTY SIX

The car ride was silent except for the sound of the air conditioner violently blowing through the Range Rover's vents. I stared out the window at the pavement baking in the July sun and tried to think of a way to ease the tension.

"I wonder if Emma finally got a car for her birthday last week," I pondered aloud.

Jonathan said nothing. He continued to stare at the hot asphalt, switching lanes to pass a slow semi-truck.

"She's always wanted a Camaro," I mumbled.

"I don't know," he finally broke his silence as we merged off of the freeway.

I looked at him, his face saddened, his eyes puffy from a bout of crying that morning. I felt terrible for him. I reached over and patted his hand resting on the console.

"What will I do if he dies?" he asked me, still staring ahead.

"He will be fine," I replied. "He will be just fine."

We took the elevator to the intensive care unit on the third floor. We were greeted by Mrs. Caroline and Adrienne when the elevator doors opened.

Mrs. Caroline immediately pulled Jonathan into her arms and sobbed onto the sleeve of his white shirt. I looked down at my feet and shifted awkwardly at the pain they were sharing in that moment.

"Claire," she released him and grabbed me. I patted her back and told her that everything would be okay.

We sat in the brown chairs in the dim waiting room as Mrs. Caroline reached for a box of Kleenex on the table. Adrienne sipped her coffee and fiddled with her cell phone.

"Triple bypass?" Jonathan quietly asked his mother.

"Yes," she nodded, wiping the running mascara from her eyes. "I'm not surprised, Jon. You know he eats meat for dessert. He hasn't exercised since Carter was in office."

"I thought he was doing better. I thought you were both eating healthier," Jonathan shook his head.

"Son, he's a sixty-year-old man. I can't force him to eat the right foods. If we have salad for dinner, he eats the salad. Then he cooks a burger and fries at midnight and eats three bowls of ice cream. He's always been a big man, Jon. You know he loves his food," she argued.

"I know, but he told me that he'd cut back on the red meat."

"He did, son. And he replaced it with a slab of bacon for breakfast and two pork chops for dinner."

"Can we see him?" I asked.

Mrs. Caroline nodded.

"Dr. Felsenthal is going to let us know when we can come back and see him. They are scheduled to start the surgery at noon."

"Why didn't you call me when he had the heart attack, Mother? I should have been here," Jonathan said.

"I didn't want to worry you," Mrs. Caroline sniffled.

"But he could have died. I don't care that it was three in the morning. He could have died. I should have been here when the ambulance brought him in."

"Sweetheart, he was talking and joking in the ambulance. He was in pain, but I knew he wasn't going to die. He knew he wasn't going to die. He told me to let you rest. He told me to call you this morning. I didn't want you rushing up here in the middle of the night. You needed your rest," she reasoned with him.

"So he just woke up in pain?" I asked watching Adrienne sigh at her phone and flip it closed.

"He was eating," she scoffed. "He was eating a pan of chocolate brownies, watching John Wayne. He managed to walk upstairs and wake me. He's never had a heart attack, but we both knew what it was. Still, I knew he wasn't going to die. You needed your rest."

"Where's Casey?" Jonathan looked to Adrienne.

Embarrassment covered her face as she sipped her coffee again and shot her eyes at Mrs. Caroline.

"He isn't feeling well," Adrienne mumbled.

"He's hung over." Jonathan stated.

"He will be here soon," she nodded while hiding behind the Styrofoam cup.

"He's at home nursing a hangover while our father is lying in intensive care? That's what you're telling me?" Jonathan bellowed.

"Calm down," I patted his knee.

"Worthless," Jonathan rose to his feet and began pacing in the empty waiting room. "He's worthless. Always has been."

"Claire is right. Calm down, son," Mrs. Caroline sighed.

We had been waiting nearly an hour when we heard the door open. We all turned, expecting to see Casey wearing his sunglasses, ball cap and gripping his own cup of coffee, but instead we saw the doctor entering the room with a caring smile on his face.

"Caroline," he said, walking towards us as we all stood.

Mrs. Caroline extended her hands to the doctor.

"Dr. Felsenthal, is he okay?" she hoped aloud.

"He's stable. You can see him before we prep him for surgery," he looked at each one of us, nodding his head and casting warm eyes upon us. "Two at a time."

"Jon, you and Claire go ahead," Mrs. Caroline said.

"Are you sure?" Jonathan asked.

"Go," she insisted.

"Jonathan, you should go alone," I began.

He ignored me and grabbed my hand and pulled me through the door to the nurse's station as Mrs. Caroline stayed behind with Dr. Felsenthal and spoke about the surgery. A heavy set nurse showed us the way to the room, and when we entered, Mr. Marsh's appearance startled me.

He didn't look good. He looked sick and frail. His skin was pale, his eyes were tired, and his hair was thin and dirty and stuck to his head. He was always a big and strong man, but he suddenly seemed thinner, older, weaker.

"Dad?" Jonathan asked over the sounds of the heart monitors and machines as we entered the room.

"There's my boy," Mr. Marsh tried to lean up in the bed. "Get in here."

Jonathan let go of my hand and nearly sprinted to his father's side. He pressed his stubbly cheek against the old man's shoulder, and he held on. He held on to his father as if it were the last time that he would see him.

"Boy, quit your sniffling. I'm going to be fine," Mr. Marsh said while winking at me.

Jonathan lifted his head and casually wiped his eyes as Mr. Marsh motioned for me to come to him.

"Aren't you pretty as always?" He kissed my cheek. "And you smell good, too."

"Thank you," I blushed and pulled away from him.

"Are you feeling okay?" Jonathan asked.

"I'm fine, Jon. Seems all those steaks and baked potatoes have caught up with me, but I'm fine. I was a little scared last night though, I have to admit."

"Why didn't you call me, Dad? I don't care what time it was, you should have-" Jonathan argued.

"I wouldn't call you out of bed with that pretty young thing to come watch these monkeys jump up and down on my chest for half an hour. Hell, I knew I would be alright. It wasn't much of a heart attack anyway," he sneered.

"But if something had happened, I should have been here," Jonathan shook his head.

"Horse puckey. I just told you that I knew I would be alright. Hell, your mother wouldn't have let me die without saying goodbye. You know what a stickler she is for manners," he laughed. "These fellas are going to fix me up good as new. I'll be climbing deer stands and shooting at eight points in the fall."

"You've got to eat better. This calls for a complete lifestyle change, you understand? Healthy eating, exercise, the whole nine. You can't go through this again," Jonathan demanded.

"Yeah, yeah," Mr. Marsh dismissed the thought. "Where is that brother of yours? Hugging a bottle of Jack Daniels I suppose?"

"Who knows?" Jonathan sat down in a small chair and pulled me into his lap.

"What will we do with him, Jon? Speaking of lifestyle changes, he sure needs one. I may need a new heart, but your brother will need a new liver soon. You've got to talk to him. I've got to talk to him. The boy needs Jesus."

"Don't worry about him right now, Dad. He will get his come to Jesus meeting soon enough," he said.

"Claire, darling, how have you been?" Mr. Marsh changed the subject.

"I'm doing fine, Mr. Thomas. Worried about you, but doing fine," I smiled.

"Don't worry that pretty little head a bit. I'm going to be just fine. I'm too damn mean to die," he laughed, his large belly jiggling beneath the blanket.

I chuckled softly as Jonathan slid his arms around my waist.

"I'm glad you kids found one another. I sure am glad," Mr. Marsh watched us sitting together in the chair, seeming so in love, and his face became brighter. "I didn't think Jonathan would love again. That worried me so. I'm glad I don't have to worry about that anymore."

I smiled and looked to the floor as Jonathan patted my leg.

"Be good to her, Jon. Always make her feel beautiful. Make her feel special. Sometimes I look at your mother while she's reading her love stories or watching her soap operas, and I just have to tell her how beautiful she is. A woman needs to hear that. And a man needs to say it," he nodded.

"Okay, Dad," Jonathan replied.

"Be good to him, Claire. Make him feel appreciated. Caroline still makes me feel appreciated. I'm not that young baseball player anymore, and I'm not busting my ass working two jobs anymore, and I'm not the mayor of Houston, Texas anymore, but she still makes me feel appreciated. A man needs to feel

~ 182 ~

respected. Do that for my boy, Claire. Do that for me," he winked at me again, his voice sounding tired.

"I will, Mr. Thomas."

"Did I tell you I worked two jobs?" he asked as I shook my head. "Oh, yes. I wasn't born into money. I was raised in a little wooden house in the backwoods of Robertson County. My daddy worked in a saw mill all his life. Junie and I both worked hard. We were poor, Claire. We were damn dirt poor.

"And when my mama died of the cancer, Junie dropped out of school and did all the womanly duties around the house. My daddy was damn near heartbroken, and he could barely find the will to go to work, but he went. And he made me stay in school. He told me I was going to be something someday. He told me I wasn't going to work in no damned saw mill all my life.

"So, I stayed in school. And I played a lot of ball and worked a lot in that saw mill, and I graduated, and I made it to college on a baseball scholarship. And I continued to work hard. I played more ball, I worked in a factory, I cooked at a diner, I studied, and I worked some more. It was hard, but by God, I did it. And then I met Caroline in all her glory. There she was with a silver spoon hanging from her mouth, but she took a liking to a damn dirt poor boy like me. She liked the way I looked in that baseball uniform. And she thought I was smart. And she liked that I worked so damned hard, cause she hadn't ever seen a man work that hard in all her life.

"She was born rich, and her daddy was born rich, and her brothers were all born rich. She didn't know a man could work so damn hard and get his fingernails so dirty, and still know how to open a car door for a woman and treat a lady right. And, by God, that oil-rich girl fell in love with that damn dirt poor boy.

"I'm not ashamed that I borrowed the money from Caroline's father to start the car lot. I'm not ashamed that I spent twelve years pushing used Chevys on farm boys. I paid every cent back to her old man. I worked hard at that job. And before I knew it, Caroline was pushing me into politics. Hell, she said I could talk the paint off a post, and I could argue like a damn lawyer, and I could lie like a used car salesman, because that's exactly what I was. And she was right. I made it. I started out on boards and committees and so on and so forth, and before I knew it, I was the mayor of Houston, Texas. And I did a damn good job at it.

"My daddy saw me become the mayor of Houston, Texas. He lived long enough to see me fulfill my dream, and his, and I made my daddy proud. He died a happy man because his boy had made it, and I can do the same, boy. You've made me proud."

Jonathan shook his head, looking away from the tears in his father's eyes, and he said, "You're going to be fine. You're too mean to die. You just said so."

"I'm proud of you, son. You weren't born with that silver spoon in your mouth. Your mother was rich, your granddaddy was rich, but I raised you to work hard and make something of yourself. You are the one that transformed that used car lot into the most successful luxury car showroom in the state. That's you, son. That's what *you* did. We may have provided you with a good education, and spoiled you here and there, but you've never relied on us for handouts. You're a self-made man, Jon. You're a good man. You've got you a good woman, a beautiful home, money in the bank, and you've done all that yourself. I'm proud of you. I just want you to know that."

"I know that, Dad. I know," his voice trailed off.

"And your damned brother, he doesn't have the damn sense of a shit fly. He's over there drinking his ass to death, relying on you for income, keeping that girl around for a decade, never putting a ring on her finger. I'm disappointed in your brother, Jon. I sure as hell am. I don't know where he gets it," Mr. Thomas looked away from Jonathan, his head shaking, his fingers rapidly tapping on the bed sheet.

"You can't worry about Casey right now. You've got to focus on getting well. Focus on that eight point in the fall," Jonathan replied.

"Hell, he's never done anything right. He hasn't even shot an eight point. I remember him sighting in on that big buck several years ago. Hands were shaking so bad from not drinking that he missed that damn deer by a mile. Thank God for you, Jon. Thank God my first born knows how to work hard. You've always done the right thing, boy. You've always taken what you want. You've known how to get what you want. I'm proud of you," he repeated.

There Jonathan was, with a stolen woman sitting in his lap, proving that his father was right about one thing. Jonathan had taken whatever he wanted. But his daddy was wrong in praising him for always doing the right thing, when I was living proof that he hadn't.

I also agreed that Jonathan was a hardworking and intelligent. I didn't doubt that he'd grown his business, or that he'd worked tirelessly all of his life. He'd also worked hard to research me, steal me from my family and my home, create my new identity, and keep tabs on my family. He was, indeed, a clever hard worker.

If only Mr. Marsh knew that his precious boy was a kidnapper, a liar, a dark and evil man. His youngest son may have been a screw up, a drunk, a lazy bum, but I was fairly certain that Adrienne stayed with Casey out of love, and some sort of respect, instead of fear.

"Thomas?" Mrs. Caroline stuck her head in the door. "May I see you now?"

"Get in here, you beautiful woman. Of course you can see me," Mr. Marsh grinned. "May I see you? That's the question."

Jonathan and I stood. I hugged Mr. Marsh first, and then I moved out of the way so his son could tell him goodbye.

"I love you, son," he whispered as Jonathan pulled away.

"I love you, old man."

"I'll see you both soon. I want a rib eye waiting on me when I come out of surgery," he joked.

"Salad, Dad. Salad," Jonathan chuckled.

"Oh, hell. That's bird food. I want a juicy steak. Medium rare."

"Bye, Dad," Jonathan touched his mother's arm as we left them alone.

"Are you okay?" I asked as we walked back to the waiting room.

"I think so," Jonathan put his arm around me. "He'll be fine, you think?"

"He's going to be good as new. He was in high spirits. He looked good," I lied.

"I'm so glad you're here with me," he said. "You're a good woman."

I said nothing.

"And you're beautiful," he kissed my head as we entered the waiting room to see Casey and Adrienne speaking to Aunt Junie.

"Well, look what the drunk cat dragged in," Jonathan said sternly.

"Don't start with me," Casey sipped his coffee.

His eyes were bloodshot, his face was stubbly, and his hair was a mess on his head.

"Did you have a good time last night?" Jonathan left me standing alone as he approached his brother sitting in the chair.

"As a matter of fact, I did," Casey stood to face him.

"Boys," Aunt Junie began.

"It's nice that you were out partying while our father was having a heart attack, you worthless piece of shit," Jonathan shouted.

"Jonathan," I rushed to him and tugged on his arm.

"You think you're so much better than me, don't you?" Casey scoffed.

"I know I am," Jonathan stated confidently.

"This isn't the place for this. Adrienne?" I looked down at her for help.

"Casey, sit down," Adrienne said, nervously.

"You've always been worthless," Jonathan growled.

Casey stared at him, hurt and shame evident on his face.

"And you've always been an asshole," he said. "I don't need this."

Casey pushed Jonathan out of his way and shoved though the waiting room door.

"Jonathan? Go after him," I said.

"Let him go. He's got more important things to do. There's a bottle of whiskey waiting on him somewhere," Jonathan sat down in the chair. I sat beside him as Aunt Junie shook her head and Adrienne dug into her purse for her cell phone.

"Surgery went well. He's going to be fine," Dr. Felsenthal's words prompted us to all heave sighs of relief.

"Thank you, God. Thank you, Lord," Aunt Junie lifted her hands to the sky and began to pray.

"Now, we're talking at least six weeks of recovery time, Caroline. The recovery time is critical," Dr. Felsenthal pushed heavy silver glasses up his nose. "And his diet has to change. Our nurses will go over all of this with the both of you, but I want you to realize that a new lifestyle begins for him today."

"I understand. Thank you so much," Mrs. Caroline reached out and wrapped her arms around the tall skinny doctor.

Dr. Felsenthal nodded and left us alone in the waiting room.

"Told you," I smiled and nudged Jonathan.

He pulled me into his arms and laughed.

TWENTY SEVEN

I sat at the kitchen table on that August afternoon, gazing out the back window at two birds hopping along the patio. They looked miserable in the heat as the scorching sun blazed upon them. I looked beyond them to the refreshing pool, and I wondered if the birds had enough sense to know that relief was only thirty yards away.

I looked back to the stack of papers on the kitchen table. I sipped my water and my head began to spin at all of the preparations that had to be made for the fundraiser in September. I had to find a caterer. I had to send out the invitations. I still had so many numbers to crunch.

What did I know about throwing a fundraiser? What did I know about saving a dilapidated library on the east side of town? What did I know about rallying people together and starting a movement and a desire to write checks and save the books and restore the historical building?

I was the wife of a prosperous man. Fundraising was expected of me. Here I was living in the lap of luxury with all the time in the world. I was expected to rally troops together for the greater good. I was expected to dress in fancy clothes and assemble all of the affluent people of Houston to pull out their checkbooks and help sick children, homeless pets and derelict libraries. This was my job.

But I didn't want this job. I wanted to be in Nashville carrying out my business degree. I wanted to own a tanning salon or a quaint clothing boutique downtown. I didn't want to plan parties and stand before a large group of people and beg them to help me save a library.

"Dad looked good today," Jonathan interrupted my thoughts as he walked through the kitchen door.

"Oh, good," I cleared my throat and looked away from the stack of papers.

"I think he's finally on board with eating better. He hasn't thrown any apples across the room in nearly a week," he chuckled as he searched through the refrigerator.

"That's good," I laughed, once again focusing on the papers before me.

"How's the fundraiser coming?" he sat beside me and guzzled his bottle of water.

"I'm nervous, Jonathan," I confessed to him. "What if I make a mess of this?"

"Nonsense. You will do fine. You'll be an old pro at fundraising before you know it. This is your first one. It's a learning experience."

"It's just so much to do," I thought out loud, my mind cluttered.

"Are the other ladies pulling their weight?"

I nodded.

"Cybil and Lacey have been great. I'm just nervous, that's all."

"It'll go off with a bang, Claire. You're too beautiful to make a mess of anything."

He'd taken his father's advice about telling me how beautiful I was at every opportunity. By this point, it had become incredibly annoying. I burned dinner, but I was beautiful. I lounged on the couch in pajamas, but I was beautiful. I had a huge zit on my chin, but I was beautiful. I was going to screw up this fundraiser in a disastrous way, but I was beautiful.

"Thank you," I said.

"Casey made it to work today," Jonathan loosened his tie.

"He did?" I asked curiously.

Casey hadn't come to work since the argument in the waiting room five weeks ago. Adrienne said he'd been drinking constantly, wandering around for hours at night. They could barely pay the bills, relying solely on her teaching salary. She had asked Mrs. Caroline for financial help, just to pay a couple of credit card bills, but Mr. Marsh refused to let them borrow any money.

"He hasn't been there in weeks, Claire, and he waltzed in like he was just there yesterday. He actually assumed that he still had a job," Jonathan laughed.

"You fired him?" I asked.

"Why, hell yes I fired him. He hasn't been there since July and even before then he couldn't sell a camel to a nomad. Why do I need him there?" Jonathan scoffed.

"I don't know," I shrugged. "He's still your family."

"He's nothing to me, Claire. He's nothing," Jonathan argued. "He's nothing but a disappointment to our entire family. He hasn't even been by to see Dad since he's been out of the hospital. That's not family."

"What will he do for money?"

"Who knows? Who cares? He's dead to me," he stated. "I've got to get out of this suit. It's 102 out there. And it's nearly 80 in here. You've been moving the thermostat again."

I rolled my eyes as he left me alone in the kitchen to worry over the fundraiser. I didn't know if it was the best time for a drink since we'd just discussed his alcoholic brother, but I shuffled to the kitchen counter and poured myself a glass of wine. Then I went to the hall closet to get my jacket as the air conditioner roared to life.

The hotter it was outside, the colder it was inside. The AC propelled frigid air upon me as I huddled into the fetal position beneath the heavy covers, my teeth chattering. I was so cold that my bones ached, my head hurt and I contemplated getting up to put on another sweatshirt, maybe two. I needed an electric blanket. It was the middle of August in Texas, but I needed an electric blanket.

It was so cold that I couldn't sleep. I looked over at Jonathan sleeping peacefully in only pajama pants. He wasn't even beneath the sheet, his bare chest exposed to the frosty air.

As I watched him breathe, expecting to see puffs of warm breath escape his lips, the doorbell rang. I startled and looked at the clock on the bedside table. It was 4:22 AM.

"Jonathan," I removed my hand from beneath the mounds of blankets, and I shook his arm. "Someone is at the door."

Jonathan sat up in the bed, and he listened for the sound again. It rang once more, and he stood to his feet, mumbling angrily.

"Mr. Jonathan, your brother is at the door," Ernesto called from the hallway over the ringing of the bell.

"What the hell does he want?" Jonathan shuffled out of the room, leaving me alone in the freezing bed.

"I don't know. I just saw him through the window," Ernesto explained.

I rolled out of the bed, my arms wrapped around my cold body, and I slid down the hallway where I could see the entry way.

"What do you want?" Jonathan shouted as he threw open the door.

I could see Casey leaning against the doorframe, a goofy grin across his face. He was obviously drunk. There were grass stains on his khaki shorts, and his Nirvana t-shirt was muddy.

Casey began to laugh hysterically as he reached around in the pocket of his shorts. He pulled out a small gun, and I immediately covered my eyes with my frozen hands, my heart pounding in my chest.

I heard a scuffle, expecting the sound of a gun shot at any moment, expecting to leave Jonathan dead in the foyer as I ran into the hot night and found a way home to Tennessee. Instead, I heard the sound of Casey's drunken body hit the floor.

"He's gone crazy, Ernesto. He's lost his ever- loving mind!" Jonathan shouted as I looked to see Casey lying motionless on the floor next to my piano while Jonathan rubbed his knuckles.

"You barely hit him. He's so drunk that Mrs. Claire could have knocked him out," Ernesto hovered over him and retrieved the gun from Casey's hand. "It's not even loaded, Mr. Jonathan."

"The stupid son of a bitch didn't even load the gun? Well, my God, Ernesto. What will we do with him?" Jonathan massaged his temples, shut the front door, and headed towards the kitchen.

"What's going on?" I walked into the living room, my hands shaking from anxiety.

"My damn brother came here to kill me I guess, but the dumbass didn't even load the gun," he said casually.

"You say that like it's a normal thing," I looked at Casey

still lying on the floor, Ernesto still examining him.

"He's pulled some stunts, but this beats all I've ever seen," Jonathan flipped through the phone book on the kitchen counter.

"He needs help, Jonathan," I joined him in the kitchen, wondering if hot cocoa would help my circulation.

"And that's what he's about to get," Jonathan mumbled, still looking through the book.

"He's got pills in his pocket, Mr. Jonathan," Ernesto called from the foyer over the shaking sound of a pill bottle.

"Lovely," Jonathan said sarcastically.

Ernesto entered the kitchen.

"Ernesto, do you have an electric blanket?" I asked, eying Ernesto's sweat pants and heavy shirt.

"Just one, Mrs. Claire," Ernesto replied quietly, "I can't sleep without it, though. You know they say heat rises upstairs? Well, it doesn't."

I shook my head in disgust that poor Ernesto and I were both forced to live in a meat locker.

Jonathan grabbed the cordless phone from the kitchen wall and began speaking in Spanish. I'd never heard him speak the language so quickly and fluently.

"What's he saying?" I asked Ernesto.

Ernesto shook his head as if it weren't my business.

"Gracias," Jonathan finally said, the only word that I comprehended.

"Who was that?" I asked.

"An associate," Jonathan replied, as I mouthed the words with him, knowing that would be his reply.

"Of course it was. So, what's your associate going to do about your brother?" I asked.

"He's going to take him to get some help," he put down the phone and sighed.

"Can't you just call a rehab facility yourself? Why have *your associate* get involved?" I asked.

"He's not going to a traditional rehab facility. I'm not putting that public shame on our family. He's going to get help.

That's all that matters," Jonathan replied and poured himself a glass of iced tea.

"I don't understand," I shook my head, my head throbbing from the cold.

"You don't have to understand, Claire," he said. "Jorge is going to take Casey somewhere and rehabilitate him. That's all that matters. He will return a new man."

Ernesto chuckled.

"Well, if anyone can rehabilitate him, Jorge can."

"Right?" Jonathan laughed as they obviously shared an inside joke about Jorge.

"I'm going to bed," I was frustrated with it all. "And turn off the damn air conditioner."

"Put on a coat," Jonathan called as I disappeared into the frosty bedroom.

When I woke the next morning, Casey had been removed from the foyer. Soon after waking, I put on my bathing suit and headed straight for the warmth, the heat of the backyard. I needed to defrost.

"Did you sleep well last night?" Ernesto joked as I sat on the steps in the shallow end of the pool, welcoming the sweltering sun.

"Well, between the ice sickles on my toes and the attempted murder, no, Ernesto. I did not sleep well. What about you?" I grinned.

"Another day in Marshland," Ernesto rolled up the legs of his khaki pants and sat at the edge of the pool, letting his feet soak in the warm water.

"Why do you stay here, Ernesto? You're really a good man. I know you are. Why do you live here, this way? Being an accomplice to crimes? Freezing all of the time? Being *an associate*?" I questioned.

"Mr. Jonathan has been good to me. He pays me well, puts a roof over my head. I could be doing much worse. I've never been mixed up with the right people. I guess you could say Mr. Jonathan saved me," he answered.

"If he saved you, I can't imagine what he saved you from."

"That's not for you to know, Mrs. Claire," he slowly kicked his feet in the water.

"Where did Casey go?" I squinted at Ernesto, the sun baking my body.

"You enjoy asking questions, don't you, Mrs. Claire?"

"I just want to know where my alcoholic brother-in-law is. I'm concerned, that's all. He's obviously gone somewhere. Just tell me what you would tell Mrs. Caroline or Adrienne," I said.

"Well," Ernesto pulled his aviator sunglasses from his shirt pocket and put them on. "Casey has gone to Palo Alto, California, where he will take part in an extensive rehabilitation program. It's imperative that he have no contact with family or friends for at least sixty days. He will come home when he is fit, and he sends his love," Ernesto replied robotically.

"So, he's being tortured by some Spanish guy named Jorge in California?" I clarified.

"It's for his own good, Mrs. Claire. Mr. Jonathan sent him there out of love. Mr. Casey needs tough love. That's what this is," Ernesto reasoned with me.

"Tough love," I murmured.

TWENTY EIGHT

When I entered the critical care waiting room, I saw Jonathan in a recliner, separated from his mother, Adrienne, Aunt Junie and Uncle Jim on the other side of the room. I'd never seen him look so disheartened. His head rested on his left hand as he stared blankly at his shoes. He looked like a sad child. He looked helpless.

"Claire," Mrs. Caroline rushed to me and pulled me into her arms.

I could feel her warm tears on the sleeve of my cotton shirt.

"What happened?" I asked, still staring at Jonathan.

Surely he'd known that I'd entered the room, but he had yet to shift his eyes my way.

"He just fell, Claire," she sobbed. "He fell in the hallway. He wouldn't respond to me. He just fell."

I held Mrs. Caroline close to my body and took in the flowery scent of her hair. I looked around the room and my eyes fell upon Aunt Junie's face. Her eyes were swollen and red as Uncle Jim massaged her tense shoulders. I watched Adrienne looking at Uncle Jim consoling his wife, and she seemed envious of their love. Jonathan continued to stare at his feet.

"They'll fix him up," I reassured Mrs. Caroline. "Everything is going to be fine."

"No," she pulled away from me and shook her head.

"Don't say that. He will be fine," I nodded.

She nodded as well, but I could see in her teary eyes that she didn't believe me. She returned to her seat, and I walked towards Jonathan. He never turned his eyes or his head my way. He just continued to stare at his shiny black dress shoes. His paisley tie had been loosened, and his black jacket was lying across his lap.

"Hey, you," I sat beside his feet on the long reclining chair.

"Hey," he mumbled, never making eye contact with me.

"He's going to be okay, Jonathan. He's too mean to die,

remember?" I grinned and touched his leg.

Jonathan said nothing. His stare was so empty, yet so full of pain. I didn't know what to say or do. I didn't want to feel compassion for him, but in that moment, no matter what he'd done to me, my heart ached for him.

He reached for my manicured hand.

"He's not going to make it."

"No, Jonathan," I said.

"What will I do?" he whispered. "What am I supposed to do without him?"

I was at a loss for words. I'd been separated from my parents, but I didn't know what it was like to lose a parent to death. I could only imagine that the pain was excruciating. I crawled closer to him, and I pulled his head onto my shoulder as he began to cry like a child.

Not very much time had passed when the doctor entered the waiting room and informed us that Mr. Thomas had left this world. The scream that bellowed from Mrs. Caroline's lungs caused me to jump. As my heart pounded from the startle, I watched Aunt Junie fall from the chair and onto her knees. Uncle Jim knelt beside her, pulled her close to him, and his own tears fell onto the top of her gray head. I was watching Adrienne cry softly into her tissue when Jonathan sprinted from the recliner and ran out the door.

I was left there, unsure whether to chase my husband or let him grieve. I was unsure who I should console. I was unsure what to do, or if I should do anything, but I was surprised when I felt a lone tear stream down my nose. I didn't know if I had cried that tear for Mrs. Caroline or Mr. Thomas or Jonathan.

I decided to leave the family there to mourn, and I walked down the hospital hallway in search of Jonathan. It took nearly fifteen minutes, but I finally found him sitting on a bench outside the main entrance.

"Jonathan?" I slowly approached him.

He looked at me, his nose red and his cheeks soaked. A small laugh escaped his lips as I sat beside him on the bench.

"We used to ride horses at Aunt Junie's house. I got thrown off this Palomino when I was just a kid. I was lying there, crying and screaming, and Dad rode up on his horse, slowly and casually. He just looked down on me lying there, writhing in pain, and he said, 'Get up, boy.' Then he rode off. That was it. I could've been lying there with a broken leg, and he just told me to get up," his smile faded. "He was hard on me. He was always hard on me. He was tough."

"He loved you, Jonathan. You know that. He was just telling you how proud he was of you," I said.

"I know," Jonathan looked to his hands. "He made me. My dad made me the person that I am today. He's the reason for all of my success. He's the reason I'm tough. He's even the reason you are sitting here. He always told me that if I wanted something, I should have it. He instilled in me that I'm entitled to what I want. I'd never have had the courage to take you if it weren't for my father."

I sighed and watched a new mother sitting in a wheelchair, a car seat on her lap as she waited on her ride to take her home and start a new life. I was taken back to the cold December day when Vaiden was born.

"How am I supposed to live without the man who taught me how to live? What am I supposed to do?" he interrupted the vision of my precious newborn bundle.

"You'll get through this," I took his hand into mine. "We'll all get through this together."

He draped his arm around me. I continued to watch the new mother as she happily gazed at the little blessing on her lap. My eyes released tears once again. For my daughter. For Jonathan.

"Who is going to call Casey?" Mrs. Caroline blew her nose into a Kleenex as we all sat around the living room that evening.

"I will do it," Jonathan volunteered.

"I want to call him, Jonathan," Adrienne spoke from behind her coffee cup.

"I just can't do it, Jon. I cannot tell my baby that his father is dead," Mrs. Caroline shook her head and wiped her eyes.

"I need to do it," Jonathan said again.

"Well, is he going to be able to come home for the funeral? Is he allowed to do that?" Adrienne inquired with agitation in her voice.

"He should be here, Jon," Mrs. Caroline sighed.

"I think he should stay and continue getting help. He's only been gone a week. He's not well," Jonathan paced beside my piano.

"Jonathan! He can't miss his father's funeral!" I exclaimed.

I knew it wasn't my place to voice an opinion, but I also knew it wasn't right to keep Casey hidden away in some California desert while his family mourned this loss.

"Claire is right. He should be here, son. He can go back right after the funeral. We will all keep an eye on him and make sure he doesn't touch a drop of alcohol," Mrs. Caroline said.

"Okay," Jonathan sighed. "Okay."

He disappeared to the back of the house, and I noticed Adrienne glaring at me.

"Where is he, Claire? Where is he really?" she asked.

"What?" I asked.

"Casey. Where is Jonathan keeping him hidden? Why can't we communicate with him? Why can't we know where he is?" she demanded.

"He's in treatment, Adrienne. I know as much as you do. Don't come to me for answers, because I don't have any," I sighed loudly and crossed my legs, disgusted with it all.

"I know you're missing him, Adrienne. I am, too, but he's in a good place. Jon says he's getting the help that he needs. That's all that matters," Mrs. Caroline nodded at Adrienne. "We don't need to know where he is. Communicating with him will just interrupt his treatment."

"My uncle was in treatment and we visited him every Sunday, sent him letters and stayed in contact with him.

Communicating with him didn't interrupt his treatment. He's been sober for fourteen years."

"Adrienne Brown, are you trying to start an argument? Are you daring to start an argument with me on the very day my husband of nearly forty years has died? Are you?" Mrs. Caroline growled.

"No," she shook her head. "I just want to know where Casey is."

"He's getting help. Now shut your damn mouth," Mrs. Caroline gritted her teeth.

I smirked at Mrs. Caroline's brazenness, which I'd never seen before. I vaguely heard Jonathan speaking in Spanish from the back of the house, and I knew he must have been on the telephone with Jorge.

"Mom?" he entered the living room a few moments later. "Casey wants to speak with you."

Mrs. Caroline grabbed the phone from Jonathan's hand and began crying.

"Sweet Casey. He's gone. Your daddy is gone," she bawled as I left the living room.

I hid in the kitchen for a few moments and then retrieved the largest wine glass from the cupboard. I filled it to the brim and slid out the back door and grabbed the pack of cigarettes that I kept hidden behind a landscaping rock. I settled into a lawn chair near the pool and I inhaled the smoke and gulped the wine, not caring who saw me, not caring when I heard the sound of the French doors opening and closing behind me.

"I know you smoke," he said. "You don't have to keep hiding them in the landscaping. How many packs have the sprinklers ruined?"

"Two," I replied as he sat in a lawn chair next to mine.

"May I bum one?" he asked.

"Seriously?" I asked.

"My dad just died," he shrugged as I handed him the pack and a lighter.

"Should I light it for you?" I grinned.

"Maybe," he lit the cigarette and smoke escaped his nostrils.

"No coughing?" I sounded impressed.

"Oh, come on, Claire. I smoked throughout college. It isn't as if you've been hiding some hard-core addiction from me," he flicked the ashes to the brick patio.

We listened to the crickets chirping and the wind whipping through the mossy trees as I glanced at him. His sadness, his loss, was still so apparent.

"Listen," I paused. "I know I've been telling you this all afternoon, but I'm really sorry about Mr. Thomas. I mean, I'm not with my daddy anymore, but just knowing that he's alive in the world makes something seem right. I miss him terribly, and I've been torn away from him, but I can't possibly imagine the pain that you're feeling."

He nodded.

"Thank you, Claire."

"I'm here for you, Jonathan. Really, I'm here if you want to cry or talk or whatever. I'm here," I said, and I meant it.

"I know," he stared at the burning cigarette.

"So," I changed the subject, "is baby brother going to tell Mom about his non-traditional rehabilitation?"

"Nope," Jonathan shook his head and watched the fountain interrupt the stillness of the pool water.

"How can you be sure?" I asked before sipping the wine.

"If he tells anyone about his treatment, he won't be allowed to come to the funeral. It's that simple," he replied.

"Hmmm," I muttered. "You can blackmail anyone, can't you?"

"It's a gift," he shrugged.

"Apparently."

"Speaking of the funeral," he cleared his throat, "I don't think you should come, either."

"What?"

"You can't come, Claire. Don't you know that?" he said.

"He was my father-in-law. Why can't I come?" I shifted my weight in the lawn chair.

"My father was the mayor. He has a lot of noteworthy friends. He's a personal friend of the President. He knows every law officer in the city of Houston, maybe even the state of Texas. Of course you can't go," he answered.

"You think I'm going to tell? You think I'm going to confess all of this to someone at your father's funeral?"

"That's exactly what I think," Jonathan said.

"That's ridiculous. I thought we were past all of that. I thought you trusted me," I argued.

"It never crossed your mind, Claire?"

"I've been to charity events and parties with these people for nearly a year now. I've never squealed before, have I?" my tone was irritated.

"It's too high profile. I don't like the idea of you running around with law officers while I'm comforting my mother and too bereaved to keep an eye on you. You aren't going," he shook his head.

"So, what will you tell everyone? Won't people wonder why your supportive wife isn't by your side at your father's funeral? You're the one so concerned with appearances and what this town thinks of us. Won't that make me look like a terrible spouse?"

"You'll be sick. You'll be stuck in the bed with a temperature of 104 and a raging case of strep throat," he said as he threw the dead cigarette to the ground. "You should probably start coughing when you come back inside the house."

"I loved your father, Jonathan. I can't believe you won't let me pay him the respect that he deserves," I angrily shook my head and looked away from him.

"That's sweet," he stood from the lawn chair. "But you're not going."

I heard the French doors open and close again, and the cigarette burned the tip of my finger. I threw it beside Jonathan's on the ground, and I finished the wine.

I would never cause a scene at Mr. Marsh's funeral. I would never speak of Jonathan's crimes during such a mournful event. It had crossed my mind, but I would never actually do it.

TWENTY NINE

I watched the heavy raindrops fall into the pool on that cool September morning. My knees were pulled close to my chest as I sat in the wicker chair on the back porch, my coffee cup resting on my knee. A family of robins huddled together at the opposite end of the porch, shielding themselves from the cold drops of water.

I was worried that my hair was going to frizz, just has I had worried 365 days before. I knew it would look terrible for dinner with Jonathan that evening.

As I sat on the back porch of my beautiful home and watched the Bermuda grass become saturated with rain, I imagined my mother was lying on the couch, surrounded by wads of tissue, studying my wedding photo and not believing that I had been gone for a year. My father was probably yelling at *The Price is Right* contestants, trying to keep his mind occupied.

Had Vaiden forgotten me? Had she forgotten the piggyback rides and the nights we cuddled in the bed and watched *Blue's Clues*? Had she forgotten her mother? Was I even a memory to her?

I was sure that Nathan had moved on. I'd been gone for a year with no sign of ever returning. He would be finished with school in just a few short months, and it would be time for him to really begin his life, without me.

I thought of the young girl who shopped in the mall that day. Wasn't she silly to feel so safe and secure? She was certain that she'd met the man that she would marry. Her future had been outlined in a journal that set on her chest of drawers. She was confident in so many things, she knew so many things, but she was completely oblivious that her future and everything she had known, everything that was familiar, would be taken from her before she reversed out of the mall parking lot that day.

Jonathan and I sat in the restaurant that evening, my hair curling around my face, as we waited on our meal. I sipped my wine and noticed the small lines around his eyes. He had aged since his father had passed away. He was as handsome as always, but he had aged in only a few short weeks.

"Are you nervous about the fundraiser tomorrow night?" he asked as he tapped his fork on the white linen tablecloth.

"Yeah," I shrugged. "But there's nothing more I can do."

"I'm sure everything will turn out fine," he continued to play with the silverware. "I'm proud of you for working so diligently on it."

"Thank you."

The silence resumed as I continued to watch him stare blankly at the table. Not only had he aged since Mr. Marsh passed, but he was noticeably depressed. He would lock himself in his office and later exit with red eyes and puffy cheeks. He said little at dinner. He looked at the television, but it was obvious that his mind was elsewhere. He tossed and turned in the bed for hours, only to eventually get up and pace the house.

And I grieved for him. Here was a man who had wronged me in so many ways, but I grieved for him. My heart ached at the pain that he was experiencing. I wanted to make him better. I wanted to take his pain and couple it with my own, and I wanted to toss it away. I wanted both of our hurts to disappear.

"Do you know what today is?" I asked, wondering why he hadn't mentioned the anniversary earlier.

"No," he glanced at me and then his eyes returned to the table.

"September 4th?" I asked. "You know, a year?"

"Is it?" his eyes finally locked with mine. "It's been a year?"

I nodded.

"Wow," he sighed. "Well, I don't know if congratulations or condolences are in order."

I kept silent and pressed the wine glass to my lips.

"For what it's worth, thanks," he took a sip of his water.

"For what?"

"Thanks for cooperating," he replied. "And thanks for being a good wife."

I shrugged.

"Sure."

My black gown dragged the ballroom floor as I presented my largest smile and mingled with the guests at the fundraiser. I thanked them for their donations and for their kind words about Mr. Thomas. I thanked these people for actually showing up and making me look successful to my husband and all of Houston, Texas.

I stood before the crowd of 200 people and weaved a lie about my love of books. I gave them a history lesson about the library, and how the building had served as a safe haven for the wounded in war and the hungry in the Depression. I urged them to dig deep into their pockets and help save the building and my reputation. Then I exited the stage to the sound of applause, and I grabbed my fifth glass of champagne.

"You did great," Jonathan greeted me after my speech.

"Thanks," I smiled and gulped the alcohol.

"I'm proud of you, Claire. I'm proud to call you my wife," he put his arms around me.

I closed my eyes and took in the scent of his cologne. I wrapped my arms around him, careful not to spill the champagne on his expensive suit. I felt safe there with him. Funny how I'd been terrified of him for so long, how he was the epitome of all that was wrong and evil in my world, and now I felt secure in his arms.

I pulled back and kissed him on the lips.

"What was that for?" he asked me, surprised.

"You're my husband, aren't you?"

"Am I?"

"Of course you are," I winked at him and returned to my guests.

I leaned against a stall in the beautiful bathroom as Mrs. Caroline cried. She was struggling so with Mr. Thomas' death. She still spoke to him as she walked through the house. She made his favorite meals. She set his place at the table for dinner. And she sniffled in the bathroom mirror after the fundraiser because she knew how proud her husband would be of his daughter-in-law.

"You need to go home and get some rest," I hiccupped but tried to hide my buzz.

"I just can't stand it, Claire," she shook her head and wrapped the silk shawl around her shoulders. "I can't stand being there alone."

"I thought Aunt Junie was staying with you?"

"She was, but she can't live there. She had to go home to Jim. She has her own life, you know. I just hate being alone," she whimpered.

"You are welcome to stay with us at any time, Mrs. Caroline," I offered.

"You're sweet, but you kids have your own lives, too," she reached out and touched my arm. "Maybe I should get a dog?"

"Maybe," I smiled while noticing my glazed eyes in the mirror.

"You look tired, honey. *You* should get home and rest," she motioned for me to follow her out of the bathroom.

"I have a few things to finish here and then I will," I looked around the ballroom littered with dirty dishes and empty glasses, proud that the fundraiser had been such a success.

"Everything was lovely, dear," she turned to kiss my cheek. "I'm very proud of you and for you. You're responsible for the restoration of that beautiful old building. That's something to be proud of."

"Thank you, Mrs. Caroline," I smiled.

She left me alone in the ballroom. I examined the mess for a few moments, and I sighed. Jonathan entered the large double doors and walked across the burgundy carpet to me, his white shirt un-tucked from his pants, his black jacket across his arm.

"Did you see your mother?" I asked.

"I walked her out," he nodded. "Do you want another drink?"

"Sure," I ignored the pounding in my head and the burning in my stomach.

Jonathan went behind the bar as I sat on a stool.

"Are we allowed to be here?" I asked, observing the empty building.

"We are allowed to do what we please," he said as he poured the liquor and handed it to me.

"What is it?" I examined the brown liquid in the glass.

"It'll put hair on your chest," he began mixing his own drink.

"You like hairy chested women?" I took a sip and made a sound that I'd never made before.

Jonathan laughed.

"It's good, eh?"

"Whiskey?" I asked as he nodded. "Well, my sinuses have cleared, that's for sure."

He walked from behind the bar and sat next to me on a barstool.

"So, success feels nice, doesn't it?" he nudged my arm.

"Yeah," I sipped the bourbon.

"You were a real leader. I saw the way Cybil and the other girls looked up to you. You really headed this thing. That's great."

"It's funny. I've never thought of myself as a leader. I've always followed. I followed my mom, my dad, my friends, Nathan. I didn't know I could be a leader," I confessed.

"Well, you are," he clinked his glass against mine, "and a damn good one."

"Cheers," I poured the warm concoction down my throat.

"Is it safe to say that you enjoy my company?" he asked.

I shrugged.

"I don't know, maybe."

"I think you do. By God, I think you just might love me, Elle Holley," he flirted.

"I don't know, maybe."

"Let me ask you something," he turned towards me on the stool.

I faced him, my dress hung on the heel of my shoe.

"Let's say someone kidnapped you, okay?" he said.

"Okay?" I hesitated.

"Let's say someone took you from me. And let's say you escaped. Would you come to Houston, Texas or would you go to Nashville?"

"Are you serious?"

"I am. Tell me. Where would you go?" he asked again.

Without a doubt, I'd go home to my daughter. But I was surprised at the sound of my thoughts, the content of my thoughts, as I spoke them into the dim, quiet ballroom.

"I miss Vaiden. I miss her so much that I can feel it. It aches. I miss her so much that I literally ache," I ran my finger around the rim of the glass. "And my mother. My God, I miss my mother's voice and the smell of her Liz Claiborne perfume on Sunday mornings."

"I know you do," he said.

"I could tell you all of the people, the things, that I miss terribly, but you already know," I shook my head and emptied the glass into my mouth. "But, I don't know."

He watched me attentively.

"I can't explain it. I feel something for you that I never thought I'd feel."

I was shaken at my own words.

"I think I do, I do," I stuttered. "I do love you, Jonathan. I've come to rely on you and depend on you. You're all I have, and I've come to accept that and even be okay with it. I think I would do everything in my power to get home to Vaiden, but I also think that I'd miss, I'd miss you once I returned home," my eyebrows raised at my realization.

"You wouldn't forget me the second you saw Nathan and fell back into your old life?" he asked.

"I don't know," I shook my head. "I told you on the cruise that I'd fallen in love with you, and I confess to you that that wasn't entirely true at the time. I don't think I knew it then. I didn't know it then, but some feelings were starting to grow for you. Now that I've become familiar with you and watched you mourn your father, I think, I think I've really fallen in love with you. I can't believe it myself, but I think it may be true."

"Well, by God. That's amazing."

"By God, that's psychotic. I've fallen in love with my kidnapper. Is that possible?" I didn't want to believe it.

"I guess so," he quickly pulled my face to his and I tasted the whiskey on his lips. "Let's go home."

"Okay," I nodded and slid off of the barstool, my high-heeled shoe finally coming free from the elegant ball gown.

He slipped his hand into mine as we walked across the grand room.

"You look beautiful tonight, as always," his fingers squeezed mine, "but may I make a suggestion?"

"A suggestion?" I looked to him.

"Boobs. We've got to get you some boobs."

THIRTY

I held the ice packs close to my chest as my breasts throbbed with pain. I mumbled expletives and tried to find a comfortable position in the bed, to no avail. I searched for the remote beneath the heap of blankets, annoyed at the sound of Andy Griffith calling Don Knotts an idiot in the most polite way possible.

"Knock, knock," Ernesto appeared in the doorway. "Are you ready to eat?"

"No," I growled. "I'm ready for another Mepergan and Southern Comfort."

"Those things don't mix, Mrs. Claire. You know that," he walked over to the bed and handed me the remote.

"No, Ernesto. Pain and I don't mix. I can't believe I got these stupid things," I glanced at my swollen breasts bulging under my sweatshirt.

"You'll be back to your old self soon," he said. "Call me when you're ready for dinner."

"I need a pill, Ernesto!" I called after him. "Ernesto!"

He left me alone as I muted Sheriff Taylor. I continued wrestling with the covers, wishing I could have a shot of whiskey and a pain pill.

"Knock, knock," Jonathan said.

"What's with all of the knock, knock stuff? Either knock or don't, but don't say knock, knock. It's annoying," I snapped.

"You have a visitor," he sat on the edge of the bed.

"I'm in no mood for Cybil's jokes, Jonathan. I don't want any visitors," I grumbled.

"It's not Cybil. It's Casey," he patted my foot beneath the heavy quilt.

"Casey?" I whispered.

"I was shocked myself. I knew he was discharged today, but I had no idea that he'd pay me a visit as soon as he made it back to Houston. He asked Jorge to drop him off here. He hasn't even been home yet. I was outside when they pulled up. He's waiting out back by the pool. Said he wanted to see you while he was here," he grinned.

"What?" I asked. "Is he okay? Is he, you know, rehabilitated?"

"Oh, he's rehabilitated. Will you see him?"

"I guess," I shrugged. "He's aware that I've just had my chest filled with silicone, and I'm a little out of sorts?"

"Yes," he laughed. "I will get him."

I tried to sit up in the bed and prepare for Casey's visit. I pulled the blankets close to my chin so that the bulging of my breasts wouldn't be obvious.

"Claire?" Casey poked his head in the door.

"Casey, come in," I cleared my throat.

The curtains were drawn, and the room was dim, but I immediately noticed the change in his appearance. He had gained weight. His hair had grown long and shaggy, but it suited him. He was clean shaven, and most importantly, his eyes weren't red. They were bright and blue.

"You look great," I said.

"Thank you," he sat where Jonathan had been sitting minutes before.

"How are you doing?" I asked him, amazed at the glow in his face.

"I'm great, Claire. I'm really great," he beamed. "Jonathan saved my life."

"Oh, Casey, that's so wonderful. I'm so glad everything worked out for the best," I smiled. "I know you must be glad to be home. Adrienne and your mother have missed you terribly."

"I've missed them. I saw them at Dad's funeral, but being torn from them afterwards really motivated me to get well," he replied.

"I'm so sorry I had to miss Mr. Thomas' funeral. I wanted to see you," I said as Jonathan entered the room and quietly sat in the oversized chair next to the bed.

"I just wanted to apologize to you, Claire. I wanted to apologize for anything I may have done to embarrass you or frighten you while I was drinking. I know that episode with the gun must have terrified you," he shook his head. "I'm so sorry for that."

"Nonsense," I grimaced at the pain shooting through my chest. "That wasn't you. That was the alcohol."

"No, it wasn't me," he glanced at Jonathan. "I haven't been me for a long time. I just wish Dad could see the progress that I've made."

"Dad would be damn proud, Casey. I know I am," Jonathan said.

Casey nodded and grinned.

"Well, Claire, I won't keep you. Jonathan told me that you got a new pair of girls. I can't wait to see them."

Jonathan and I laughed as Casey blushed.

"That came out so wrong," he said. "I'm sorry."

"Have you been drinking, boy?" Jonathan stood, still laughing. "Maybe the alcohol wasn't the cause of all of your crude talk?"

He chuckled and stood.

"Feel better, Claire."

"Thanks, Casey. Good seeing you," I called as he followed Jonathan out of the room.

I hadn't noticed it before. I was so taken aback at Casey's healthy face and the clean hair that I hadn't noticed his limp. I wanted to call to him and ask what had happened, but I already knew. Jorge was the cause of the gait.

"He beat the hell out of him, didn't he?" I asked Jonathan as we relaxed in bed and watched television that night.

"Who?" he asked, completely aware of what I was referring to.

"Jorge beat the hell out of Casey," I stated.

"Oh, the limp?" Jonathan glanced at me and then returned to Morgan Freeman on the screen.

"Yes, the limp, Jonathan," I scoffed.

"He acquired that limp while rock climbing. The rehabilitation center offers rock climbing as a way to reestablish trust and confidence in the addicted individual," he answered.

"Cut the crap, sweetheart," I rolled my eyes.

"If you knew Jorge beat the hell out of him, then why did you ask?" he glared at me. "He's well, and that's all that matters. Didn't you see that today? He's a new man. So what he wobbles a little when he walks? At least he isn't still on the slow train to hell."

"Tough love," I mumbled.

"Damn right, tough love. Tough love works. It worked on me. It worked on Casey. And if you keep talking like that to me, it's bound to work on you," he joked.

"Shut up," I hit him in the face with a pillow.

THIRTY ONE

I gasped, and the aroma of the aged books filled my lungs. I choked on the dusty taste as my vision became blurry. I pressed my palms into my eye sockets as the blurriness was replaced with wetness. I squinted through my tears and looked in shock at my father's obituary on the computer screen.

I pushed away from the table and stumbled through the library. I staggered out the door and into the blinding sun and humidity. I didn't know how my legs were even working, but I managed to make it across the empty parking lot to my car and collapse onto the seat.

I stared ahead, my mouth open, my heart beating rapidly, and I had the overwhelming urge to vomit all over the leather steering wheel. I was in shock. Tears had wet my eyes only moments before, but now they were gone. My eyes were dry because I was in shock. I refused to believe that my father had been dead for nearly ten years.

I remembered that I had spoken to my daddy on the telephone on September 11, 2001. That was the last time that I'd heard his voice. I struggled to remember the last time that I had seen his face and felt his arms hold me in an embrace. I tried to remember the way I jiggled against his big belly when he held me in his arms and laughed.

Jonathan had taken me on Tuesday, September 4th. I hadn't seen my daddy that morning. He was running errands while I watched Mama wipe purple jelly from Vaiden's elephant shirt. I hadn't seen my daddy since the night before.

He was relaxing in his recliner while watching *Law and Order*. He loved *Law and Order*. He loved the theme music, the drama, the way a heinous crime could easily be solved in under an hour.

"Night, babies," he loudly called from his plush chair as Vaiden and I walked up the stairway.

We passed Emma's room, and Vaiden ran in to give her a hug. Emma scooped Vaiden into her arms, but she never paused in her phone conversation about a girl at school who had dyed her hair green.

Vaiden crawled into her white toddler bed, and I tucked her under the paisley print quilt. We said her prayers, and I kissed her and turned out the light. As I walked across the hallway to my bedroom, I had a thought.

She needs new pajamas. Those Dora pajamas are too short. I can skip English Lit tomorrow. I will go to the mall and get my baby some pajamas.

I had no idea that would be the last night in my home. I was oblivious that seeing my father sitting in his chair and watching his crime show would be the last time that I would ever set eyes upon him.

I'd been staring at the same chipped brick on the side of the library building for nearly ten minutes, reliving the last night that I had spent with my family. I remembered the spaghetti that mother had cooked for dinner, the phone conversation with Nathan as I sat on the side of the bed and picked at a frayed hem on my nightgown, the faint sound of the *Law and Order* theme on the television downstairs as I drifted off to sleep, excited about playing hooky the next day, excited about shopping instead of discussing Edgar Allen Poe.

The shock began to wear off. The shock that my mother was a widow, the shock that my sister had mourned my daddy's loss ten years ago, while I didn't have a clue, wore off. And I began to scream and weep and hyperventilate in the driver's seat of the Land Rover.

Daddy had died on September 19th. Of course I couldn't remember what I was doing on September 19th in 2001. I knew it was only two weeks since I had been abducted, but I wanted to know what I was doing at the exact moment when my father drew his last breath. I wanted to know where I was, what I was wearing, what I was speaking, feeling, thinking when my family learned that my daddy wasn't coming home.

The obituary informed me that he had died in a car accident. Where was the accident? What had happened? Was he so distraught over my leaving that he couldn't concentrate on the road? I wanted and needed to know the specifics.

My mind frantically searched for memories, and I remembered the photo that Jonathan had shown me so long ago to prove that my family was safe. Vaiden was on her tricycle, Nathan's truck was muddy, Emma looked bored and Mama looked sad. She looked sad. I had thought she looked sad over my disappearance, but she wasn't just mourning my loss in that photo. She was also mourning the loss of my father.

I had thought nothing at the fact that daddy wasn't in the picture. I just assumed he was inside the house yelling at the television, or that he was possibly out searching for me. I had no idea that he was dead.

I hated Jonathan for not telling me, and yet I was thankful that I didn't know when it had happened. If I'd known that daddy had passed away and I couldn't be there with my family, I would have been hysterical. There in that plush girly bedroom in Houston, Texas, I would have died from heartbreak.

I continued to sit in the parking lot, sweating from the scorching sun beating onto the black SUV, and I knew I had to drive home and give my mother the hug that she'd needed from me for so many years. I knew I had to throw caution to the wind. I couldn't worry about the police officer that I'd seen earlier. I had to hold my mother and my daughter in my arms.

Whatever wrong that I'd done in this lifetime, I'd paid for it and then some. I'd been held captive for a decade. I'd missed my daughter's milestones. I'd missed the birth of my sister's child. I'd lost the love of my life to my best friend. And I'd been absent from my family when my father left this world.

I would shove the officers out of my way and run as fast as I could up the steep driveway to be reunited with my family. I would confess *everything* to the police. I'd let them handcuff me right there, and I'd spend the rest of my days in jail if I could just hold my family in my arms for a mere second.

I quickly reversed out of the library parking lot, and I headed to the camper to retrieve my things. After that, I was destined to go home, and I was determined to stay this time.

THIRTY TWO

The Land Rover suddenly halted, and I threw open the door as dust from the gravel flooded my face. I left the car door open, and I sprinted to the camper. I opened the bathroom cabinet and grabbed the binders that contained all of my information, the notebooks that had been locked in Jonathan's safe for so long, and I threw them into an empty duffel bag.

I stuffed clothes on top of the books, and I frantically looked around the camper for anything that was detrimental to the stories that I had been feeding Clarence and his family.

I left what little food that lined the kitchen shelves behind, and I tossed my belongings into the back of the car. I saw Mrs. Dora swatting at flies as she sat in her lawn chair and dug inside a potato chip bag.

"Mrs. Dora?" I called to her, my voice cracking, my eyes on the verge of pouring tears.

"Yeah, honey?" she turned her head towards me, a small pool of sweat setting on her temples.

"I've got to go," I was unsure of exactly what to say, but I continued to hold back my sobs.

"You've got to go?" she asked. "Where to?"

"I've got to get home," I anxiously shifted my weight from one foot to the other as she stood and watched me.

"Is something wrong, Charley?" she witnessed my odd behavior, my quivering lip, the sorrow in my eyes.

"Is Mr. Clarence around? I wanted to let him know that I need to leave," I continued to rock back and forth, as if I were about to urinate on myself.

"He and Paul Walter went fishing this morning. Charley, are you okay?" she sat the bag of chips on the chair and began to approach me.

I backed away, unable to hold my tears any longer.

"Charley?" she watched them pour from my eyes.

"He's dead," I sobbed as I squatted down in the dirt and rested my head on my knees. "My daddy is dead."

"Oh, sweetheart," she walked to me.

She was unable to lower her heavy body to the ground next to me, but she bent over and rubbed my back.

Moans poured from my lips, tears poured from my eyes and snot poured from my nose. I opened my eyes to see the small pool of mud beneath me from the salt and the snot.

"Get up, now. Stand up here," Mrs. Dora stood up straight, her back obviously in pain, and she pulled on my arm.

I stood as well, and she wrapped her large and heavy arms around my body. My arms hung limp at my side, my knees buckled, as I rested my chin on her soft shoulder and continued to cry.

"Did you just find out, dear?" she spoke kindly.

"Yes," I wailed. "He's gone. My daddy is gone. I have to go home."

"Of course you do, honey," she rocked with me. "Oh, I'm so sorry. I know this hurt. I've been through this hurt. I know how horrible it is," she whispered into my ear as my eyes stung from the briny tears. "Girls need their daddy. It hurts when a girl loses her daddy."

"I have to go, Mrs. Dora," I backed away from her and dragged my forearm across my messy face.

"You can't drive back to St. Louis like this, Charley. Let me drive you, honey," she offered.

"No!" I exclaimed. "No, Mrs. Dora, I need to be alone. I will be fine."

"Are you sure? I will be glad to take you home," she rubbed my arm.

"I have to go," I backed away from her. "Please tell Mr. Clarence thank you for everything. Thank you all."

"Keep in touch, Charley. Please?" she called to me.

I nodded and ran full speed towards the car. I sped down the gravel drive and crossed the Tennessee River, counting the seconds when my family would be in my arms.

THIRTY THREE

Cybil was telling the sordid tale of Jennifer McAlister walking in on her husband and their Swedish nanny, but I wasn't listening. I was busy watching Casey as he sat at a table across the room. He was sipping a glass of ginger ale as Adrienne laughed loudly in his ear. He shifted his eyes about the room, and he nervously bit his fingernails. Whatever happened to him in Palo Alto, California had turned him into a timid man. A sober man, but a timid man.

"Isn't that unbelievable?" Cybil continued.

"Terrible," I sipped my wine. "Just terrible."

"I mean, the nanny. Of all people! The nanny! And little Colby was asleep upstairs. I just can't imagine," she scoffed.

"Terrible," I repeated. "Just terrible."

I left Cybil and some other ladies to discuss Jennifer's marital problems, and I headed towards Casey. I wanted to make sure he was okay. I knew he must have been having a hard time sitting at the country club where he'd shot whiskey so many times before.

I felt a tug on my arm, and I turned to see Grant standing there.

"Hello, Claire," he winked at me, a glass of scotch pressed to his lips.

"Grant," I replied.

"They look good," he nodded towards my breasts.

I felt my face become flushed, and I immediately began to examine the room to see if Jonathan was witnessing our conversation.

"I could see them from across the room," he continued.

"What do you want?" I asked in an annoyed tone.

"Well," he gulped the rest of his drink, "I have a proposition that I'd like to discuss with you."

"What's that?" I finally spotted Jonathan, and his eyes were focused on us as he pretended to laugh with the group of gentlemen that surrounded him.

"Well, you're aware that you're married to a murderer, correct?" Grant spoke softly.

"If you say so," I said.

"I've been thinking that it's time to do something about him. If you don't want to end up dead, then I'd like you to help me come up with a plan."

"What?" I asked, stunned.

"Suzanne's been weighing heavily on my mind for the last several months. I'm growing angrier and angrier about the whole situation. It's time to do something," he shifted his eyes.

"You're going to go to the police?" I questioned.

"No," he laughed. "Claire, I'm an attorney. I know better than anyone how the judicial system works. This thing would hang around in court for years without substantial evidence, and he'd walk free. I'm going to take this into my own hands. And I know you can help me."

I couldn't believe what I was hearing. I was in shock that this man was plotting the murder of my husband in a country club full of people.

"You really think this is the best place to discuss this?" I looked around the bustling room of socialites.

"No, I think we should discuss this in further detail later. I just wanted to let you know my thoughts."

"Why tell me? I could run and tell him right now. Why do you think I want my husband dead?" I whispered.

"Because you know what a monster he is. You know what he's done. I'm sure he's abused you in some way, too. You were too sick to come to Mr. Thomas' funeral? Sounds to me like you were held up in the house with a black eye because you probably said the wrong thing at the wrong time to an unstable Jonathan. Am I right?" he smirked

"You are absolutely wrong. He'd never lay a finger on me. I'm shocked that you think I would go along with this!" I exclaimed.

"No, you're not. I saw your face that night behind the pool house. You weren't surprised at the information I gave you. And you harbor your own secrets about Mr. Jonathan Marsh, I know it."

"You're psychotic," I shook my head. "I have a good mind to tell him every word you've said."

"You won't," he replied. "You know I'm right."

"I know you're crazy," I said. "If you'll excuse me, I need a drink."

"We'll talk later," he called out as I walked away.

Jonathan pulled me into his arms as Glenn Miller played throughout the country club.

"I like Glenn Miller. Did you know he went missing? He just vanished," Jonathan pressed his hand into the small of my back.

"Yeah," I gulped as Grant's words replayed in my mind.

"Are you going to tell me what he said?" he asked, reading my mind as usual.

"Yeah," I gulped again.

"You stormed away from him. You looked mad. Are you scared to tell me what he said?"

"I'm not scared," I said as we swayed to "Moonlight Serenade".

"Tell me," his tone was strict.

"He said he could see my boobs from across the room," I gritted my teeth while eyeing Grant in the corner with a beautiful unknown woman.

Jonathan chuckled.

"What else?"

"Jonathan," I sighed.

Daily I thought of how Jonathan had torn me away from my child and my parents. I reminded myself of the terror that I'd felt for so long while in his presence. I reminded myself of all of the evil things that he'd said and done to me, but somehow, someway, I'd grown fond of him.

Maybe it wasn't love, but it was something. I had begun to care about him and his family. I finally felt comfortable in his presence. I overlooked all of the evil that had been done to me, and I laughed with him and held him in the dark and some sort of bond between us was born. I told myself that I was brainwashed, and maybe I was.

I knew that telling Jonathan what Grant had said would cause a war. It would be a war, and I would be right in the middle of it. But if Grant was the vile man that Jonathan and Ernesto had made him out to be, and if he had really harmed those women and ended Suzanne Simmons' life, then he deserved a war.

"He told me you killed Suzanne," the soft lighting cast shadows on Jonathan's hair as we danced. "And he told me you hurt all of those women."

Jonathan remained silent as I glanced up at his strong cheek bones.

"He said it's time for you to pay for your wrongs," I stated.

"He did?" Jonathan was angry.

"He did."

"That son of a bitch told you this? He told *my wife* this?" his pacing began to speed as we moved around the dance floor.

"He said you'll end up killing me, too. He wants me to help him," I closed my eyes, hoping Jonathan wouldn't drop me to the floor and proceed to shoot Grant Mallory right there in the country club to the soundtrack of Glenn Miller.

He didn't. Instead, he began to laugh hysterically.

"What?" I sneered.

"He has no idea what he's done. He has no idea," he shook his head.

"Jonathan."

"Do you see that woman he's speaking with over in the corner?"

We turned and I saw him and an older blonde woman. She wore a beautiful red gown and a sparkling diamond broach.

"I see her," I answered.

"That's Suzanne's mother. Mother said she's in town for the weekend," Jonathan said. "There he is, talking to his victim's mother, only minutes after bringing up her death, pinning it on me and revealing his plans to harm me to you, to my wife."

I was at a loss for words.

"He has no idea what he's done," Jonathan repeated.

"I don't know about this," I shook my head and peered from the back of the Land Rover to Grant's large home on the hill.

"Think of what he's done. He's killed someone, and he's blaming it on me. Not to mention he wants to kill me as well!" Jonathan exclaimed from the front seat.

"Mrs. Claire, he's evil. This has to be done," Ernesto spoke from behind the steering wheel.

"Look, Ernesto talked to a guy. It's all figured out. All we have to do is-"

"I don't want to know," I stuck my fingers in my ears.

"Just stick to your part of the plan. Ernesto and I will take care of the rest," Jonathan reached to the back and touched my hand.

"What happens when the tire blows or the brakes quit or whatever it is, and he speeds out of control and hits some innocent bystander on the freeway? We'll be responsible for that, too, Jonathan! We can't do this," I spoke quickly.

"Look where he lives, Claire," Jonathan looked out the dark, tinted window. "He lives in the middle of nowhere. Did you notice the curvy and narrow road that we had to travel to get all the way back here, hmmm? There's nothing for miles. He'll end up in a tree or the swamp. No one else will be involved," he promised.

"I can't believe this," I whispered and beat my fists into my knees.

"Just stick to the plan," he repeated.

"You can do this, Mrs. Claire," Ernesto reassured me.

"Why didn't you let whoever took care of Roger do this? Why can't one of your associates do this?" I begged Jonathan.

"This is too personal, Claire. Now go."

I knew he was tired of talking. I knew it was too late to back out now.

I stepped out of the car and slowly shuffled up the long, dark and damp driveway. Leaves crunched beneath my shoes. The wrought iron front door grew closer, and my heart pounded in my chest.

I rang the bell and shifted on my feet. I wanted to run down the driveway and dive into the Land Rover that was hidden at the bottom of the hill. I wanted to speed home, drink some Jack Daniels and go to sleep.

"Where's your car?" Grant threw open the door and examined the driveway.

"It's hidden in a bamboo cut-off down the road. I walked the rest of the way. I didn't want anyone to see me here," I spoke my rehearsed words.

"I live in the middle of the damn bayou, Claire. No one is going to see you here," he opened the door wider, and I stepped into the beautiful home.

"Wine?" he asked as I took in the stunning décor and followed him to the kitchen.

"Yes," I said.

I sat my purse on a stool and we stood awkwardly at the kitchen counter and sipped the red wine. I didn't know what to say. I could sense that he didn't either.

"So, I assume that your being here means that you're in? Or do I need to check you for a wire? Were you sent here as a spy?" he asked me, seriously.

"No," I said, my arm pits sweating profusely beneath my turtleneck.

"Let's have a seat," he motioned for me to relax on the couch in the adjacent room.

He sat in a high back chair across from me and began to speak, "Here's what I'm thinking."

"Grant, wait," I sat my wine glass on the end table. "You're absolutely certain that Jonathan killed Suzanne? You're absolutely certain? There's no doubt?"

I'd been trying to locate Laura Leighton and the other abused women for weeks, with no luck. They had married, their names had changed and the phone book produced no clues. I had just wanted to hear from one of them that Grant was responsible for their injuries and their fear. I didn't care that Jonathan wouldn't be pleased that I'd gotten involved. I just wanted to make sure that we were punishing the right man.

"Yes, I'm certain. I wouldn't be doing this if I weren't certain. He's got to be punished, Claire. You know he's dangerous. You know he deserves to be punished," he nodded.

"Why would I think he's dangerous? I don't think he deserves this," I argued.

"You know he does."

"No, I don't!" I shouted. "You're talking about my husband. I don't think-"

"I know he took you," Grant's eyes left mine and shifted to the hardwood floor.

The silence in the room was deafening. I was unable to blink my eyes. I was unable to breathe. All I could do was look like a stupid deer caught in headlights.

"I know he took you," he repeated.

"What?"

He bobbed his head.

"How?" I spoke quietly.

"I was with him in Miami. I was there when he saw you for the first time. You had a little girl. He went on and on about how beautiful you were," he said softly.

My arms began to shake, the lightheadedness set in and my mouth continued to drop.

"When I first met you at the Marsh's, I knew. Your hair was long and blonde, but I knew it was the same girl that we saw in the airport months before. I can't believe he didn't think I'd remember," he confessed.

I was still unable to speak.

"I don't know who you are. I don't know your real name. I don't know where you're from, but *I know* you don't belong here. You know he deserves this," he stood from the chair and then sat beside me on the couch.

"I-I" I stuttered.

"You can go home. If you help me do this, you can go home," he softly touched my shaking hand.

I stood and began to pace the dark mahogany floor.

Here it was. Here was my chance to be free. I could help him plot Jonathan's death. I could have him help me locate the associates. I could warn him that Jonathan was outside. I could tell him not to drive the Porsche parked in his driveway. I could save his life, and I could regain mine.

I remembered Ernesto's words at the park on my birthday. I remembered the humidity hanging in my hair, the ice cream melting down my arm, and I remembered the candid look on Ernesto's face as he warned me about Grant's wicked ways.

I remembered the fake nightmare and my screams slicing through the frigid night. I remembered the honest pain in Jonathan's tone as he described the hurt and the theft and Suzanne's death.

Grant had known for so long that I'd been taken. He'd known since the first moment that he laid eyes on me that I didn't belong here, and he'd done absolutely nothing to help me. That, in itself, was evil.

"I came to Houston on my own," I stopped pacing and looked into his eyes. "You're wrong. I belong here."

I couldn't believe these words or the fact that I was defending Jonathan Marsh. I had to have been in love, or brainwashed, or delusional or stupid. This was my chance to be reunited with my daughter, but I was too crazy to take it.

"You had a child in your arms. Was that your child?" he stood and faced me.

"I don't know what you're talking about," I turned away from him so he couldn't see the tears in my eyes.

"He's brainwashed you," he walked around to see my face. "You're crying. He's brainwashed you!"

"He has not!" I shouted. "I know you killed Suzanne! I know *you* were the one who did all of those terrible things to those women. I read a letter from Laura Leighton. She said *you* were dangerous! She begged Jonathan for help! I know you're the evil one. Jonathan didn't kill anyone!"

"My God, Claire, or whoever you are. You believe him? You actually believe him? You found a fake note that he planted, and you believe it?" he scoffed. "You're just as crazy as he is!"

"I'm not crazy!" I shouted. "Maybe I don't belong here, but he doesn't deserve to die for something that *you* did. I was only kidnapped! Suzanne Simmons was killed!"

"So he did take you?" he grabbed both of my arms.

"Let go of me," I pulled away from him. "You did nothing to help me. You could've gotten me back to my daughter. You could've contacted the police or helped me. You could've done something. You did nothing!"

"I'm doing something now!" he exclaimed. "I'm trying to help you!"

"You're trying to pin your crimes on him," I stomped into the kitchen to find my purse.

I knew this meeting hadn't lasted long enough for Ernesto and Jonathan to fulfill their part of the plan, but I couldn't bear to stand before Grant Mallory for another moment. I had to get out of there.

"Claire!" he called to me as I rushed towards the front door. "I'm sorry you've gotten messed up in this. I can help you go home. I can help you. Claire."

"I am home," I said before I turned and walked out the front door.

I saw the Porsche parked on the damp driveway, but I didn't see Jonathan or Ernesto. I ran as quickly as I could down the hill to the Land Rover hidden behind a thick row of bamboo.

"Go!" I screamed once I was inside the car.

"Baby, what happened?" Jonathan turned in his seat to face me as Ernesto started the car and sped down the desolate road.

"He knows, Jonathan. He knows you took me," I choked on my rapid breath.

I was unsure why I was telling him this. He didn't need to know. I just couldn't stop the words from being spoken.

"He what?" Jonathan bellowed. "How?"

"He was with you in the airport!" I shouted angrily at him. "How could you be that stupid? You're supposed to know what you're doing! You created me! You created a person out of thin air! How could you be so stupid?"

"I didn't think he would remember you! I mentioned you once. He only saw you for a few seconds. How would he remember that?" he looked at Ernesto, confusion in his tone.

"Well, he did!"

"What did you say?" he asked me. "Claire! What did you say?"

"I told him it wasn't true!"

"You did?" he cocked his head. "You expect me to believe that you didn't run into his arms and make plans to get back to Nashville?"

"Well, that's what a sane person would do, but obviously I've gone bat shit crazy. No, I didn't do anything. I ran out of the house," I wiped my damp eyes and swallowed the snot running down my throat.

"He's got to go, Mr. Jonathan," Ernesto watched the curving road.

"Yes, he does," Jonathan faced the dashboard and rapped his fingers on the console.

"What? I thought you'd already taken care of that. The Porsche?" I leaned into the front seat.

"We didn't- we couldn't- There was no time to figure it out," he groaned. "It's not like we tamper with brakes on a regular basis. We aren't Grant Mallory."

"So what are you going to do?"

"Jorge," Ernesto said.

"Jorge," Jonathan repeated.

THIRTY FOUR

I watched Grant's mother sit at the dining table, her face pale and her eyes empty. She twisted the tissue in her hand so tightly that I was sure blood would fall from her fingers onto her black dress pants.

Grant's grandmother held a shaking coffee cup to her lips, drips of the dark liquid splashing onto the pine table. A young girl rested her curly head on the old woman's shoulder.

I couldn't help but to feel responsible for all of the pain and suffering that was taking place. I looked away from the grieving family to Jonathan speaking quietly with an unknown man. He caught my gaze and motioned for me to follow him out the back door of Grant's parents' home. We walked deep to the back of the property, the leaves crumpling beneath our shoes.

"You can't let this get to you," he pulled me close as the cold wind blew the dead branches above our heads. "I see you staring at his family. You have to ignore that."

"I can't."

"You have to," he rubbed my arm as I pressed my face deep into his black jacket. "I just remember Suzanne's funeral. I remember those faces and those tears. I remember the tears that I wept that day."

"This is all so terrible," I cried softly. "We shouldn't have done this."

"Don't say that. He got what he deserves, and you know it," he let go of me and wiped the tears from my eyes with his thumb.

"It wasn't our place to do this. He would've gotten what he deserved in the end. Karma would have," I began.

"Don't tell me about karma, Claire. Listen, it's worked out perfectly. The police think some scorned client broke in his house. Grant was always representing shady people. They have a guy in custody that served a few months in county, and they assume he's pissed he got any time at all. See? If that guy gets pinned for this, then we've gotten rid of two worthless people," he made it seem like we had really done the right thing.

"I guess," I wiped my nose.

"Let's go back in for a few minutes and say goodbye to everyone," he straightened the white boutonniere that he and the other pallbearers were wearing.

I followed him inside and watched Grant's mother snivel on his shoulder.

"You were the best friend he ever had," she moaned through her cries.

I swallowed the vomit that threatened to escape from my lips, and I gave her a sorrowful smile.

I was drunk by 8 o'clock on Christmas morning. I sprawled on the floor in front of the tree, the bottle of whiskey in my hand. I drank to forget Vaiden's fourth birthday. I drank to forget Grant's murder.

"Claire, this is ridiculous," Jonathan entered the living room and began picking up the shreds of wrapping paper that I'd strewn all over the floor. "It's not even noon! My family will be here this evening. How am I supposed to explain you sleeping off a hangover?"

"I don't care," I burped and held a scarf that he'd given me that morning.

"You've turned into a drunk, Claire! Do you realize that you've turned into my brother? I've had enough!" he barked angrily and left me alone on the cold floor.

I woke to a kick in my thigh. I opened my tired eyes and saw a large man hovering over me, the Christmas tree twinkling behind him. He pulled his large boot back and jolted me in the thigh again.

"Feliz Navidad. Get up," he instructed.

"What?" I coughed and rubbed my stinging leg. I looked around and realized I must have passed out on the living room floor.

"Get up," he reached down and yanked me by the arm.

He was tall and muscles bulged beneath his leather jacket. A scruffy, patchy black beard covered his tan face, and a long greasy ponytail draped over his shoulder. His eyes were black, and a hairless scar slashed through his right eyebrow. He chewed on a toothpick and a gold tooth flashed as he spoke.

"Your husband says you're struggling with the alcohol demon," he threw me to the couch as I massaged my sore arm.

"You're Jorge?" my voice was hoarse.

"I am," he nodded and continued to stand over me as I pulled my robe closed over my flannel pajamas.

"I've heard such good things about you," I cleared my throat and looked to the bottle on the floor.

He sat so close to me on the couch that I could smell his warm, phlegmy breath.

"Have you witnessed the change in your brother-in-law?" he asked, the tooth shining.

"I have," I replied.

"I'm offering you an invitation to go through the same treatment. I would love nothing more than to spend sixty days with you," he gave a malicious grin. "I guarantee once I'm done with you that you will never be drunk on Christmas morning again."

"Thank you," I sighed. "But I think I will pass."

He forcefully clutched my arm again.

"Do you think this is a joke?"

I shook my head, my heart beating rapidly.

"If you don't stop this drinking, I will take you to the desert, and I promise you'll experience terror that you didn't know existed. Do you understand? Your drinking ends today," he growled. "Not another drop. Not at a party, not at home. Alcohol never passes through your lips again. Do you understand? Tell me you understand."

I now knew why Casey had transformed into such an intimidated man. Sixty days with Jorge could scare the hell out of anyone. I'd only been in his presence for three minutes, and I was about to urinate and vomit, simultaneously.

"I understand," I said as he loosened his grip.

He gave a large smile, another gold tooth exposing itself.

"Good," he whispered. "That's very good."

I wanted to ask if he'd killed Grant, but I knew the answer.

He stood and peered down at me, still smiling.

"Merry Christmas, Mrs. Marsh," he nodded and walked towards the foyer.

"Pleasure to meet you," I called to him.

When I heard the front door close behind him, I sighed loudly and relaxed my sore and hung over body.

THIRTY FIVE

I sat sideways on the piano bench and tapped my bored fingers on the F and G keys. My eyes moved from the door to the clock, as I waited on his arrival.

"Mrs. Claire, go to bed!" an agitated Ernesto called from his room upstairs.

"In a minute," I replied, still touching the keys.

"I can't sleep with that noise!" he shouted.

I sighed and closed the piano lid. I shuffled into the kitchen and poured myself a glass of tea. I removed the heavy robe and sat it on a kitchen chair, and I went onto the back porch, where the hot, July night heat welcomed my cold body.

Adrienne had given birth to her second baby boy a few days before. Jonathan and I had the same argument that we'd had with her first, nearly three years ago. Jonathan wanted children. I didn't. But my lack of desire didn't stop him from trying. Dozens of negative pregnancy tests prompted Jonathan to send me to every fertility clinic in Texas. He was distraught and irate to learn that the problem didn't lie with me. The fertility problem was his.

Adoption was out of the question. There would be too many questions and too many people checking our background. It would be too risky, and besides, Jonathan wanted a baby of his own. He wanted to pass along his father's genes.

For the last several years, Jonathan walked around angry most of the time. He was angry that his sperm was useless. And he was always angry with me. He was convinced that I was the problem, even though I'd had a healthy baby girl nearly twelve years before. He told me I must've been barren. Kidnapping a fertile woman who would someday go barren wasn't part of his plan.

I hadn't spoken to him since the night before when he'd arrived home drunk with a prosthetic belly that he'd picked up in some costume store downtown.

"Wear it," he demanded and threw the heavy plastic stomach at me.

"You're out of your mind," I laughed and heaved it to the floor.

"If you can't get pregnant, I at least want to see what you'd look like pregnant. Wear it!" he commanded.

"You wear it. I can get pregnant just fine. You're the one that's barren, not me." I spoke angrily.

He pulled his hand back and I braced myself for the blow, but instead he lowered his arm and sighed in disgust. He left me alone in our bedroom, the absurd fake belly lying at my feet.

I hadn't spoken to him since. But I was sure he was with Camilla.

Cybil and I sat on her back porch and overlooked the koi pond as I fanned myself with a sheet of paper and sipped the lemonade.

"You're awful distant today. What's wrong?" she studied my tired face, the noticeable crow's feet surrounding my eyes.

I groaned.

"We had the baby argument again."

"Oh, Claire," she clicked her tongue. "I'm sorry."

"I said some things I shouldn't have. I was ugly to him. I know how difficult it is for him to accept the fact that the problem lies with him, and yet, I pointed it out again," I was ashamed of myself.

Cybil said nothing. Instead, she shook her head and poured a splash of Vodka in her orange juice.

"You weren't such a mean old cow when you had a drink now and again," she joked.

"I haven't had a drink in years. Have I been a mean old cow all of this time?" I sipped the sugary lemonade.

"No," she stirred the orange juice. "But you have your moments."

"You drink all of the time, and you're still a mean old cow. What's your excuse?" I playfully punched her in the arm.

"Yeah," she shook her head. "You and Jonathan will get past this. You always do."

"I don't know, Cybil," I watched the fish darting back and forth. "It's pretty bad this time."

"What else is going on?" she inquired.

"He finally came home last night. I waited up for him, and I was going to apologize. He didn't say a word to me. He just got in the bed and went to sleep. He'd been with Camilla," I felt my stomach churn at the words.

"No, Claire! No!" Cybil exclaimed.

"I know it was her. He had that funny smell. It's always a mixture of acetone, and, and bubble gum. Or something," I couldn't put my finger on it.

"What a peculiar one," Cybil shook her head. "She's so ugly, too. I don't know why he doesn't quit messing around with her, with that weird hair and those gaudy tattoos."

"Even worse, I've been going to that horrible Hillary over at West End Cutting because I refuse to let my husband's mistress do my hair. My highlights look terrible," I complained and ran my fingers through the brassy locks.

"I thought he was done with her, Claire. He promised, didn't he? Didn't he beg your forgiveness in St. Croix? I thought he was doing better."

"I thought so, too. At least it wasn't Paige Palmer or Jennifer McAlister this time," I picked at my fingernails.

"That Jenny McAlister, humph. She ought to be ashamed after that fiasco with her Swedish nanny years ago," Cybil gritted her teeth.

"I'm the laughingstock of Houston, Cybil. Everyone knows he runs around on me. I've looked like a damn doormat for the last five years," I swallowed the lump in my throat.

"No you don't, honey," she took my hand in hers. "He's just an asshole. He's cut from the same cloth as the many other assholes, even my asshole. Everyone knows about Andrew's affairs. That's just part of the glamorous life that we lead."

For the first time in so long, I thought about Nathan. I wondered if he was a husband, and if he was a faithful one or if he was an asshole. I was certain that he must be a good husband. I was certain that if my life had played out the way it was supposed to then I wouldn't be heartbroken and betrayed in this way.

"I need your help," I turned to her.

"What?" she lit a cigarette.

"I need you to help me get some finances in order. Can you do that?"

"Finances in order? For what?" she asked.

"If I leave him, Cybil, I'll have nothing. I need money."

"Honey, if you leave him, some judge will grant you whatever you want. The cheating husband never fairs well in court," she reassured me.

"I'm not talking about court. I'm talking about leaving, just leaving."

"Running away?" she asked.

"Yeah, running away," I nodded.

"You can't do that. Where will you go?"

I knew where I would go. I would run straight to Pine Hills Drive in Nashville, Tennessee. And I would take my daughter into my arms and never let her go.

I hadn't attempted to contact my family in nearly a decade, and I didn't know if Jonathan's threats from years before still held true, but I'd grown tired and brave enough to finally attempt to get home. I'd been betrayed by him too many times.

"I have family in the southeast. Please help me, Cybil. I could leave without the money or anything, but I have family who could use the cash," I thought of Nathan's modest agriculture salary and Vaiden's college fund.

"Just take the money out of the bank and run, if that's what you want to do," she argued.

"I don't want to do that. He will be furious if I do that. He will come looking for me. If you hold some money for me for a little while, he won't think that I've stolen from him. He'll be angry that I've left, but he won't be angry that I'm a thief, too. Let me just give you a little money here and there for the next few months, you know, under the table. Just hold it for me for a while. I will contact you and get it later."

"I don't know, Claire," she shook her head. "I don't know if I want to get wrapped up in this."

"I'm not asking you told hold ten million dollars for me, just a few thousand here and there. I don't want much," I begged her with my eyes.

She exhaled loudly and thought it over.

"Okay."

"Thank you."

"How are you going to casually give me thousands of dollars without him knowing that it's missing?"

"The fundraiser and charity account. He has no idea. I will tell him it was spent on catering or something. I will make something up. It will look like the money has gone towards my countless fundraising, but I'll be giving it to you. He won't know," I promised. "Keep it in a mason jar under the bed. I don't care. Just hold it for me."

"What will I do when you're gone? You're all I have, Claire," she batted pouty eyes at me and threw her cigarette into the ash tray.

"I love you, Cybil," I spoke genuinely. "You've been the best friend I've known."

She smirked and wiped the corner of her eye.

THIRTY SIX

I sat at the dinner table and listened to Ernesto and Jonathan's conversation about the storm brewing in the Gulf of Mexico. Ernesto was concerned about his family in Mexico City. He was thinking of making a trip to see his ailing mother for a few weeks.

"Whatever you need to do, Ernesto. Take as much time as you need," Jonathan agreed and chewed his meatloaf.

"It would only be a couple of weeks. My brother says she isn't doing well," Ernesto replied, his eyes dejected.

"You should be with them. Shouldn't he, Claire?" he gave the conversation to me.

"Yes," I nodded and sat my fork on the empty plate.

"Why are you so quiet?" he asked.

I shrugged as I thought of my plan to escape while Ernesto was away. It would be the perfect time, although I hadn't given Cybil but a small amount of cash.

"Ernesto, will you excuse us?" Jonathan asked.

Ernesto took his dishes to the kitchen and disappeared upstairs.

"What?" I asked, preparing for an argument.

"I just wanted to apologize," he pushed his plate away and looked at me.

"For what?" I asked.

"You know I've been with Camilla. I'm sorry," he shifted his eyes to his hands. "I've done you wrong, Claire, and I'm sorry. You know I love you."

"I know."

"I've just been so angry with you for what you said, but I've come to accept that it's my fault we can't have children. I'm sorry for taking that out on you. I wanted to hurt you for what you'd said, and I knew being with Camilla would cause you the most pain," he spoke remorsefully, and I believed him.

"Thank you," I stared out the dining room window to the crepe myrtles blowing in the heavy gray wind.

"Do you still love me?" he asked.

I remained silent.

"Claire, I love you. You're everything to me. I'm really sorry. From the bottom of my heart," I could hear his voice cracking.

"You'll do it again," I looked at him. "You always do."

"I won't, baby," he shook his head. "I won't. I don't love those women. You're the only woman I love. What we have could never be replaced."

I felt my lip begin to quiver, and I knew a full crying spell was about to ensue. I stood and walked to the kitchen sink.

"You know, you took me, Jonathan. You took me from my family, and you took me from a man who was *always* faithful to me. When you took me, you told me that you'd give me everything that I wanted. And you did in the beginning. And I contently lived with that. But now, now you do nothing but tell me how useless and barren I am, although I'm not, and you sleep with any woman who will have you. You haven't held up your end of the deal. I've done *everything* I was supposed to do! I haven't contacted my family or run away! You haven't done your part!" I shouted irately as the water splashed the bits of meatloaf and mashed potatoes down the drain.

I watched him sitting silently at the table for a few minutes, and then I turned and went into the bedroom.

I threw my wedding ring into the jewelry box, and I shuffled around in the chest of drawers for the silk gown that I'd gotten in St. Croix months earlier.

"Go home," he called quietly from the doorway.

"What are you talking about?" I asked, still looking through the drawers.

"I've kept you long enough. You aren't happy here. I've failed you. Go home."

I stopped searching for the gown and turned to him.

"That's it? I can go home?" I scoffed.

"Go," he nodded.

~ 241 ~

I stood soundlessly for a moment, trying to process his instructions.

"What about my family, Jonathan? You'll call off *your associates?* I don't have to live in fear or worry about them? I can just go home?" I said sarcastically.

"I won't hurt your family," he continued to stare at the floor. "Go home."

And I believed him.

I was dumbstruck. I wanted to retrieve my largest suitcase and eagerly start throwing clothes inside of it, but something kept me from sprinting to the closet. It was Jonathan. It was my feelings for him. It was my concern for him and what he would do once I was gone.

"I've never done anything right," he watched the rug beneath his feet. "I'm not a good man, Claire. I've hurt so many women, Suzanne, innocent people, your dad. I'm sorry."

"Women? My dad? I don't understand," I slowly walked towards him.

"But I only did what I thought was right," he refused to look up from the floor.

"You said my dad. What does my dad have to do with this?" I stood before him.

He said nothing.

"Jonathan!" I shook his arm. "What are you talking about? Did you kill Suzanne? Did you do something to my dad? Jonathan!"

And he still said nothing.

"Jonathan!" I screamed again, still furiously shaking his limp arm.

"You've been good, Claire. You don't deserve what I've done to you. You don't deserve the cheating and lying. You can go home," he finally looked at me, his eyes wet with tears.

"What about my daddy, Jonathan? What does he have to do with this?" I begged him.

"Nothing," he wiped his eyes. "I've just broken his heart by taking you. Your dad, your mom, your daughter, your boyfriend. I've wounded a lot of people by taking you."

"Suzanne? What did you do to Suzanne? What women have you hurt?" I begged him.

"I wasn't good to her, either. I've never been faithful to anyone, Claire. I'm not a good man."

My eyes fell to the floor, too, and I sighed.

"If I go home, what will you do?" I asked.

He shrugged helplessly like a child.

I found myself crying, as usual. And they weren't just happy tears because I was finally allowed to go free. I was mourning this loss, this marriage.

He turned and left me there, and I stood silently for several minutes, looking around the dim room. Finally, I walked to the closet and packed my suitcase.

I stood at the foyer, next to my beautiful baby grand piano, and I watched Jonathan sitting soundlessly on the couch.

"Jonathan?" I walked to him and looked down at him, his head in his hands.

"Go!" he barked.

"Jonathan," I sat beside him and pulled him into my arms. "I love you."

"You don't," he said. "You shouldn't."

"Maybe I shouldn't, but I do. I've actually had some wonderful times here with you," I kissed the top of his head. "You've been my life for so long. I love you. I've loved you for a long time."

"Then stay," he looked at me, his cheeks soaked with tears.

Maybe I would go home and be reunited with my family, and maybe, for some ungodly reason, I would keep in touch with Jonathan Marsh. I would visit him. We would speak on the phone. I would remain friends with my ex-husband and kidnapper.

"Then stay with me, Claire!" he begged. "If you leave, I will kill myself. I will!"

"Jonathan."

The tears ceased to fall from his eyes, and he was suddenly overtaken with lividness.

"I will kill myself. And then I will kill you. If you try to leave, I will kill you!" he sprang from the couch and rushed to the bureau in the corner.

"You just told me I could go!" I shouted at him. "What is wrong with you?"

Jonathan turned from the bureau and pointed a gun at me. It was small and silver and I assume it was the same one that he'd pressed into my side at the gas station in Wynne, Arkansas ten years before.

"I swear to God, if you walk out that door, I will kill you. I'll kill your family. I'll never cheat on you again, Claire! I told you to go, but I can't bear to see you leave. I can't live without you, do you understand that? The only way you're leaving this house is in a hearse, do you understand!" he screamed frantically, spit escaping his lips, sweat forming on his brow. I'd never seen him so hysterical.

My heart began to pound, and I prepared to die. I knew, in that moment, he was crazy and desperate enough to shoot me and then stick the gun in his own mouth. I closed my eyes and pictured Vaiden, in her pink elephant shirt with the glob of purple jelly, because I wanted her face to be the last that I'd see.

"Mr. Jonathan!" I heard Ernesto call from the catwalk above us.

I opened my eyes and saw him standing there, a gun of his own pointed down at Jonathan.

"Mr. Jonathan, put it down," he said calmly. "You aren't going to shoot anyone. Mrs. Claire isn't going anywhere. Now put it down."

"Ernesto, stay out of this. This isn't your concern! Don't do this!" Jonathan continued to point the gun at me.

"Put it down, Mr. Jonathan. I'm your friend, you know that. You aren't thinking clearly right now. You have to put the gun down!"

As Ernesto spoke, Jonathan jerked his arm towards him and fired the weapon. I gasped loudly when I saw Ernesto hit the floor.

"Jonathan!" I screamed.

I saw the look on his face, and it horrified me. He was scared and sickened. He looked at me, stunned, ashamed, and in an instant, without saying a word, he put the gun in his mouth and pulled the trigger.

I fainted. When I saw Jonathan hit the floor, his head covered in blood, I fainted. I'd never fainted before, and it was the oddest experience that I'd ever encountered. Everything went black, and I woke up on the wool rug, in front of the couch, unsure if I'd dreamed the entire thing.

"Mrs. Claire," I heard Ernesto's kind voice as he hovered over me and slipped his hand beneath my head.

"Ernesto?" I asked, hoping and praying that none of this had really happened. "Oh, Ernesto, you are okay?"

"He missed, Mrs. Claire. I'm fine," he said. "Are *you* okay?"

"Yeah," I said as I sat up and saw Jonathan's body on the other side of the living room, limp and covered in blood.

Ernesto held me close to his shaking body. We both rocked back and forth and together we wept.

"I loved him, Mrs. Claire," he cried into my ear.

"I know you did."

"He was out of his mind. He'd never try to harm either one of us. He was out of his mind!" he moaned.

"It's my fault. I said horrible things to him. This is my fault," I continued to weep, my stomach nauseated and my vision blurry. "I put all of the blame about not having a child on him. I didn't even want a child with him."

"No," Ernesto said as we pulled away from one another. "No, Mrs. Claire, don't blame yourself."

I tried to regain some sort of composure, and we sat silently for a few minutes, wondering what we should do.

"We need to call the police," I wiped my wet face.

"No, not yet."

"Ernesto," I began.

"I'm not going to do that to Mr. Jonathan. I'm not going to let Houston, Texas know he struggled with demons. No one is going to know he did this to himself. No one is going to know."

"Ernesto, we can't cover this up. Someone probably heard the shots, anyway!" I argued.

"Mrs. Claire, if you loved him at all, please don't let him be remembered this way. Please," Ernesto begged.

I exhaled sharply and looked at his body once again, my heart broken for the man who had hurt me, yet loved me, for so long. I wouldn't let him be remembered this way. I wouldn't expose him for the things he had done. I wouldn't let his ailing mother know that he'd stuck a gun in his own mouth and pulled the trigger. I wouldn't let the socialites whisper about his demise in the dark corners of the ballrooms and the country clubs. He wouldn't be remembered this way.

"Okay," I agreed.

I followed Ernesto around the house like a helpless puppy dog as he spouted orders.

"You need to go home, Mrs. Claire," he searched the kitchen drawers.

"Home? I should go home?" I asked, bewildered.

"Yes," he said, still searching for something. "If I create a murder scene here, you'll be the first suspect. You know they always suspect the spouse. I don't want you to go through that."

"I can't just leave, Ernesto."

"You can," he looked at me. "You can finally go home."

"What will the police think? They'll think I killed him and ran. They'll come looking for me!" I exclaimed.

"No, they'll think that someone killed him and took you. I can make it look that way," he reassured me.

"They'll still come looking for me, Ernesto. It'll be a manhunt if they think I've been kidnapped," the words seemed surreal.

When I was actually kidnapped ten years before, the search only seemed to last a few days. But I knew this would be different. I wasn't just some missing nobody from Nashville, Tennessee anymore. I was well known. I was important. I was the wife of an extremely wealthy and prominent man. This would be a field day for the media.

"Yes, they'll look for you, and they'll find you," he continued looking through the drawers.

"I don't want them to find me!" I shouted.

"They won't find you alive, Mrs. Claire," he stated.

"You're going to kill me, Ernesto?" I asked, a knot forming in my throat.

"No," he was annoyed at my ignorance. "They're going to find a body, but it won't be yours."

I followed him into the living room, Jonathan still lying on the floor, as he carefully removed the gun from his hands.

"You're going to stage my death? Claire Marsh's death?" I watched him point the gun at Jonathan's chest.

"Yes," he looked to me. "And I have to shoot him again. It has to look like a murder, not a suicide. He can't just be found with a gunshot wound to the head. It wouldn't take forensics three seconds to figure that out."

"Someone will hear all of this, Ernesto. The neighbors? There have already been two shots fired. Someone had to have heard!" I worriedly looked towards the window.

"No, they didn't, Mrs. Claire. No one heard a thing. I have to shoot him again. No one will hear. I promise," he calmed me.

"I can't watch," I ran to the bedroom and slammed the door, followed by the sound of a lone muffled gunshot.

"Come out, Mrs. Claire," Ernesto opened the bedroom door moments later. "You have to go to the lot and get another car. Do you know where the security cameras are and how they work?"

"Yes," I was trembling.

"You have to leave your Jaguar here so it'll look like you were abducted, okay? Get to the lot. Walk, ride a bicycle, skate, I don't care, but get there and get another car. You can't be seen on the cameras, though. That's extremely important. No one can know you were there this evening."

"I can do it," I convinced myself.

"I will stay here and tend to this mess. Go and hurry."

When I returned an hour or two later, the stolen Land Rover concealed in the garage next to my Jaguar and Jonathan's Range Rover, Ernesto had a small suitcase, a pillow and the prosthetic stomach piled by the back door.

"Are you sure we're doing the right thing?" I searched his face for answers.

"Mr. Jonathan wouldn't want people to know it ended this way. You know his ego," he grinned at me.

"What about my family? Will I be safe to go home? The associates?" I asked.

"You and your family will be safe, Mrs. Claire. The Santos' live across the street on Pine Hills. I will contact them and explain everything."

"They live across the, in the Barkley's house? The house that was for sale when I left?" I finally pieced it all together.

"Yes," he replied. "Saul Santo, his wife Desi and their three children. Vaiden and the youngest Santo girl are friends."

"Oh my God," I shook my head in disbelief. "That's where the photos-"

"They are no longer your enemies, Mrs. Claire. I will contact all of them. You don't have to fear anyone," he reached out and touched my arm as I sighed in relief.

"Thank you, Ernesto," I reached for his hands and held them in mine.

"Once I finish here, I'm going to a lady friend's this evening. That's my alibi. I will phone the police when I return in the morning. This will look like a breaking and entering. It will appear that you've been taken, and your body will be found in a few days."

"Where will you get my body? Why will they think it is me? Matching dental records?" I asked. "You won't kill someone, Ernesto? Where will you-"

"That's not for you to worry about, Mrs. Claire," he squeezed my hand. "I've packed only a few things in your suitcase. It can't appear that you left on your own. Your purse and cell phone, all of that is still here. Take that prosthetic stomach. Maybe you can use it as a disguise as you make your way home. Maybe you should dye your hair for a while?"

I tugged at my blonde mane.

"I put all of the documents from Mr. Jonathan's safe into your bag. The police won't find anything to link you to Elle Holley."

"I just go home? I can just go?" I wanted to hear it again.

"Yes," he nodded, "but wait at least a day or two before returning to Nashville, okay? Give me time to contact all of Mr. Jonathan's associates. Give it a few days for the dust to settle, and then, yes, you can go home."

"I can go home," I wanted to say it aloud again.

"You can," he said.

"Oh, thank you," I hugged him.

"I will miss you, Mrs. Claire," he tightened his arms around my back.

"Bye, Ernesto," I pulled away and looked at him with tears in my eyes.

"Go be with your daughter," he let go of me.

I grabbed my belongings by the back door and sped down of the driveway of the River Oaks home for the last time.

THIRTY SEVEN

"I've hurt so many women, Suzanne, innocent people, your dad. I'm sorry," I kept replaying Jonathan's words as I neared Nashville.

I'd only known of my father's death for a few hours. I was still in such despair, but things began to make sense. As I sped down the interstate, I pieced together a time line.

Had my father been punished that September day in 2001 because I'd tried to contact my home from Camilla's beauty salon while Jonathan was in New York? Had Jonathan been responsible for my father's automobile accident, the same way he was responsible for Suzanne's?

Had Jonathan fooled Ernesto and me into believing for so many years that Grant Mallory was a killer? I was responsible for Grant's murder. Was I guilty of the death of an innocent man? I wasn't completely convinced, but maybe so. Maybe, I didn't know, Jonathan was the bad guy all along, not just a kidnapper, but a murderer.

I was thankful for the convenient truth. I was relieved that I'd spent ten years with Jonathan Marsh and never truly known how malicious he may have been. To me, he was the kidnapper who became my husband, my lover and eventually my friend. I wanted to remember him the latter. I didn't want to know the absolute truth, so I shunned the idea that he was responsible for so much destruction, devastation and death. I would train myself to forget it.

I would even train myself to forget the kidnapping, the beating that nearly left me dead and the countless betrayals. Instead, I would remember the trips to exotic islands, the intimate moments; Clint Eastwood spaghetti westerns late at night and the mid-day breakfasts in bed. I would remember the parties, the sails on the yacht and the good that I did through my charities and fundraising. I would remember the walks on the beach and the kind words spoken in the dark. I wouldn't remember the bad or the what-ifs or the probabilities. Remembering those things would do me no good.

The Land Rover pulled up the steep driveway, all of my senses in overdrive. I slowly exited the car and carefully observed the cracks in the concrete where I'd tripped and fallen on my skates as a child. I touched the rough river birch trunk that butted up to the house. I breathed in the Nashville air, the freshly cut grass and it was if I could taste home on my lips.

I was home.

I stood before the kitchen door, unsure if I should just open it or knock first, but I reached for the knob and turned it before thinking the decision through.

I stepped into the kitchen, and I took in the smell of my home for the first time in ten years. It was the same familiar smell, but I couldn't describe it. It was just the smell of home.

I was home.

And there was my mother, entering the kitchen from the living room. *My God, my mother.* Her once medium-length, dishwater blonde hair was now silver and bobbed right below her ears, but her face was the same. She had hardly aged at all. Her skin was tan from working in the garden, as it always was during the summer months.

She wore a white blouse and navy shorts, her clothing covered with that same ragged plaid apron that I tugged on as a child while I begged to lick the spoon covered with icing. Her feet were bare, her toenails painted the normal shade, her favorite shade, of pink.

I was speechless as I examined her from head to toe, the kitchen door still open, the heat and bugs of the summer entering the house. I wanted to form some words or run to her arms, but we both stood there, paralyzed.

Then she fell to her knees. She didn't just falter or stumble, but she suddenly fell hard to her tanned knees, and her arms reached for me.

"Elle," she whispered, tears and moans only seconds away from escaping her eyes and her lips.

"Mama," I whispered back, and I ran into her arms and joined her on the beige linoleum floor.

"Praise God," she sobbed into my ear, her hands cupping my face. "Where have you been, my darling?"

"Where's Vaiden?" I focused my eyes on my mother's beautiful face.

"She's across the street with a friend," Mother drew me to her shoulder and rested her face on my head.

"The Santos girl?" I asked, frightened at the mere mention of their name.

"Yes," she pulled away and looked to me, confused. "You know Mariana Santos?"

"No," I shook my head. "Yes. I don't know. It's such a story, Mama. You'll never believe it."

"Oh, Elle, my God, your father-he-" we wept together.

"I know, Mama,"

"How did you know, Elle?"

"I have to see Vaiden first, Mama. I'll explain it all, but I have to see her," I stood and helped my mother to her feet as we both wiped our wet faces with our hands.

I wanted to ring the Santos' doorbell and see Saul's face and personally meet the enemies who had kept watch on my family for so long, but I certainly didn't want to share the intimate moment of reuniting with my daughter in their presence.

"I will go and-" my mother was interrupted at the sound of the kitchen door closing.

"Nana, who's parked in the driveway?"

My back was to her, and although I hadn't heard her speak since she was a toddler, I knew the voice belonged to my daughter.

My mother covered her mouth with trembling hands and nodded towards me. My heart pounded in my throat, the same way it had when Jonathan Marsh had taken me from the parking lot so many years before. I exhaled and turned around to face her. *My God, there she was. There was Vaiden.*

I couldn't believe who I was seeing. She wasn't the toddler who sat in the booster seat watching *Blue's Clues* on the day I was taken. She was a tall, thin, beautiful twelve-year-old girl. I immediately saw Nathan in her caramel eyes, and I felt dizzy as I studied every inch of her face and every mole on her tan arms. Her legs stuck out of denim shorts and her toenails were a bright shade of purple.

After standing silently and relishing in her beauty, I dashed to her and grabbed her. I soaked in the smell of her fresh hair, and I wailed onto her shoulder, unable to speak.

"Mama?" she asked.

The words wouldn't come, so I just nodded my head while I continued to embrace her. She wrapped her arms around me and softly began to whimper.

"I'm home, sweetheart," I finally managed to speak between rapid breaths. "Your mama is home."

THIRTY EIGHT

We sat at the kitchen table for hours, and I carefully told them my story. I told them how I'd skipped English Literature to buy Vaiden pajamas, how a stranger entered my unlocked car, how I'd been forced to live a luxurious life, how I'd had a beautiful wedding and traveled halfway around the world on lavish vacations.

I didn't tell them the bad things. I didn't tell them that the Santos family was affiliated with Jonathan, or that Grant Mallory was murdered in his home because Jonathan had convinced me that he deserved to die. I didn't tell them about my excruciating beating or the affairs or how I suspected that Jonathan was responsible for Daddy's death. I only told them what they needed to know. I left the really evil things locked away in my mind, determined to train myself to forget them.

"It sounds like you've been on vacation for the last ten years," Vaiden shook her head.

"Sweetheart, I thought of you every moment of every day. I wanted so badly to come home. I know it sounds like I was living a wonderful life there in Houston, but I wasn't allowed to come home. He told me that he would harm you if I came home. I couldn't take that chance."

"Is he going to hurt me now that you're here?" Vaiden's beautiful eyes, Nathan's eyes, were wide with fear.

"No, honey," I promised her and squeezed her hand. "No. He can't harm you now. He took his own life a few weeks ago. He's not going to hurt you. He's not going to hurt anyone again."

"Why, Elle? Why did he do that?" my mother peered over her glass of iced tea.

"We," I tried to think of a way to explain, "He was just, I don't know. He was severely depressed."

"You were married to him for so long. Did you love him?" Vaiden asked so innocently.

I didn't know how to respond to the question. I knew how absurd it would sound if I actually answered it truthfully.

"I," I stuttered and sighed.

My mother noticed the obvious distress on my face as I struggled to answer, so she graciously changed the subject.

"Why did it take so long to get home if he's been dead for weeks?"

"I had to make sure it was safe. His death has been all over the Texas news. I saw a report about it on the national news the day after I left. Remember? Remember when I called you?"

"I remember. I was so frightened and confused, Elle," Mama said. "But I was so happy to hear your voice. I haven't known what to think for so long. I was so worried, but so relieved that you were alive."

"Was he famous? Were you kidnapped by a famous man?" Vaiden didn't understand. I barely understood, so I couldn't imagine her young mind trying to comprehend it all.

"He wasn't famous, honey. He was just very well known in the area. His father was in politics. They were very popular people in Houston. When he died, everyone in Houston knew about it."

"I want to see him," Mama said. "I want to see the man who took you from me."

We stood from the old, familiar kitchen table where I had hurriedly eaten Pop-Tarts before school, and we walked to the computer in the living room.

"I'm so proud of you for joining the 21st century, Mama. How does it feel to own a system?" I smiled as I turned on the monitor.

"Your father would be beside himself. You know how he felt about all of this technology," she stood over me as I typed on the keyboard.

"Here," I said after clicking an article on the *Houston Chronicle* website.

"Elle," she gasped, "he looks harmless, like a, like a wonderful man. He's so handsome," she pulled her glasses from the top of her head, put them on and examined the photo of

Jonathan and me, "and you look beautiful, Elle. Look at that blonde hair."

I studied the photo of the two of us arm in arm at last year's Feed the Children Benefit while my mother began to read aloud.

"The search ends for Houston, Texas socialite Claire Marsh. Marsh's husband, Jonathan Marsh, son of former Houston mayor Thomas Marsh, was found shot to death in his River Oaks home on Thursday, August 8th. The charred remains of Claire Marsh's body were found four days later on the banks of the Buffalo Bayou near Memorial Park. Police believe Claire was abducted and also murdered by her husband's killer. No charges have been filed."

"They think you're dead?" Vaiden asked.

"This is too much for her," I quickly turned off the computer and stood up. "You shouldn't know anymore. Just know that I am home now. That's all that matters."

"And thank God you are," Mama began crying again as she pulled me into her arms.

"Elle!" I heard frantic screams from the kitchen.

I was barely off the couch before my sister had bounded on top of me and squeezed me until my ribs hurt.

"Look at me! Is it you? You're here? You're alive? You're here?" her hands were trembling as she gasped for air and studied my face.

"I'm here," I quickly nodded. "I'm here."

"Your hair, Elle! My God, this hair!" she tugged at the short orangey strands.

I gasped at the police officer entering the living room, a badge on his chest and a mop-topped toddler in his arms.

"This is my husband, Chad," she pointed to him, her upper body rapidly expanding.

"You're the cop?" I laughed. "You're the police officer! I saw you walking up the driveway! I saw you!"

I giggled uncontrollably. I actually jumped up and down with joy and then I rushed towards him, as he darted frightened eyes at my sister. I gave Chad an awkward hug and pulled sweet fat Knox from his arms. I studied the baby boy's blue eyes and covered his cheeks in kisses. He, too, thought I was psychotic, and he screamed for his mother.

I told my story again, especially careful not to reveal too much to my brother-in-law, the police officer. My mother seemed just as shocked to hear the drama unfold the second time as she did the first.

When our emotions had leveled out a bit, I sat in the living room with my family. It was as if time had stood still, as if the house had been waiting on my return. The furniture was new, the television had been upgraded, the walls were a different hue of beige, but it was the same living room where we'd played Twister, where I'd danced to MTV videos after school, where I'd watched *Law and Order* with my father. The comfortable floral couch was gone, the cattail arrangement in the corner was gone and my father was gone, but this was my living room. I was so glad to be back in this room, and I couldn't stop smiling.

"You know Nathan married Sarah Beth?" Emma broke the silence as we held hands on the couch.

"I saw it on the internet," I shrugged. "I couldn't expect him to wait on me. I didn't expect him to wait on me. I just vanished. What could he do?"

"I'm so sorry, Elle," Emma squeezed my hand. "You've been through so much."

"No," I said. "I'm sorry I haven't been here for so many milestones, through dad's death. I should have been here. I would have been here if I thought it was safe."

"You're sure it's safe?" she glanced at her husband.

"Everything is fine, but we can't talk openly about this. I don't want people to know that I was Claire Marsh. The police think Claire Marsh is dead. We have to keep this a secret. It's imperative that we stick to the original story. I've been married to some guy named Michael Kee in Miami. I left on my own. I wasn't kidnapped. This has to be kept a secret. Does everyone understand?" I looked around the room at my family as they all agreed.

"Chad?" Emma glanced at her husband.

"I understand. I won't say anything," he promised as Knox slept soundly on his uniformed chest.

"Why do we have to keep it a secret? Everyone will think you just left me. I don't want people to think that," Vaiden raised her head from my mother's shoulder as they sat across from the couch on the love seat.

"We can't help that, baby. If I have to look like a horrible mother, then so be it. It's better that way. Jonathan can't hurt us anymore, but I don't want anyone to know I was his wife. I don't want to relive that nightmare any longer. Claire Marsh is dead. The past is dead. This has to be our secret, okay?" I held up my pinky finger and she held up hers.

"Okay," she said.

"Oh, what a day," Mother sighed. "What a strange, beautiful, exhausting, wonderful day."

"Chad, you can take Knox home. I'd like to stay here longer if that's okay," Emma looked to her husband.

"Absolutely," the young-faced man in the uniform replied. He carefully stood as not to wake his sleeping son. Emma dug through her purse on the floor and then stood to hand him the keys.

"Take the van," she said. "I can have Mama drive me home later or I may just stay the night. I'll let you know," she ran her fingers through her precious little boy's soft hair and she kissed her husband. I fought many sentiments at the sight of this because I was in such awe that my sister wasn't a kid anymore.

"Elle," Chad said as I rose to my feet. "I've heard so much about you over the years, and I'm certainly glad you're home safe. I didn't think I'd ever get the chance to meet you, but it turns out God had other plans. I'm sure thankful for it."

That's when I knew my sister had married a good man.

THIRTY NINE

Emma and I shared popcorn at the dining table, and she filled me in on the decade's gossip. We picked up right where we had left off, as if I'd only been at church camp or at the beach for spring break. Mother walked through the living room with a load of laundry, Vaiden sprawled across the couch and listened to music on her headphones, Mrs. Lancaster called to see if Mother could bring a peach cobbler to the church homecoming next Sunday. It was so normal, yet so surreal.

"Sarah Beth and Nathan both work such long hours in the summer, with the farm and the produce market and the greenhouse. Vaiden is a huge help around the place, too, but she likes to stay the night with Mama a lot while on summer vacation. She stays with Nathan's parents and Chad and me some, too, but she loves being here the best. She's such a precious girl, Elle. She's never any trouble. She's got the kindest heart and the best manners, and she can sing like a bird. Her "Amazing Grace" brings grown men at the Methodist church to tears."

I beamed with pride. I knew she would turn out to be a wonderful young lady. She was such a good baby, so content, so caring at such an early age. I wasn't surprised she had turned out this way.

"How has she dealt with me being gone? What did she think happened to me?"

Emma sighed, "Oh, Elle. She and I have talked about it countless times over the years, and I've always let her know how much you loved her. I knew, Mama knew, we all knew that something was preventing you from being here. Vaiden knew it, too, deep down that you loved her with all of your being. She knew you'd be here if you could. She didn't believe that you'd abandoned her. We wouldn't let her believe that. That's why we were so scared that you were dead, Elle," Emma began to cry. "We've hired private detectives all over the country. We've put up posters and fliers and scoured the internet. We've interviewed every Michael Kee in the world, I think, and you were nowhere to be found. I'd convinced myself that you were dead. Mama had, too. Daddy was sure of it, even in the beginning. He knew, we all knew, Vaiden and Nathan knew that you wouldn't just run away with some stranger. When we got the wedding photos of you, we knew it wasn't right. We could see that your smile wasn't genuine. We knew they must have been Photoshopped or taken right before something terrible had happened to you. We knew it couldn't be true. Vaiden told all of her friends that her mama was dead. And," she shook her head, "we really believed it. We've mourned you for so long."

I reached across the dining table and grabbed my sister's arms. "I'll never leave you again, Emma. Never again."

Vaiden still had the same room at Mama's house, only Dora the Explorer had been replaced with peace signs and photos of her friends. As I waited on her to get out of the shower that evening, I sat on the edge of her bed, looking around and shaking my head in disbelief. I glanced through her open door to my old room across the hall, which had been mostly untouched since I'd left. The same lime green quilt covered the wrought iron bed, and a Dave Matthews Band CD still sat on my chest of drawers.

"I always call Daddy and Sarah Beth before I go to bed. Do you want to talk to them?" she startled me as she walked into her bedroom with clean hair and a Hannah Montana nightgown. I knew the Hello Kitty t-shirt that I'd bought weeks earlier was entirely too babyish for this pre-teen with purple toenails.

My heart began to pound at the offer. What would I even say?

"Sarah Beth has been a good mother to you?" I asked as Vaiden removed the sparkling studs from her ears and placed them on her nightstand. She sat by me on the bed.

"Yeah," she nodded.

"Did you know that we were the best of friends when we were young?" I smiled at the beautiful girl sitting next to me.

"Oh, yes. She's told me all about you. She told me that you

got caught toilet papering your teacher's house one time," Vaiden laughed. "She said you turned as white as the toilet paper you were holding when your teacher shined a flashlight in your face."

I smiled, "Yes, I did. You don't toilet paper houses do you?"

"I did once," she shrugged. "I got caught, too. That's why Sarah Beth told me the story."

I smiled.

"We were so close. I loved Sarah Beth," I thought aloud.

"I love Sarah Beth, too" Vaiden pulled the covers down and slipped her purple toes under them.

I knew Sarah Beth had been a wonderful mother to my daughter. She'd married the love of my life, but she'd been a good friend to me by loving my child as her own. She'd taken care of Nathan and Vaiden when I couldn't. I'd never hold a grudge for anything she'd done. Instead, I'd thank her for it.

"Do you want to talk to her?" Vaiden reached for the pink phone beside her bed, unaware of how awkward it would be for me to speak to my best friend at that moment, my best friend who had married my love and served as a mother to my child because everyone thought I was dead.

"I don't think so, Vaiden," I patted her leg beneath the blankets. "Why don't you skip calling Sarah Beth and Daddy tonight? I don't think you should have to explain to your dad and Sarah Beth that your mother is back from, well, back from the dead."

"Yeah, that's pretty heavy," she said as I grinned at her language. "Maybe you or Nana should call and let them know I'm okay and that I'm going to bed."

"I think that's a great idea," I agreed.

I turned off her light, stroked her dark blonde hair and watched her quickly drift off to sleep. I was content to sit on the edge of the bed and study her for hours, as I thanked God that I was home. Mother interrupted my gaze when she cleared her throat from the doorway and motioned for me to come into the hall.

"That warms my heart," she said. "Seeing you and your

daughter reunited warms my heart."

"Mine, too, Mama," I squeezed her hand.

"We haven't discussed this yet, but should I call Nathan? Do you want me to tell him tonight, or would you rather wait until morning?"

"Let's call him," I eagerly nodded.

"Nathan, dear, it's Judith. Vaiden is fine, she's just so worn out from today and she went to sleep without calling first," Mama spoke into the receiver as I sat across from her at the kitchen table, nervously rapping my nails on the arm of the chair.

"Yes, son, she's had a busy day. We ran errands all morning and she went swimming at the Santos' and then Elle came home," Mama and I smiled as she bobbed her head. "Yes, honey, Elle. She's home, Nathan."

Mama's eyes were becoming damp with tears, and she repeated it again, "I think you should come over, Nathan. Elle is home."

"What will you say?" Emma asked as I stood in front of the bathroom mirror and brushed the lackluster orange strands of hair.

"What do you say in a situation like this?" I looked to her for advice.

"I have no idea, Elle," she admitted. "Maybe you should ask him if he likes your hair. I don't know."

"Oh, this hair," I mumbled in frustration. "I had such beautiful hair. I hate for him to see me this way, ten years older with ridiculous choppy hair. I hate- "

Mother entered the bathroom and interrupted my complaining.

"Nathan's here," she said as Emma and I looked to one another wide-eyed. "He's waiting outside. You know he always waited for you outside."

Nathan and I had our best conversations in my driveway. We'd sit on the tailgate of his truck for hours, watching the Barkley family live their lives through the open windows across the street. We would count how many bowls of ice cream fat old man Barkley ate while watching *Gunsmoke* in his recliner. We laughed at little Mickey Barkley running through the house in his underoos while his mother chased him with pajama pants.

"Emma, don't spy on us!" I exclaimed as I rushed down the stairway, my sister and Mama in pursuit.

"Why would I do that?" she laughed because it was a known fact that she always spied on us. Many nights Mama would pry her peeping eyes from the kitchen door as she watched Nathan and me hold hands and count the stars and dream of our future.

I exhaled and opened the kitchen door. I stepped into the garage and suddenly felt like a teenager again, as I eyed the unfamiliar Chevrolet truck sitting in the driveway. Nathan always drove a Chevrolet.

I slowly shuffled my bare feet across the garage, and into the driveway, praying the moon wouldn't cast such a bright glow on my haphazard hair and the bags under my eyes. I was so incredibly nervous that I would say or do something stupid. It felt eerily similar to our first date so many moons ago.

The driver's side door of the truck opened, and he appeared. His Ducks Unlimited hat was shining beneath the street lamp and casting a shadow on his face. His tall, thin body stood frozen fifteen feet before me.

We stood still and stared at one another, unsure of how to react or what to say. In my heart, my gut, I wanted to hurry to him. I wanted to hold this man in my arms and never let him go. I wanted to feel the stubble of his chin on my cheeks and smell the sweet scent of his skin. I wanted to kiss him the way we kissed when we thought Emma wasn't watching us from the kitchen door. I wanted to act on these powerful instincts, but I knew a married man stood before me. I knew my best friend's husband stood before me.

"Nathan," I began.

He rushed me, with his arms outstretched. I was paralyzed with nervousness, but he picked me up off the ground and his mouth found mine. I closed my eyes, pressed my hands to his face and savored every moment of his presence, every finger that wrapped around my waist, every breath that he breathed into me, and I never wanted this moment to end.

"My God, Elle," he exhaled into my ear. "Is it you?"

I nodded, my face wet again with tears, my nails digging into his white t-shirt.

"I never thought I'd see you again," he whispered as his grip around me tightened. "I-I thought you left me. I thought you were dead. I don't know what I thought."

"I would never leave you," I pulled away and examined his face.

He was the same sweet, southern boy that I'd fallen in love with when I was only fourteen. He still looked like that young kid tripping in his roller skates, only manly stubble covered his cheeks and small wrinkles had formed around his beautiful brown eyes. One look at that face, one kiss from him again, and I was certain he was still the love of my life.

"Tell me! You're home to stay? You have orange hair," he touched my head as I grinned. "What's going on, Elle? I thought you left us. Ten years, Elle!"

I could feel his heart pounding beneath his shirt as I tried to explain.

"I would never leave you and Vaiden. You know that. I was taken, Nathan, kidnapped. I've been forced to stay in Houston with a man for ten years."

"I was just in Houston a few months ago, Elle! I was- My God, I cannot believe. You're here? Who took you? What son of a bitch took you? How did you get home? Vaiden, what did she say? Why didn't you call me earlier? How did you get home?" the questions kept coming, his breathing heavy, his handsome face covered in disbelief.

"I'll explain it all," I promised.

"Sarah Beth, Elle. Oh my God, I married Sarah Beth, Elle. How was I supposed to know? What was I supposed to do?" he spoke as if he was guilty, his eyes darting in shame.

"I don't care, Nathan," I pressed my face against his. "Just hold me."

"My God, Elle, I can't believe this. Where have you-"

"Later," I said as I held him close. I looked over his shoulder to the Barkley's house across the street.

There, in the front window, was Saul Santos. His silhouette was still, the light from his living room television casting shadows behind him. He raised his right hand to the glass. It was his way of letting me know that I was safe.

"Mama, the movie is about to start!" Vaiden called to me from the living room.

"Okay, give me just a minute," I replied as I sat on the toilet, staring at the small pink plus sign on the bathroom counter.

It seems Jonathan Marsh's sperm were fine after all.

Acknowledgments

I'm not winning a Grammy for "Most Explicit Rap Album", but I have to thank God first and foremost. I have to thank Him for the passion that He instilled within me to write and the patience and guidance that He gave me in completing and publishing this novel. I'm nothing without Him. I'm nothing without His love and mercy.

I also have to thank my family and friends for their unwavering love and support.

Jason, my heart, everything I write, I write for your approval. Thank you for not running away, with arms flailing, as I droned on for hours upon hours upon years about this book. Thanks for telling me things I didn't want to hear, although I needed to hear them. Thanks for being on my team. I love you immensely.

Mama and Carmen, you mean more to me than you'll ever know. I'm unworthy of your steadfast praise in everything I write. Thank you for being so publicly proud of me. You are my heart.

Mrs. Kristi, thanks for always being proud of me and proud for me, too. Mrs. Cathy, thank you for your kindness and encouragement and being my biggest fan. Natalie Ann and Bennett, thanks for letting Mama write when you'd rather I play Monopoly. Or feed you.

I also want to thank some wonderful friends who read this book when it was newly written- chocked full of grammatical errors and the word "sob" was overused. Jamie, Kristen, Summer and Chris- your initial feedback on this novel lifted my spirits more than you'll ever know. To have such supportive and genuine friends gives me the warm and fuzzies. I'll always remember your kind words, compliments and support in my endeavors. God bless each one of you.

This was written entirely to the soundtrack of Ray Lamontagne. I have to acknowledge him here. His lyrics-astounding poetry set to beautiful melodies- were the driving force behind my inspiration to write this book. You can't help but be inspired to make something, create something, when you listen to "Jolene" and "Empty". They aren't songs. They are stories.

Thanks to all of my blog followers and Facebook fans. Your likes, shares and support astound me every day. I've always had a (loud, sarcastic) voice, but I never knew anyone would like it. I can't believe you people do. I'm humbled and amazed by your generosity and kind comments. You've brightened some pretty dark days.

I'm also incredibly grateful to the amazing January 11th Birthday Crew, Brandy Kemp and my oldest and dearest friend, Carrie Anne Yearwood, for using your incredible skills and God-given talents to create the cover for this book. I've got friends in low places, but you aren't among them. You're in high places. You're rock stars, both of you. Also, Mr. and Mrs. Huddleston and the beautiful Kendall Davidson, I am so appreciative of you for putting a face and a setting to my story.

Special thanks to Rachel Rofe, who provided the essential tools (and a heaping helping of encouragement) to actually make this book possible.

And thanks to you, whoever you are, for reading this book. By purchasing it and (hopefully) leaving a positive review for it, you are helping to make this girl's lifelong dream come true. It's a beautiful thing. And so are you.

Now, everyone meet me at McDonald's. Dinner is on me.

About the Author

Susannah B. Lewis is a freelance writer, blogger, humorist, aspiring best-selling author, wife of one and stay-at-home mother of two. She contributes pieces to *The Huffington Post, Hahas for Hoohas* and *Your Tango*. Her work has been featured in several humorous e-books, *Southern Writers' Magazine, The Humor Daily, The Funny Times* and Erma Bombeck's Humor Writers, among others. When she's not putting pen to paper, bandaging boo-boos or spraying Shout on unidentifiable stains, she enjoys reading, playing the piano and teaching her children all about Southern charm.

Read her humor blog, Whoa! Susannah (www.whoasusannah.com) and follow her on Facebook (www.facebook.com/whoasusannah) and Twitter (www.twitter.com/whoasusannah).

Made in the USA
Lexington, KY
17 October 2017